MELODY IN TEA

by

MARY FLANNERY

-LARGE PRINT-

I ndílchuimhne

ar mo

mháthair, Kathleen,

Éilín, Íde, Tomás & Bríd, Donnchadha

agus m'aintíní agus m'úncailí uile

Má tá tae ar fáil ar Neamh,

caithfidh go bhfuil sé thar barr!

Contents

ACKNOWLEDGEMENTS

I am very grateful to everybody who encouraged me. A special word of thanks to the people whose wonderful memoirs I read, to be able to 'feel' what it was like to live in a Tea Garden in India or Pakistan in the mid-twentieth century. Thanks especially to the people of the *Koi Hai* website. To Buddy McDougal for her heartwarming memoir *'Two Leaves and a Bud.'* To David Mitchell for *'Tea, Love and War'*. As this is a work of fiction, you may shake your head here and there, but there's no story without conflict, or – *suspense!*

Thanks to my dear Dad Patrick, as always positive and encouraging, and to my Aunts Nancy, Mary, Carmel, Anne and Eileen and to my Uncle Brendan. You all enriched our childhoods and gave us a love of family and laughter, over many cups of tea of course…

I've been blessed with four wonderful siblings. Eileen, Larry, Caitríona and Síle, love you lots. A special thanks to Síle for correcting and polishing my Dedication *as Gaeilge.*

As always a big Thank You to my husband and best friend Liam, for tolerating my inhabiting another world and for pecking away at the keyboard for hours on end. I know this began as a short story, but my characters demanded more...

Camellia Sinensis

"Two leaves and a bud"

INTRODUCTION

In the 1990's, among the Christmas gifts we received was a CD from my parents, called *'The Most Relaxing Classical Album in the World...ever!'*

It lived up to its name. And among the selections, I found a track I found myself looking forward to in particular. It was particularly tranquil, but suggested deep emotion and, perhaps, sadness.

I listened to it last thing at night, and in that strange transitory world between waking and sleeping, I found myself with a procession of images that surfaced with the 3-minute track. A story of love and loss perhaps – a young woman emerged in my mind, poor and sad, in a cold flat in winter, whose mind and heart were far away, in a land of brilliant sunshine – and the love she had left there.

Frances' story took on a life and I had to write it down.

GLOSSARY

Amah
Nanny or female maid (East Asia)
Ayah
Nanny or female maid (India)
Baksheesh
Money into the hand as alms or a bribe or a tip
Banglat
Bungalow – can be 2-storey or more
Basay
Home
Bearer
Housekeeper/House Servant
Boro
Big or Most Important
Boro-memsahib
Boro-Sahib's wife
Boro-sahib
Most important sahib; the boss
Box-Wallah
Tradesman or Businessman
Chappati
Flat Bread
Chit
Handwritten note
Chokidar
Security Guard
Chota Peg
a small whiskey, preferred by Europeans

11

Dacoit
Thief
Dhobi
Washerman or washerwoman
Dhoti
Hindu man's wear; a long tunic with baggy trousers
Go-down
Warehouse, can be large or small
Hartal
Industrial Strike
Khub
Very
Lungi
Muslim man's sarong-type garment
Memsahib
The Sahib's wife; also form of address for her
Pani-Wallah
literally water-bearer but also kitchen helper
Sahib
Form of address for a man usually used with Europeans
Shalwar-Kameez
Woman's long tunic over trousers tapering at ankles
Shundur
Beautiful
Tig
OK; all well
Sola Topi
A hat from the pith of the sola plant

NOTES

Just a few things about Historical Fiction.

A writer of historical fiction takes a reader on a trip to another time. Hopefully the reader will enjoy this little 'holiday', but just as *'The Past is a Different Country'* he or she may find some attitudes and opinions of the characters surprising, even troubling.

The characters can't be anachronistic; i.e. they can't have 21st Century values in their time in history. Even characters you are supposed to like may have the values and thoughts of their own times.

Conversely, the writer's own opinions and values might slip in even unknown to her, giving her character a 21st century viewpoint that was uncommon then! I have tried not to do this, unless there is a plausible explanation for the opinion, but if something slipped in, forgive me!

It would be anachronistic to spell Calcutta as *Kolkata*. Under British rule, it was spelled Calcutta, and this spelling was maintained for a long time after that. There are other instances of this in the text where spellings altered later. It is pronounced *Kalikata* in Bengali.

The tea-gardens often employed people who were not of the area, giving rise to a variety of languages spoken.

tea garden
with
shade trees

MELODY IN TEA

CHAPTER 1

English Weather

*I*t was the rain. Icy English rain, pouring with hardly a pause for four days now. It hammered at the window, morning, noon and night. Frances twitched back the curtain and peered out the window of her ground floor bedsit. Florian Lane provided a shortcut from the tube station to Meadow Street, and though the pavement was rutted in places, people on their way to work in that vicinity found it worth stepping around puddles to shorten the time in the elements. The people she saw hurrying along the streets this February Monday morning, city people with

15

umbrellas, men in bowlers and greatcoats with collars pulled up around their ears, shop assistants and secretaries with hairdos safe in headscarves, were they all as disgusted as she with the deplorable weather? Their faces, when she managed to glimpse them, seemed set and impassive, and she wondered if they had ever heard that there were places in the world where even in winter the skies caressed people with golden rays instead of lashing them with icy rain.

Why would anybody in their right minds want to live in England? Was winter here ever going to end? Her bedsitting room numbed her with its biting cold. She pulled on her dressing-gown – a pink candlewick, and thank God - warm! A Christmas present from Aunt Margaret. She plugged in her two-bar electric fire and within moments a blast of hot air warmed her toes. She put the kettle on for tea, and made one-sided toast under the grill of her small, chipped cooker.

Two slices, thinly spread with strawberry jam, was her breakfast, partaken on a small table covered with a crimson cloth from Sundarpur – a piece of bright, happy workmanship that was out of place here.

She bit into her toast and drank her tea. Jenny's wireless was loud, as usual. Jenny could not exist without her wireless on. At this time of morning a smooth male voice spoke unintelligibly though the wall that divided the old high-ceilinged parlour (the house had been a family home) into two flats, interspersing his monologue with popular songs. Jenny had the better half of the room; it boasted a decent fireplace. But Frances' door to the main hallway was the original one, solid wood, painted white. Jenny's doorway had been hacked out of the wall and fitted with some cheap wood. Jenny complained that it let in draughts, but Frances had no sympathy – Jenny had a real coal fire. They had the same wallpaper, a serpentine pattern in blue, probably pre-

World War One. The same carpet ran through the divided room, so hard, threadbare and discoloured that the original shade was in dispute. Both rooms had cheap, secondhand kitchen fittings knocked into them. The flats had a window each; the old curtains had been left there; rich maroon velvet, but every time they were opened or drawn, the girls coughed with the dust, and collaborated as to how best to ask the penny-pinching landlady to take them down and clean them, fearing that clean they would be appropriated for better rooms, or that their rent would go up.

'How much is that doggy in the window! Yip! Yip! The one with the waggely tail!' Frances knew she would hear this ever-popular song if not in the morning as her neighbour ate her breakfast, then in the evening as she got her tea ready, and Jenny always turned up the volume and sang along, which she found amusing, as Jenny was tone-deaf. Frances did not dislike

contemporary music – 'Que Sera Sera',
when that was played, also fairly often, she
too sang along, the words having some
meaning for her, she supposed. But she did
not own a wireless herself. At night, Jenny
forgot to turn hers off sometimes as she fell
asleep, delaying Frances' dropping off, but
not in an unpleasant way that would make
her complain – the selection was mellow,
'Mona Lisa' or 'Stranger in Paradise'. She
liked hearing it even if the romantic music
made her a little melancholy…a figure often
surfaced…a man…tall, with a mop of
coppery hair, a wave falling over his
forehead; deep green eyes and an
expression steady and intelligent, a man you
could depend on, and now lost to her.
Sometimes she heard classical pieces,
soothing, suitable for late-night listening,
and she wondered if they would ever play
'Gymnopédie'.

And last night, they had! She'd been almost
asleep – but the first soft chords gently

nudging her consciousness jerked her awake. As if summoned, she'd sat up suddenly in the chilly darkness and pressed her ear to the wall. It had been over too quickly – about three minutes at most – but she could hear clearly enough to know it was the orchestral arrangement – and she smiled in delight as she had heard the oboe coming in. Hugh was right – the oboe was perfect for that part! It had a plaintive sound. When the last notes died away, she had snuggled deep underneath the blankets to hug it in her memory, trying to block out the piece that followed it. She wanted to keep those three minutes of aural pleasure, to cling to them, for it brought beloved memories to her, beloved memories from faraway in India, and again she heard Hugh's velvety touch on the piano. Memories seized her –evenings on the verandah – the happy sounds of children, watching sunsets over the Sundarpur Hills, and Gymnopédie. She'd fallen asleep thinking of Hugh. She'd woken up thinking of him. She clung to the memory as one would a fading dream. But everything was in the past now. Hugh was past. And her late husband, Alec…though life with him had been difficult, she was conscious often that she owed him her life in India and he'd brought her to a home she'd loved. She remembered her first glimpse of the bungalow– its blue wall peeping shyly out of a forest of flowering trees and jungly palms, and it had only enchanted her more when it came into full view. No, she reminded herself as one would remind a friend whose memories were rose-coloured, it was a company bungalow, and never hers.

'I was a memsahib once,' she said aloud to the gloomy, tiny bedsit, but perhaps it was to herself, to remind herself that she had once been a woman with a husband, a home, leisure and sunshine, even if she had been – she could admit it to herself now – unhappy for the last years. She poured herself a second cup of tea, spattering a few drops on

the tablecloth, as she wasn't really concentrating. She quickly got the dishcloth, wet it under the cold tap and gently dabbed the stain.

If she hadn't had this tablecloth, with swirls of exotic flowers and plants delicately embroidered in gold, and a few other textiles and ornaments salvaged from what was left of her other life, Frances Whittier would sometimes find it difficult to believe that she had ever been to India, ever been the wife of a manager of Localsh Tea Company, and for seven years had lived a life completely different from this one. That life had ended in the unexpected death of her husband, and with his death, she had lost her home also.

'I do wish that doggy's for sale!' Over. Until this evening. The smooth voice of the presenter was heard again.

The short piece which had delighted her in the dead of night replayed itself in her mind - the thoughts rushed her as she munched her toast and swallowed her tea, then finishing quickly, she brushed the crumbs off the tablecloth with her hand and quickly plunged the dishes into a basin of cold water, took her washbag and towel and went up to the bathroom.

CHAPTER 2 King's Cross 1949

She'd first met Alexander on the 10:54 from King's Cross to Stevenage. She'd been going on a short trip to see Aunt Margaret – her mother had insisted – it wasn't fair to a young person like herself to have to stay in day after day, night after night, looking after a sick woman. Mrs. Wells would look in twice a day, and the doctor would visit daily. So Frances had packed a small bag and got the bus to Kings Cross. She found her train, settled herself in a seat and began to look around. Almost immediately her eyes met those of an approaching passenger, a well-dressed man in a grey pin-striped suit and a straw Panama, who asked, in a rather polished accent, if the seat opposite hers was free. She said yes. He swung a suitcase onto the rack above and sat down, took a folded newspaper from inside his suit jacket and began to read.

For want of something to do, she studied him as the train moved off. He was tanned, as brown as if he had been in the garden all summer long. He had a neat, dark moustache like David Niven. His suit was expensive. His tie was silk; the corner of a probably perfectly ironed handkerchief peeped from his pocket. His eyes, when he lifted them from the paper briefly to glance out the window, were pale blue. Nothing spectacular, she thought, in his appearance - except a certain air of confidence – almost loftiness, and his tan almost certainly did not result from hours spent tending roses. She thought rather that he must have spent the summer in the South of France. That fit better with his demeanor, his superiority. He was aged about thirty.

He looked up, and she quickly averted her gaze to the window. She tried to look nonchalant but she knew she blushed slightly. Had he seen her observe him? She hoped not. But she felt him watching her for a moment.

'Excuse, me' he said with a smile, leaning towards her a little. 'Do you mind if I smoke?'

'Not at all,' she responded. He lit an Embassy cigarette and resumed reading, only to lower the Times again after half a minute.

'What do you think is in this newspaper?' he asked her, still smiling. She thought it rather forward of him to address her so casually. Was he going to try to 'chat her up?' The appraising look he gave her as he awaited her response told her so.

She floundered for a witty reply, besides the word 'news' which she was sure he would think sarcastic or simply stupid. Some girls could carry off sarcasm as humour and men loved it, but she could not. It would just sound mocking, not flirty at all. She wished she could flirt. But she had not the foggiest idea how to go about it. So she said, rather helplessly: 'I don't know.'

'The first flight of the *de Havilland Comet*,' he said. 'Do you know what that is?'

She blushed. She felt that she was definitely being 'chatted up'! It was a new experience and she felt flattered.

'No, I have no idea.' She wanted to add that a comet was a star or something, but he began to speak again.

'A passenger jet plane. I would like to try one of those, yes, faster than one of the old P&O tubs, I should think. A lot faster.'

'You have travelled, then?' she ventured.

'Indeed, yes,' he said, and hearing the clank of a trolley, exclaimed: 'Ah, here's the tea!'

He paid for hers, insisting as if it was a great honour to do so – and she ventured to ask him if he had spent the summer in England. He told her that he was in the middle of a leave from India where he worked 'in Tea.'

'What will you think of British Railways tea?' she asked with interest. 'I see you don't take milk or sugar!'

'Oh, goodness, no. Would you put milk or sugar into wine?' He took his cup.

'British Railways *Camellia Sinensis,* I shall tell you all in a moment,' he said. He moved the cup to and fro a few times in front of his face. 'Poor grade. No nose at all.' he took a sip and appeared to swish it a little around his mouth with a slight frown before swallowing.

'Woody. Over-infused, or infused for too long. But one cannot expect a quality cup of tea on a train. Of course it's not ours,' he added, smiling. 'Our tea – Localsh Tea - is exclusive, a blend of leaves from three varieties of bush, withered, rolled, dried, sorted and graded until we have a top-quality product. There is hardly a tea-drinker in England who knows anything of what goes into producing an excellent grade of tea.' He sipped again, grimacing. 'Have you ever wondered about it?' he asked.

She shook her head.

'I can't say that I have, but I'm sure there's so much I don't know!'

'But I thought young people knew everything,' he teased her gently, and she laughed.

'I know that my mother and aunt can't wait for tea rationing to end. With the War over for four years, they can't understand why we still have rationing.'

He began to talk of rationing and other related matters and as they left the houses behind them and whizzed by green fields and farms, he asked her about herself.

She felt at ease with him, and talked
willingly, and at the end of her journey, he
said that as he had such a short time in
England – four months – it would give him
immense happiness if he could meet her
again. He was being forward – she must
forgive him that – but could she take pity on
a man on home leave from a distant outpost
of what had once been the British Empire?
His time was so short – he had so few
friends left in England – if it wasn't too
much trouble for her or she didn't think he
was being presumptuous – ? Frances felt
very flattered at the attention and awed by
the petition. She had never had a boyfriend –
the mistresses at her school made sure that
the girls had no opportunity to distract
themselves with boyfriends. Her summer
had been spent with her ailing mother. Why
not meet Alexander Whittier again? They
could go for a walk but wait – Alexander
had a splendid idea! When was she returning
to London? In three days? His destination
was farther to the north but he was returning

to town in a few days – why should they not get the train down together from Stevenage again? It seemed like a very good proposal, and she stepped off the train in a dream, and paused on the platform and looked back, looked for him through the window, almost not believing what had happened. He was evidently looking out for her, was smiling and gave her a warm wave of his hand.

And that was how she had met Mr. Alexander Whittier, who had told her to call him Alec. Not Alex, he had said. He seemed rather particular about that. By the time she alighted at the station, she had told him quite a lot about herself, that she had been to St. Anne's School and left only last June – that her father had been Headmaster of a small Catholic school in Croydon and that he was dead; that she was an only child, and that her mother was in poor health and she spent almost all her time looking after her. He listened, absorbing all with interest.

But when she related her meeting to Aunt Margaret over a cosy tea later, the latter had asked her what *she* had found out about Mr. Whittier. She had to admit that besides his working for a tea company in Assam in northeast India, which he told her bordered East Pakistan, he had not told her much about himself at all.

Everything happened very quickly after that. Although she knew that Alec was of a class superior to her own, it had been quite astonishing that his brother was a Baron, the Right Honourable Lord Delarbrey, as Alexander – himself an Honourable – put it. What could he see in her? She wasn't beautiful, though her mother had told her that her brown eyes were very expressive and warned her about 'wearing her heart on her sleeve'. Her mousy hair was cut in a short bob, and she sported a little fringe over her forehead. Her skin was clear. She and her friends had decided face shapes one day after coming across an article in a discarded copy of *Vogue*. It had seemed dreadfully important at age sixteen to know what shape ones face was, and it was unanimous that Frances' was the only heart-shape, while the others had ovals and rounds.

But she hadn't come out of the top drawer. Though she spoke very well, at least as well as *he* did, due to her father's making her recite poetry in impeccable English, the difference in class must be obvious to him. She was half-Irish and Roman Catholic! But why would Alec not have a girlfriend of his own – rank? A girl who hunted and would be at home at cocktail parties and was a regular at the Dorchester? A girl who had been presented at Court. Frances' family was very middle-class - but careless, contented people - her parents had mixed with aspiring writers and thinkers – dreamers, Aunt Margaret called them, with cynicism.

But Alec seemed to love her innocence about the world he came from. Her ignorance of fine wines – indeed any wines at all (for he confessed to being a connoisseur) - and her inexpensive but tasteful jewellery and handsewn dresses seemed to charm him. As did her curiousity about what life was like outside England, and he seemed to love nothing better than to tell her about Assam and its vast areas of tea estates watered by the Brahmaputra River, and Darjeeling in the north, at the foot of the Himalayan mountain range, the lower slopes of which were also cultivated in tea.

They were walking in Kensington Park one fine Sunday and Alec began to talk of himself. He had worked for Localsh Tea Company for ten years. He had begun as a junior assistant just after the War began, and had worked his way up to senior manager, second only to the Superintendent on the estate. He had received the promotion to senior manager just before he left for England on his leave. The tea estate extended over five miles of low hillsides, almost as far as the border with East Pakistan. At one end was a factory, where the picked tea was processed. Mostly, their workers were Indians – but Europeans managed the estate. They were housed in bungalows on the site, near the factory but quite away and apart from where the Labour lived. Very nice spacious bungalows, five in all, allotted on the basis of rank. He was at present housed in the bachelor's bungalow, - *the chummery* - along with another chap, Tom. Married men had their own bungalows. He had, however requested a bungalow of his own, and it had been granted to him along with his promotion, and upon the expectation that he would soon marry. The Superintendent – Alastair Jamieson – was married, and there were two other couples on the estate. He intended to return to India a married man.

Frances felt rather downcast when he told her that. He was no doubt putting her on her guard not to get too fond of him.

'And - do you have somebody in mind?' She looked at the ground, fearing the answer. The sophisticated and fashionable figure who frequented the Dorchester resurfaced in her mind, tossing her coiffed hair and looking rather contemptuously in her direction.

'I think I do,' he replied warmly.

'Oh,' she said, looking away. Then, biting her lip, and a little cross, charged: 'And – shouldn't you be with her, instead of with me?'

'Frances Mary Sullivan, are you really as modest and unassuming as you seem? I believe you are!'

She blushed to her ears, and her heart turned over as he took her hand and squeezed it. She could hardly believe her ears, for since she had met Alec, he had hardly left her mind for one minute.

When Frances told her mother that she thought that Alec might be – *might be* - in love with her, Mrs. Sullivan became both anxious and excited, and invited him to tea in their plain terraced home in Fairway Street. She used all her butter and sugar coupons to bake a cake. Alec seemed very taken with Mrs. Sullivan, and their home, their untidy parlour filled with bookcases, lamps, two long-haired cats and several sprawling armchairs, which he declared the cosiest sitting-room in England.

'Oh Frances, what *peace* it would give me to know you were settled and well-looked after!' Mrs. Sullivan exclaimed later, as Frances helped her to bed.

Her words – her urgency, almost, filled Frances with foreboding.

The following week her mother's health declined very rapidly. The doctor was called, and arranged an immediate admission to the Royal Marsden Hospital. Frances and Aunt Margaret kept a vigil by her bedside. Frances had long been averse to hospitals – the antiseptic and other indefinable smells, the odd hospital noises, hopelessly sick people on stretchers being wheeled along the hallways. She would always associate hospitals with her father's death. She feared that nothing good would come of her mother's admission either. To Frances' heartbreak, she died within three days.

Alec was a brick. After the funeral, he helped her to empty the house, for she had no way now to pay the mortgage and had to move.

'Where will you go?' he asked her.

'To Aunt Margaret's, I suppose, to begin with. She's taking Florrie and Poppie.' She stroked the latter. 'I suppose I shall be more trouble to her though, than they.'

'You don't really want to go to Aunt Margaret's, though, do you?'

She felt a little tremor go through her at his tone.

'No, I don't.' she said, hardly daring to breathe.

'Marry me – marry me and come to Assam,' he had proposed, pressing her hand in their upside-down parlour, filled with boxes and overflowing with her parents' belongings. She didn't have to think it over - not even for a moment – she was in love with him and had been from their first meeting on the train. She loved every feature of his face – it was the dearest face in the world. Every movement he made enchanted her. He was intelligent and wise in the ways of the world. She looked up to him. She was utterly in love, and her love had spilled over to the flat plains and hillsides she had never set eyes upon, all covered in tea plants as far as the eye could see.

To make it all romantic and proper, Alec took her out to a posh restaurant. The ambience was lovely but Alec lamented that the fare was plainer than he would have liked for such a special occasion. Rationing was still in place. Wasn't it outrageous that England had to feed Germany and Italy? Frances wouldn't have cared if they had had to make do with stale bread and black tea. He produced a ring and placed it on her finger. It was a beauty – an oval emerald set in a cluster of tiny diamonds.

Aunt Margaret was both intrigued and alarmed. 'You know him such a short time,' she had murmured. 'My dear, these men in Tea come home on leave to find wives. They rush things. Of course he has found a Treasure in you – but you are so young! You're still in shock after losing your mother. We never expected her to go so quickly! But are you very sure you love him, and that he feels the same way about you?'

'Of course I'm sure. I can't even imagine a future without Alec. And of course he loves me. He asked me to marry him, didn't he?'

'You are romantic, like your mother. But she was much older than you are now when she got married, and stayed here in England.

Your grandmother didn't want her to marry a Catholic. But they loved each other and it all worked out all right, and Mother came around, especially after you were born. She never dreamed there would be any children – your mother was over forty. A more doting grandmother I never saw in my life, and I thought she had doted on my three! She didn't even mind you were to be brought up R.C.'

As she gathered up the small items of sentimental value that she had decided to bring with her, Frances had a moment of doubt. It would be nice if Alec had uttered the three words 'I love you' but what did it matter, really? It was obvious that he did. She put the doubts out of her head.

She had an inheritance of five thousand pounds. Alec went to the City and put the legal work into the hands of an old public school friend who had become a lawyer. Wardo – real name Tom Edwardson - would sort it out, so all was set in motion for the lengthy business of probate. The house was sold very rapidly, thanks to Alec also - and all of the money realised from the sale was paid into his account in the Bank of England, as would happen with her inheritance when the legalities were sorted out. Aunt Margaret was now uneasy about that - but Frances said airily that she trusted Alec completely, and as they were engaged, what was there to worry about?

They were married in a Catholic chapel a week before they boarded the ship. It was a quiet ceremony; Alec's brother Lord Delarbrey and his wife Lady Helen were not present. Frances wondered if they disapproved. Her bridesmaid was Grace, her best friend. Alec's best man was 'Wardo' Edwardson. Two other friends named Reggie and Sylvester attended.

Wardo's wife Alison was a warm, friendly woman, kissing her cheek and telling her she loved her dress, her grandmother's made-over calf-length pale blue satin with lace overlay. On Alec's side also was a sprinkling of elderly aunts and uncles who looked rather bewildered at becoming related to the Sullivan clan, but who certainly enjoyed their feast – three courses, one of them an excellent roast beef - at the Savoy. Alexander it was who chose the Hotel. Nobody on the bride's side had ever eaten a meal there. Frances was sure that her friends Grace, Kathleen and Mildred were almost as smitten with Alec as she was herself. For his part, he was attentive and charming, a perfect gentleman who was able to put everybody at perfect ease.

Their voyage to India would have to be their honeymoon, Alec said, as if in some regret. But Frances could not think of a more perfect honeymoon than on board a ship. They only had two weeks to get ready, and had much to do.

Alec informed Frances she would need inoculations. She was not pleased to hear this; she hated injections and everything to do with medicine. He accompanied her to the clinic. Frances' nose wrinkled at the smell of antiseptic and she went pale as she saw the injection prepared by the one of the two nurses.

'Oh, come now, if you're going to India, you're going to meet snakes and all sorts, so you shouldn't be nervous of a little injection,' said the nurse a little snappily.

'I am sorry,' Frances gasped. 'I've always hated needles.' She felt very foolish. *'Snakes?'* she said in alarm to Alec.

'Oh don't worry, they will be more frightened of you than you of them,' Alec said.

'Indeed I would not encourage her to be unafraid of them,' said the nurse in a very bossy voice, advancing toward her holding the syringe pointed toward her like a weapon. 'That's a very dangerous approach. I was in Africa during the War. You have to be always alert to your surroundings. You have to be careful where you step. Are you ready?' A pause. 'There you are, that didn't hurt you. Oh, Mrs. Whittier!' - this said in an annoyed tone.

Frances had fainted. Alec rubbed her hands, and she didn't hear his invective unleashed on the nurse, who was now saying that she had injected hundreds of people and none of them – none whatsoever – had reacted like that, as she retreated to the other side of the room where she had drawn up the injection.

Frances came to and felt very foolish indeed.

'And she's off to India,' said the nurse to the other, with some sarcasm.

'Oh shut up, Nurse Rook. You know well you frightened the life out of that poor young girl. Jealous, you are, because she's off out of freezing England to an adventure and a warm climate.'

The second nurse hurried to Frances with a glass of water, and said:

'Don't worry, Mrs. Whittier. It does happen lots of people. We had a Colonel here last week who served under Montgomery and he didn't even wait for the injection before he fainted dead away. He hit his head on the floor. Don't mind her.' (*whispering*) she just likes to boast about how brave she was in the war, how she was always one step ahead of danger. She hates it here, she'd be happy if the war was still on and she was living in a tent under the burning sun.'

Frances put the glass to her lips with shaking hands. Alec was muttering imprecations at the first nurse and threatening to report her.

'It's all right,' Frances said. 'I'm all right now.' She still felt wretched, but she mustered her strength and dignity and they left the clinic a few minutes later. She felt much better to be away from the antiseptic smell.

The shopping began - Alec had to buy several dozen cases of wine and other 'little luxuries that made living in the outpost bearable' to take with him, and Frances had to buy light blouses and skirts suitable for the Indian climate. A last trip to Stevenage to bid everybody goodbye, and it seemed that the whole world was at Liverpool to see all the passengers away. She could just make out her three best friends in the crowd on the deck, waving frantically to her. She wished the same for them as she had – each married to the man of her dreams.

She was delirious with happiness during the voyage. They danced every night, dined in style, mingled with other voyagers to India, who as she was a Bride, made her feel unique and special. She felt cherished and appreciated in a way that she hadn't dreamed she deserved. Her engagement ring – the proof of her husband's devotion – captivated her. She had never owned anything as beautiful or valuable, but it's worth for her lay completely in her bond with the giver, not in its monetary worth. Almost every day, Alec produced another piece of jewellery for her that he had purchased before the voyage – pearl earrings, a gold filigree necklace, an exquisite diamond seahorse brooch. They were all proofs of his love.

They went ashore at Gibraltar, Marseilles and Port Said, and at each place novelty and fascination awaited her as Alec guided her around the boisterous, alarming but captivating bazaars. She'd had no idea of anything outside of England, and this new world was one astounding surprise after another. She related all to Aunt Margaret in letters, and acutely missed her mother, longing to tell her about the ship, the ports and the voyage. But Alec's love was a compensation. She thought herself very fortunate indeed, and didn't mind that occasionally he seemed a little quiet – a few times, he went off by himself on the ship and she could not find him. Once she came upon him leaning on the rail gazing out to sea. He appeared to be in a world of his own. But he was happy to see her, and they went for a game of badminton.

CHAPTER 3 Assam, India

Frances arrived at her future home at the end of the monsoon season. Alec had told her to expect that there would be a big welcome for her, again she could only think of the silly thought she had had at odd moments on board ship. Like the second Mrs. De Winter in *'Rebecca'*, she felt Alec to be her superior in every way. She thought she was too simple and ignorant for him. She'd even wondered, with more amusement than dread, if a nasty housekeeper like Mrs. Danvers awaited her in Assam. Now on this searing October afternoon the resemblance to Daphne du Maurier's dark novel struck her again – here she was, being driven up a road with thick foliage on both sides, and there would be a crowd of people waiting for her in the house, for Alec had told her they would have at least ten servants. He rattled them off for her – equivalent to the English butler or housekeeper, was the Bearer. He would be in charge of the running of the household. He would also be his valet. There would be a cook, and his assistant, the *pani-wallah*, literally, a water-bearer. A maid, called an *ayah*, would be her personal maid. Another bearer to clean the house. A *dhobi* to wash the clothes. There were two gardeners - *malis*. Two guards to mind the house, called *chokidars*, one for night and one for day. And a few more servants might come and go as necessary, and she wasn't to be surprised to see any servant bring a relative around to help him. It was the way. They wouldn't knock like the servants at Home, and came and went in and out the rooms as they pleased. Frances had no doubt she'd need to be reminded of who was who in the house and who did what. It all sounded confusing! A personal maid, indeed! She hoped the maid, and the other servants, wouldn't think her silly or inexperienced.

The few days since they had disembarked the ship at Calcutta had been filled with new sights, noises, smells and vibrant colour. The railway stations were filled with activity, clatter, confusion and din. She stuck by Alec's side as he smoothly made his way through impossibly tight crowds to find the right platform, their luggage taken care of by several coolies, who balanced the loads on their heads as if they were the weight of feathers. The heat rushed over her – she felt she was in a sauna as they jostled and pushed their way along the platforms. The smells were frequently horrible – she often held her hand over her nose and mouth. She told herself sternly to ignore them but wondered if she would be able to get used to the constant assault on her nostrils. Alec was not bothered.

Frances' eyes never left the scenes unfolding before her as they made their way in a taxi to the Great Eastern Hotel. How could she ever have thought London to be the busiest city in the world! But she was distressed to see the abject poverty and extreme undernourishment of the people. Even worse than anything she had seen in wartime, in the midst of shortages of every kind.

Localsh Headquarters was located in Calcutta, and the next day she went with Alec and was introduced to everybody there. Everyone greeted him with warmth, and he presented the office with a few bottles of wine. The new Managing Director, Mr. Billingsworth, was away, so his bottle of Burgundy would await his return.

'Bit of a waste, really.' Alec said regretfully to Frances. 'I've heard that Billingsworth is a bit of a bumpkin. Some kind of dark bitter, I'm sure, is his poison. But never mind. He will know he has not been forgotten by the Honourable Alexander Whittier.'

They travelled First Class on the Assam Mail train with a cabin to themselves. It was very hot. She was surprised she slept so soundly with that and all the clanking and thudding. At mealtimes, the train halted for enough time to allow the passengers to disembark to eat. Alec was very careful about choosing her food – no salads, only fruit she could peel. No pink in chicken or meat. Boiled water only or a mineral straight from a sealed bottle. And mild spices, *korma*, which she found very hot to her European palate.

Disembarking at last sweaty and grimy at Sundarpur, a middle-sized town full of rickshaws, pedestrians and bicycles, they took a bicycle rickshaw to the Planter's Club. This building with tennis courts and a football field was the meeting place of all the Europeans – as all the white people were called no matter where they were from – for miles around. The hall and bar could be busy on Saturday nights, but today there was nobody but themselves. Alec sent a man in search of a bullock cart for their luggage, and a Club employee to go with the driver to take a *Very Important Chit* to Localsh Tea

Estate's *Boro Sahib*, Mr. Jamieson, and nobody else. He sat down to write it with a little smile, and read it aloud with a satisfied air after he had finished.

'Alastair! I am in Sundarpur, and I have very happy news. As expected, I was blessed with a bride, and she accompanies me. Her name <u>was</u> Miss Frances Mary Sullivan - now she bears the title of the Honourable Mrs. Whittier. I look forward to the welcome which I am sure will be ours upon our arrival later this evening, and I have instructed the bearer of this humble note to arrange for a car to be sent down, at the convenience of Localsh Tea, to convey us both to our new home. Yours, etc, Alexander.'

Frances would have preferred he had left out *the Honourable*, but she felt that Alec knew best.

They were able to freshen up in the Club, and have cool drinks and a meal, and a few hours later a Localsh jeep met them, with

the driver very pleased to see Alec and his
bride.

'I suppose there is a big Welcome party
tonight, Nath!' Alec said with enthusiasm as
they climbed into the back.

'I do not know, *sahib*, I know nothing of any
party.'

Alec seemed surprised. For her part, she felt
relief. She felt apprehensive of meeting
Alec's colleagues and their wives, and to
walk into a large noisy party where she
would be the centre of attention, was the last
thing she wished for that evening, when she
was tired from the journey. It would be quite
all right to put it off.

They passed several little roadside bazaars,
and after a half-an-hour they wound off the
rough trunk road to go through a large
wrought-iron gateway bearing the name
'LOCALSH TEA'. The gate was opened for
them by a man wearing the traditional Hindu
dhoti - a long loose white tunic and

billowing trousers. He waved and smiled his welcome and the gate shut behind them with a loud clank-clank.

As they drove on the bumpy dirt road, Frances saw expanses of orderly bushes of deep green on either side, their tops flat as tabletops, and all the same size so that every endless row looked like long dark green tables set end to end. They stretched in rows as far as the eye could see, up and down low hillsides, with scatterings of tall trees among them, like chaperones. Alec followed her eye. 'Yes, our tea bushes.' he confirmed before she had a chance to ask him. 'The tall trees you see among them are for shade. Do you see the white trunks?' She did. 'We paint them white, to keep the spiders from destroying them. Without those tall trees, the tea would be useless.'

About a mile up a winding slope they came to a compound with large factory-type buildings – this was where the picked tea was brought and processed to be made ready for export. They passed a few Indian men who stopped in their tracks, stared, and waved to Alec.

'The news will get about that we are back,' he said, in a satisfied way. *'Sahib and Memsahib Whittier.'*

They did not stop at the factory, but continued the grade uphill, and the bushes petered out as they came to an area of dense vegetation and trees with impossibly large leaves that seemed to push back and choke everything else around them. The road came to the top of the hill, turned and dipped suddenly, revealing a view of the tops of several large houses stretching for about a mile, accessible through large imposing gateways. The first one they passed was a two-storey white mansion, with balconies upstairs and verandahs downstairs, set in an expanse of lawns and trees.

'Mr. Jamieson's, the Superintendent's bungalow. He and his wife Marj live there.'

'That isn't a bungalow!'

'Oh, we call all the houses bungalows! Or rather *banglats*, which is the word that bungalow is derived from, I expect.'

'It reminds me of *Tara* in *Gone With the Wind*. A plantation house. It's so grand.'

'Oh, not really.' He sounded a little dismissive. Frances' eyes were still fixed upon it even as they left it behind them, and she saw a short, middle-aged woman in a light dressing-gown emerge onto the upstairs verandah and plant her two hands upon the rail, her eyes following the car as it went by. A tall man came behind her and gently turned her around to lead her back in.

A little curious, Frances thought.

Just then, Alec put his arm about her with eagerness and brought his face level with hers.

'There – there's our house – see – the grey bungalow. A proper bungalow, one level. But it's so large. You'll see.'

'Not so, *sahib*! You are *Banglat* Number Three!'

'It's Number Two, Nath. The senior manager always lives in Number Two. Turn in the gate, Nath, this gate, I tell you!'

'You are Number Three, *sahib*,' Nath drove past the gate of the long grey bungalow.

'What are you doing, Nath? Turn around, I say! Didn't you hear me? Bungalow Two!'

'No sir, you cannot be Two, because *Sahib Arkins* is in Two. I took all the clothes, curtains, linen – everything – books, records – even *memsahib*'s plants – even dug up flowers - there from Three to Two last week. *Boro Sahib* instructs me to take you to *Banglat* Number Three.' They drove another little way down the hill, until, almost hidden in a copse of high trees, Frances caught a glimpse of cornflower blue.

She sensed that all the joy of the moment had left Alec. He took his arms from her. He glowered. But Frances was too excited to mind his mood, though it was the first time she had seen him out of sorts. As they turned off the road and halted at the gate, her new home came fully into view. A bungalow behind a green lawn, but not like those in England. This was the length of six houses in Fairway Street, and had a low, thatched roof. It nestled between what she was to learn were acacia and palm trees. A verandah ran along the front, she saw an ornamental balustrade, and a riotous snowy gardenia finding its way cleverly through and around the openings. She had never seen a house with more charm.

A man ran up from within to open the gate and he gave a loud greeting: '*Sahib, Memsahib!*' as he watched the car turn into the driveway. He was dressed a little differently to the man at the main gate. He wore a Western-style shirt and the Muslim *lungi*, a sarong-like garment.

Frances looked about her after she got out of the car. Past the tops of the jungly trees on the road, she saw misty hilltops.

'Well, come on in!' Alec called to her as he made his way toward the house. There were several steps which led to the verandah. Frances hurried after him, almost in a dream.

The screen door leading from the verandah to the house itself banged shut after both of them and she found herself in a large, airy room, with a strong, sweet scent, and with quaint, but charming furniture. The first item she saw was a piano directly inside the verandah door. Her eyes were drawn then to a bouquet of white lilies placed prominently upon a long table at the far end of the room, and an envelope propped against it.

But there was no time to examine it now; people were streaming into the room from another door leading to the back, these were the servants, male and female, clad in native dress, headed by the bearer. He wore all-white and his name was Anwar. They greeted the newly-wed couple with enthusiasm and Frances relaxed in their obvious joy at seeing her. The two women servants came up next to her and took the material of her dress at the shoulder between their fingers, evidently admiring it. This invasion of privacy was a little disconcerting, but she endured it; it must be their way. She smiled shyly at them. They seemed to like her on sight; that was a relief.

'Lemon water, *sahib*?' asked Anwar, after he shooed everybody off, now that they had had their adventure of meeting the new *memsahib*.

'Yes, Anwar – but I thought *Sahib* Arkins was living here, why the change? Do you know anything?' Alec had lit a cigarette and was pacing up and down.

'How would I know, *sahib*? I am told – you – *Sahib* Whittier will live here, so I get everything ready for you, and had the charge of moving all your belongings from the bachelor *banglat* for *you*. I do not know why this or that, you have to ask *Boro Sahib*. I hope you will find everything in good order, *sahib*, and nothing broken in the move.'

Frances had opened the envelope addressed to them, and read the note inside it aloud.

*'Dear Mr. and Mrs. Whittier – Welcome!
We are to get word when you arrive, and will drop in as soon as you have had time to settle in – about an hour later.
Mike and Lydia'*

'I have to see about this,' Alec was saying, 'this won't do.'

'Who are they, Alec?'

'Hmm?'

She read the note for him again.

'Mike and Lydia live in Bungalow Four – or at least they did when I was leaving for England.' He sounded a little bitter.

'It's a lovely house!' Frances was wandering into the large verandah, which she hadn't taken any notice of as she had passed through to the lounge. 'Oh it's cooler out here! Oh Alec, do come out here, I love this place!'

CHAPTER 4 Neighbours in Tea

Frances had a bath and put on fresh, clean clothes before her neighbours arrived. The Finches were a couple in their late twenties. Lydia had bright blue eyes and a dark fringe peeping from under her hat. Her khaki shirt-waist dress was old-fashioned but it had a loose and comfortable look. Her husband was a strapping fellow about six-feet two. He was in long slacks and a short-sleeved shirt and a wide-brimmed hat. Lydia carried a large plant with long striped leaves and spectacular reddish-orange flowers.

'It looks so exotic. What is it called?' Frances asked. 'I have to confess I know very little about plants.'

'I'm sure you'll learn very quickly! One does! This is a canna. It likes shade rather than full sun. It's easy to grow, hard to kill, the kind of plant I like best,' Lydia replied. 'Where shall I put it? What about in that corner?' she had a bouncy step and an easy manner and Frances took an immediate liking to her.

'Oh, and don't deadhead it. It will ruin the blooms for next year. There, how does it look? Or would you like it somewhere else?'

'I quite like it there, visible from the sitting-room too, I would say.'

'We call it a lounge, don't ask me why. Mike, the champers! We have to drink a toast!'

Her husband produced a bottle of champagne from a cloth bag.

'Oh, please sit down.' Frances realised suddenly that this was her house, and she was the hostess.

'We've been saving it since last Christmas. And I know it's coals to Newcastle; how many cases did you bring back this time?' asked Mike, grinning.

'Not enough. Dreadfully expensive. With the war over four years, one would think prices would have come down. By the way, have I been demoted since I was promoted? I seem to find myself in the junior manager's house.'

The couple looked a little awkwardly at one another before Mike leaned a little forward in his bamboo chair.

'The promotion was not a sure thing, old boy, was it? These things never are until all the paperwork is done - i's dotted and t's crossed and about ten signatures. Arkins was not altogether happy when he heard that you were in the running. He has seniority. He went over Jamieson's head.'

'And they no doubt listened to him. I was assured that post before I left. Everything except the formalities. And *Old Boro Sahib* went along with it, well I know where I stand.'

'I wouldn't take it out on Jamieson, old boy. His hands were tied. He rather had to explain to Billingsworth why you were offered this in the first place, over Arkins, and they can't have been satisfied.'

'There's one bottle of Burgundy I am sorry I parted with,' Alec said, stubbing out his cigarette. ''39 was a bad year in any case. No loss I suppose.'

'Good or bad years don't make any difference to anybody except you,' was Mike's rejoinder, while Lydia said: 'We appreciate any year we can come by.' She giggled at Frances. 'I'm afraid people drink a lot more here than at Home.'

But Alec was not to be cheered.

'And it's very embarrassing for me to arrive back with my new bride who thinks she married a senior manager and will be living in a superior bungalow, not one like this with a thatched roof and chipped paint.'

'Oh darling, it doesn't matter one whit to me!' Frances cried. 'I think everything is beautiful!'

'It matters to me.' Alec said in a rather clipped tone.

'All the exterior paint chips in the monsoon,' Lydia explained to Frances. 'And oh! This is the only house on the estate with a piano, so you are rather lucky in that way, that's if you like a piano.'

'I am very lucky then,' Frances said, even happier. 'I don't play, but I hope others do.'

Alec was silent.

'So what else has changed since I left?' he asked a little sullenly.

'Oh, we had a *hartal*. There were some agitators about the Labour. They got everybody worked up. And you know *Boro Sahib* doesn't have quite the presence you have, when they need placating. He has an imposing way, but falls short on charm. Arkins has neither. It took three days to get everybody back to work.'

'What, a *hartal*, and three days without production? That's untenable.'

'A strike,' said Lydia to Frances, in an aside. 'A *hartal* is a strike.'

Mike continued. 'The leaders were seen off, and I hope they won't be back. If they do, it will be next plucking season, so we are all right for the Cold Weather. Jamieson paid the police a bit more *baksheesh* than usual to come and arrest them. They held them for a few days, knocked them around a bit and told them to get out. *Communists*. Nobody wants communists.'

'Paid the police?' Frances asked, wide-eyed. She knew what *baksheesh* was. It referred to money given into the hand. Beggars had already asked her for *baksheesh* along the way. It appeared to mean a bribe as well.

'Oh, chaps, please don't go on about agitators on Frances' first day!' cried Lydia, then, turning to her, said:

'I'm dying to know how you and Alec met! And please do tell me about your wedding! What was your dress like? I hope you have photographs!'

As Mike and Alec continued to talk of agitators and *hartals*, Frances related all. To her delight Lydia was very eager to hear and asked dozens of questions. She thought it very romantic to meet one's spouse on a train, and was very sympathetic to hear that her mother had died rather unexpectedly, and was charmed by the account of the wedding and the voyage out.

Lydia asked Alec if he had carried Frances over the threshold and berated him when he said that he had quite forgotten! Lydia insisted he do it before they left, and they all went outside. And so to their hearty applause, and with the servants watching with loud acclaim from the side (for somebody had somehow overheard the plan and hurried to fetch everybody) he picked Frances up in his arms and carried her up the steps.

The Finches departed for their home after that. Frances went to see about unpacking her suitcases. She could not find them. She was surprised to find it had all been done, the servants had opened her cases and put everything away, and stashed the cases somewhere. Her books had been placed in the bookcase, and she was very pleased to see that there were some books there already, including a full set of Jane Austen and some modern novelists, Angela Thirkell and others.

Alec was cross to hear that Bungalow Three had no fridge. One would have to be ordered immediately from Calcutta, and would take weeks to arrive. Bungalows One and Two had fridges; it was very annoying. And – how were they to eat tonight? Thankfully Anwar had taken it upon himself to do some marketing, the table was laid nicely, and a dinner of fish and rice was placed before them, with side dishes of garlic spinach and small boiled potatoes.

They drank to their future together and took their tea on the verandah. Localsh tea, of course. The verandah was enclosed in mesh, but so fine that it in no way obscured the view of the garden, the trees on either side and the jungle across the road.

They were joined for a short time by the only bachelor on the estate, Tom Robertson, a stocky, muscular young man with a sunburned face and loud laugh who also brought a gift, a bottle of Scotch. There was no sign of the other two couples – Mr and Mrs. Jamieson and Mr. and Mrs. Arkins. Alec was offended by this, but Frances thought that they were just allowing them to settle in.

Everything was so different to an English house! Little lizards ran up the walls, cheeping. Alec said they were *tic-tics* and harmless. They ate insects so they were useful. Outside, the sun dipped behind the distant hills, and she smelled curries and fragrant flowers, all mixed together. Birds chorused in the trees. There was children's laughter, the snorting and bleating of animals, and the cackling of fowl. Alec explained that the servants and their families lived in houses around the back. She heard the sounds of drums and music from afar. Then all fell silent in the darkness. The stars seemed very near and millions of fireflies danced before her eyes.

This is my home now, she said to herself, and again, marvelled that this was not a dream.

She awoke in the darkness later to the frantic barking of a pack of dogs who seemed to be gathered all together under the window, and she shook Alec awake. They were jackals, and were not at all as near as they sounded. She found their high-pitched barking spine-chilling in the dead of night like that. Alec assured her they would not be seen or heard during the day. Before he drifted to sleep again, he said: 'If you hear a trumpeting sound, it'll be a wild elephant, but don't be alarmed, if he does get through the gate, he'll just trample a few plants and go away again.'

'What about the *chok* – the man who is on guard? Won't he stop him or frighten him away?'

'Das the *chokidar*? He sleeps. An entire herd wouldn't wake Das. Goodnight, Fan.'

73

What a strange new world I have come to, she thought again to herself after the sound died away – they must have been on the move - as she fell asleep again. Everything thrilled her, except for the mosquitoes.

CHAPTER 5 'Nuton Memsahib!'

Since she had arrived in India, Frances felt that every inch of her person was covered in mosquito bites. Even areas she thought were sufficiently covered by her clothes had itchy, red bumps. The verandah's fine mesh was not enough to keep all at bay. Persistent little pests found their way in just the same. Alec said that they loved new people and devoured them.

She woke the following morning to a loud hooter. The factory, perhaps? She turned to Alec and found that had already arisen. She had not heard a sound.

After saying her Morning Offering and dressing, she emerged into the lounge, wondering about breakfast. The dining table was bare. She ventured to the door in the back of the lounge, and found that it led into a narrow room she thought must be part of the kitchen. She saw a plain wooden table and cabinets and cupboards. Anwar came through a door opposite, and seemed surprised to see her.

'The verandah, *memsahib*, the verandah, please. This is the bottle room.'

'The bottle room, yes.' she said vaguely. Bewildered, she went to the verandah as bidden and found the small round table there covered in a white cloth and neatly laid for two.

'Where is my husband?' she asked Anwar, feeling silly that she didn't know.

'At the factory, *memsahib*! You will wait for him, yes?'

'Of course!'

'He will come very soon.'

Anwar was correct. Alec had to get up to give the orders for the day at the factory, but he returned for breakfast. They enjoyed an astonishingly good spread of tea, toast and butter, marmalade, and fried duck eggs. A plate of cut pineapple and mango was very refreshing – it was already very hot.

Alec, dressed in casual slacks and short-sleeved shirt and with a *sola topi* – a hat made of plant pith – he had purchased one for her also in the Army and Navy Stores in Calcutta, for everyone wore them - left again for work directly afterwards. He kissed her goodbye and said he would return for lunch; she should explore the house and talk to the servants about what she wanted them to do.

What she wanted them to do! She had never in her life asked anybody to do anything! Happily, they all seemed to know what to do, and Anwar proposed the menu for the day, but, he said, she needed to give him some items from the go-down.

'You know where the keys are, *memsahib*?'

Oh, no! But it was all right, he knew where the keys were, but told her that he could not help himself to any goods for the house, she had to distribute them. The go-down, she found, was a small storehouse filled with dry goods. Anwar had stocked up all he could before their arrival, he had flour, rice, sugar and salt and other basics available in Sundarpur. In Calcutta she and Alec had ordered tins of soup and vegetables, jars of preserves and other non-perishable items, soaps and other toiletries. They would arrive soon. But she drew back in horror when she saw black creepy-crawlies on the shelves. Cockroaches! Would she really have to come here every day?

The kitchen was a small, stone hut standing by itself outside the back door, with a cook named Joseph, dressed in a white vest and trousers, pounding dough on a table. Near his feet, a youth was sitting on the ground cutting vegetables on a stationary arc-shaped blade. Beside him was a basket of fruit and vegetables, obviously next to be chopped.

There was an ancient brick oven fired with sticks. Upon it, a blackened kettle hissed steam from its spout. A row of shelves held several dented, battered pots. Canvas bags of flour, sugar and other dry goods sat upon the floor. She opened one – the one containing flour, and beheld little moving creatures making merry there. She quickly closed it again and looked around. Beside her was a deep sink that may have once been white. But now it was a brown-greyish colour, and cockroaches ran around inside. Did her food really come from here? It was disgusting! When Joseph caught her eye, he frowned and said something in his own language, and his tone was a little accusing.

'He is asking you if everything is all right,' Anwar explained.

'Where do you keep the meat?' she asked, feeling that her voice was a shriek, as she espied more cockroaches around the pipework from the sink.

As if in answer, a hen clucked outside the small window. Anwar motioned her to follow him. Sure enough, there was a hen-house with three or four fowl there, and a tank nearby in which several fish were swimming. Joseph had not come outside and she could hear him thumping the dough in the kitchen. She hoped he wasn't angry with her.

Anwar next led her a little away from the house, behind a screen of trees, to a haphazard collection of small white stone huts which were the servants' quarters. Toddlers wandered about among a collection of hens and goats. Every hut had a vegetable garden and some of the women were working there. Anwar introduced her to his wife, Fatima, who emerged from the largest hut with her two small children. She had obviously been anticipating this because in contrast to the other women who were

79

wearing thin cotton saris, her sari looked very dressy and she wore lipstick and jewellery. The children were dressed up as well.

Frances greeted them with smiles but inside she felt very awkward and overwhelmed. Were she and Alec responsible for the welfare of all these people? The other women now stopped their work and stared and smiled. *'Memsahib! Nuton memsahib!'* they called. She supposed *nuton* meant new. A few months ago she was a schoolgirl. Now she felt astounded that she was considered worthy of notice and even had a certain status. She did not feel in the least comfortable. She felt very ill-prepared for her new role.

Anwar continued his briefing. Every day, a jug of milk was brought up from the Lines – the village where the Tea Garden Labour lived - and boiled. Cheese, she learned, was not to be had very often, but butter was made with the milk.

'Why are there ants in the flour?' She couldn't get her mind away from the fauna in the kitchen.

'They are weevils, *memsahib*'. Anwar informed her. 'It is always like this, always there are weevils in the flour. Every *banglat*. *Boro Mem*'s *banglat*!' He waved his hand in the direction of the superior bungalows. *Boro Mem* was Mrs. Jamieson, she knew.

Joseph came out of the kitchen and asked something rather fiercely of Anwar and hearing the reply, the cook glared. Eyes flashing, he beckoned Frances inside, picked up the ball of dough and held it out to her, speaking rapidly, gesturing wildly with his other hand.

'He wants to know if you see any weevil in the dough,' Anwar translated.

'No – no of course I don't,' Frances said feebly.

Joseph then promptly produced a fine sieve, in which a heap of weevils lay, squirming all together. Intended to reassure her, the sight made her feel sickish. Afraid it showed in her expression, she made good her escape, muttering 'I'm sorry - thank you,' while Joseph set the sieve down again with a loud clatter.

'I will bring you tea - to the verandah, please, *memsahib*,' Anwar seemed to understand her discomfort, and was maneuvering her back to her rightful place, the front of the house, where *memsahibs* belonged, well away from the work area.

After her tea, she explored a little more. The verandah went around three sides of the house. Several doors along its length led to the bedrooms. Every bedroom had a private bathroom. The water from the taps was brackish, but Alec had told her it was perfectly fine for bathing. Their own room was very large and had old, but good, rosewood furniture. The lounge had long couches cushioned in blue. The large table at the far end had ten chairs. That frightened her. Would she be expected to give dinner parties? Thank God she had a cook, though how he could cook for a dinner party in that little hut was beyond her. She knew nothing about cooking. Still, she would be expected to be the perfect hostess, and was fearful that Mrs. Jamieson most probably would be difficult to please.

Everything was different and new, there were even sheets of large canvas under the ceilings. She saw movement above it, and darkish shadows, and realised that its purpose was to keep the thatch fauna out of sight. There was an entire world above those sheets. The battle against insect life appeared to be relentless!

Trying to forget the insects, she walked about in every room. They needed curtains and rugs and other soft furnishings, and she imagined what they would be like when they were decorated according to her own taste. She expunged the kitchen from her mind. This was a sunny, delightful house. Having nothing to do after her walkabout, she went into her bedroom to arrange some things there, but Rosa, the junior bearer, was sweeping it out, so she left again. Without housework to do, what was she going to do all day? She couldn't possibly read all day, that would be utterly lazy!

As if in answer to her question, there was a friendly 'halloo!' from outside, and she saw Lydia making her way to her, in a pair of shorts and blowsy top, carrying two tennis racquets.

CHAPTER 6 Wanted: Sense of Humour

There were tennis and badminton courts up the hill, in full view of the windows of Bungalow One, so that Frances wondered if Mrs. Jamieson was looking out at her in disapproval. She wasn't sure why the *Boro Memsahib* might disapprove, but it seemed to her that she would. That brief glimpse of her that she had gotten looking from her balcony – her hands gripping the rails - her husband drawing her inside - gnawed at her. *Boro Memsahib* was unhappy. Alec had expected there to be a welcoming party last evening; and was very put out that there had not been one arranged, but in view of what had transpired with the promotion, it might not have been at all enjoyable, but very tense, so perhaps it was just as well.

'Don't push me too hard,' Lydia said cheerily as they took their sides. 'I'm older than you, *and* I'm expecting a baby!'

After three very leisurely games, she went to Lydia's home, very curious about what it was like. It was very similar to her own, but more homely. Lydia's little girl Lucy came out holding the hand of her ayah, a sweet-looking woman in a white sari. Frances liked children; her next-door neighbour had three, and she used to look after them for pocket-money.

Lydia had grown up in India, had gone Home for schooling for twelve long years, during which she saw her mother twice and her father only once. She would send her own daughter to school next year when she was six. Frances thought that was a dreadful custom, but said nothing. Apparently it was the norm. Lydia had returned to India when she was eighteen, and met her husband, a young planter fresh from Scotland. He had had to leave the Tea industry in order to get married to avoid the 10-year rule, and then Lydia's father had employed him. Many of the tea planters were from Scotland.

Frances had a hundred questions for Lydia about how to run a house, but held her tongue for now. Lydia was a new acquaintance and she didn't want her to form the opinion that she was helpless. The myriad of questions she had could wait, but she had to ask her about curtains for the windows and the weevils in the flour.

'Oh what a pity you didn't bring material with you – what is available in Sundarpur might be rather limited and – *colourful*. But never mind – you can look at a catalogue – Mrs. Jamieson had the latest one delivered the other day - and order them from *Timothy White's* in Calcutta. I will help you, it will be terrific fun.'

And insects were a fact of life in Assam. She'd get used to the cockroaches, they never climbed on you. You could sleep on the floor and they would detour around you rather than take a shortcut across your head or chest. She laughed, and Frances knew she would have to find it in her to laugh as well. Somehow she'd have to find a sense of humour like Lydia, to deal with new, annoying and especially the endless creeping things. They came with the heat, and she already loved the sunshine. It was almost lunchtime; and the men were expected home, so Frances made her way to her bungalow.

Alec was not in very good humour. He had seen Old Jamieson and had it out with him.

He'd made the excuse that his hands had been tied.

'We're invited to their house tonight for dinner,' Alec said. 'The Arkins' and Finches and Robertson will be there. Wear something nice, and good jewellery – but not the diamond seahorse – I notice you are very fond of it, but it's just asking to be lost or stolen. I think we should put that in the safe – and perhaps your emerald ring too.'

'My engagement ring!' she said in astonishment.

'It would be better,' he said. 'Wear the one I got you in Port Said. It's not as valuable.' It was indeed a very tasteful ring, an amythest. But the emerald was her engagement ring, how could she not wear it?

It was a strange request, but he knew best, so she handed over the emerald and the diamond seahorse.

'I saw the servants' quarters,' she told him. 'They live in huts! So poor! So small!'

'Much better than what the tea estate labourers have. It's actually a big thing to live in a stone house, no matter how humble it may look. Oh by the way, you have to decide the menu every day, just like in England, all right? Joseph knows how to do a lot of English dishes, by the way.' He looked down at the fish and rice and spinach. 'This is what we get if you don't give the orders,' he joked. 'Begin tomorrow.'

It was the custom to go for a nap after lunch, and she was surprised she slept soundly, and Alec thumped her playfully to wake her. He was going back to work until the evening. When he returned, it was with a bottle of Burgundy for the Jamiesons. They were, he said, on good terms again, it had been foolish of him to expect the promotion and foolish of Old Jamieson to have offered it. Nonetheless, he wasn't getting a 1945, which was a great year – a '39 would fit the bill very well. But they had shaken hands and agreed to forget it, and if Frances liked the house, he would as well.

'I love the house, Alec!' she said. 'I can't imagine anything nicer!'

'Well, you are easy to please, aren't you!' was his response, but she felt he was happy as well.

Frances put on a new white linen dress and wrapped a lightweight violet stole about her shoulders - the new ring went nicely with everything and they set off. Alec had retrieved his car from the factory shed where it had spent the summer. It was an impressive vehicle, a silver Humber, and it had belonged to the Army, but had been little used and he had bought it for a song. They drove the short distance up to Bungalow One.

'Oh dear, you are covered in bites,' was Mrs. Jamieson's greeting to her, staring at her arms, and in what Frances thought was a rather accusatory tone. 'But never mind, I suppose you don't have any Caladryl. You should always have Caladryl.'

Yesterday Frances had seen a small fat middle-aged woman, now she surveyed her at close range. She was much better looking that she had imagined. Her pointed, regular features still had prettiness. Frances could almost imagine her a Bright Young Thing of the 1920's, dancing and flirting. But after this remark she bustled away and seated herself on a sofa. Frances felt the rudeness of it.

Mr. Jamieson was also aloof, but gracious and gentlemanly. He it was who introduced her to the Arkins' as the Honourable Mrs. Whittier.

Mr. Arkins – Duncan – was a small round man with a glass of whiskey in his hand. He said nothing, only stared at the newcomer as if he had not seen an unfamiliar face for years. His wife Edith had short fair hair and horn-rimmed spectacles. She greeted Frances with a very serious *'how do you do'*, before rather flatly congratulating her upon her marriage. Then she turned to sit beside Mrs. Jamieson and they talked together in low tones, drinking sherry.

Frances was very relieved to see the Finches and Tom Robertson there.

The *Boro Sahib*'s bungalow was palatial. They even had a chandelier hanging from the ceiling. Dinner was very formal, with Royal Doulton china, and Frances hoped she was making Alec proud of her. She had never attended a formal evening dinner before, and she sensed that this was even more formal than many in England. A full silver service, a fine candelabra, and the ladies well-dressed and gentlemen in suits and bow-ties. How strange it was, here thousands of miles from Britain, in what was now an independent country, that they were so British.

'What do you think of Joseph?' asked Mrs. Arkins, leaning across the table to Frances as they were eating dessert. It was the first time either of the two women had addressed her since they had been introduced.

'I have only had dinner last night and lunch today, and they were quite all right,' Frances said cautiously.

'I should warn you. He is very sensitive. He's Christian, you know, so he will cook beef *and* pork. So don't make an enemy of him.'

'I'm sure I won't.'

'Good cooks are terribly difficult to find.'

'Thank you, I'm sure I won't find any fault with him at all.'

'Oh come now, Mrs. Whittier, we heard something,' Mrs. Jamieson interposed, flicking her eyes in her direction at last. 'Servants talk, and word gets about! Oh, what would one give to have the staff of the old days! When I came out in 1922, they were very loyal.'

'What was it you heard?' Frances asked, alarmed.

The other diners were engaged in a conversation of their own, and so it was only the three of them.

'The word was that you did not much care for the kitchen,' said Mrs. Arkins. 'Indeed, that was *my* kitchen, for four years, and while it may not have had the conveniences of every mod con you get in England, it was a kitchen I was always proud of.'

'Indeed, Edith, we had many a wonderful dinner produced from your kitchen,' said Mrs. Jamieson.

'*Thank* you, Marjorie' said Edith Arkins, turning her head decidedly toward Mrs. Jamieson. 'I wanted him to move with me to Bungalow Two, but he refused. He likes the stove better in Three. It's quite a superior kitchen.'

Frances was mortified. She felt the best course would be to say nothing, and allow the subject to drop. They trooped onto the verandah and were served tea there.

Alec was in wonderful form. He looked very handsome in his newly-pressed white suit, smoking an Embassy, regaling the company with news of England – he'd attended two of the cricket tests with New Zealand, seen weather forecasts on a television set in a Hotel, and other snippets the men were interested in.

But Frances was silent. The two older women made no attempt to engage her in conversation, and the Finches left directly after dinner because Lydia was tired. She entertained herself by soaking up the evening sounds - loud birdsong, aromas of burning incense and again the sounds of clucking hens and bleating goats. Again she heard children's happy voices. Her first day in Assam had been an avalanche of new experiences, sensations, and feelings. And a little unpleasantness with the people with whom she would have to spend a great deal of time in the future. Mrs. Jamieson and Mrs. Arkins did not like her; did not approve of her at all. It was rather upsetting, really.

CHAPTER 8 Tea Factory

Frances had already learned that what she loved most about India was the warmth that never seemed to go away, not even at night. In the morning she rose to a warm room, and if it might get just a little too hot in the middle of the day, it was very bearable. She had always been what her mother called 'a cold creature' always colder than everybody. In winter, she had suffered from chilblains. As a small child in school, where the heat was very variable, she'd even cried from the cold of her feet. Like many other people in that horrible winter two years before, she'd never been warm enough.

On her second morning when she jumped out of bed it was like jumping into a warm bath. She loved it! She didn't even need shoes when she went about; the floors were warm under her feet, and she went without until she almost stepped upon a cockroach.

It was time to explore the grounds of her new home. She walked to the gate and turning around, her eyes roved over the front of the bungalow. It had a relaxed, laid-back look, homely and welcoming. Tall, flowering trees marked the perimiter of the garden, and masses of sunny orange and yellow marigolds grew at their feet. Clusters of drooping purple orchids marked every corner. She wandered about and disturbed a colourful bird who flew out of one tree and into another, emitting a screech.

'Parakeet, *memsahib*.' She had been joined by Anwar and his little son.

The little boy was a fount of information, enlightening her as to the names of the trees and plants. In the back, there was a pineapple and a mango grove, and a row of banana plants, their large and spreading leaves creating shady areas. All in all, the back garden looked rather jungly, but in an organized way, and she thought it perfect. A fenced-off area had a kitchen garden, there was little there now – it appeared that Mrs. Arkins had ordered it picked clean before she left. Frances wondered hazily if she could become a good gardener. She was now living in the country!

Another little boy came from Bungalow Four. Smiling, he held out a note.

'Chit, chit, *memsahib*!' It was a note from Lydia. She was feeling rather tired, and could Frances come up maybe, and keep her company for a while?

She found Lydia in bed with the curtains full-drawn, waiting for Dr. Lane to come from Sundarpur. 'Doctor *Babu* – that's the Estate Doctor - is busy with three malaria cases. Oh, *Babu* is not his name – it's a title. Mike thought the surname *Babu* was very common until I enlightened him, so now I tell everybody who is new.'

'I hope it wasn't the tennis yesterday.' Frances began, but Lydia waved her worry aside.

'Nonsense, exercise is wonderful. No, it's a headache – it's the heat – I know it. I had it with Lucy. I hear a car. It might be Dr. Lane.'

Lydia introduced her to the old weatherbeaten gentleman who, just as he would in England, carried a bag. She amused herself by taking a stroll in the garden while Lydia was being examined.

'I just stayed around to see if I could get you anything,' she said after the doctor had left, in case Lydia had thought she was just being curious about her condition.

'Oh, no, I don't need anything, but thank you just the same. Actually, Dr. Lane wants me to rest a great deal, and stay cool, if that's possible. It should cool down soon, though. A little. The winter here will become like our summer in England. We call it the Cold Weather, though it isn't cold really, just nippy at night. He gave me some tablets for my head. Actually - Frances - there is one thing you could do for me – can you read to me for a bit? I am so bored. I have *Gone With the Wind,* and haven't even started it. Do you mind? You can open the curtain for light; I'm going to close my eyes.'

Frances assented readily, and settled down to read aloud. Lydia fell asleep after a bit, so she put the book down and was preparing to go, when Lydia said:

'Frances? I'm so happy you're here. I think we can be good friends, can't we? I know it can be hard to settle in. Anything you want, just ask, all right?'

'That's very kind of you, Lydia, and I appreciate it. I can come up and read you more of the book, maybe? I'm quite intrigued with *Gone With the Wind*, already! I saw the film, but it's not going to spoil it, it seems there's so much more in the book.'

'I wish I could see the film. Perhaps it will come to the Club someday. Were the dresses gorgeous?'

Frances described Scarlett O'Hara's crinolines as best as she could recall, and then she walked back to her bungalow with a light heart. She was happily married, she had a lovely home and an enchanting garden, a new and exciting life, and a new friend. She missed her mother and Aunt Margaret very much at times. But she felt very grateful for having met Alec and fallen in love with him – and he with her. He still hadn't said the 'three little words' but she was sure they would come.

In the afternoon, Alec proposed that he take her to see the factory and meet the staff there. They set off in the Humber after their lie-down.

'As you go about the Estate you will see - a light complexion here and there. It's best not to ask any questions.' he advised her.

'I wouldn't dream of it,' Frances protested, after a pause during which she tumbled upon what his meaning was.

'Because you know – bachelors get lonely, and do silly things.'

'Oh my – not you I hope!'

'I have no children. Well, not yet.' He smiled at her. 'Do you know that a planter has to have permission from the Company to get married?'

'No, I was not aware of that, it doesn't seem fair, does it?'

'It's ridiculous.'

102

'How did you ask permission? Did you telegraph?'

'I didn't ask permission; I knew I had permission before I left for Europe.'

'And how did you know you would be successful in finding a wife?' Frances chuckled.

'I was not about to return without a wife,' he said. 'But – they were expecting somebody else – Mrs. Jamieson's young step-sister. She visited here last Christmas and put her eye on me, and everybody thought it was all wrapped up. But I didn't like her at all. Well, here we are!'

Frances had no time to think about this interesting and rather serious snippet of information.

The Factory was noisy and busy, and Frances noticed that all three young secretaries, Mary, Victoria and Kitty had that light complexion which Alec had spoken of. They welcomed her with smiles;

Mary and Victoria were particularly warm. Alec showed her around with obvious pride and explained how the plucked leaf ended up dried and ready to be packaged.

The large baskets of leaves which were brought in twice per day were poured onto a large table to wither for several hours, then they were taken to a machine that 'rolled' or 'twisted' them to break up the cells in the leaf – it had to be watched carefully, for too much or too little would result in a bad taste. Timing was very important. There was a fresh, pungent aroma from the freshly twisted leaves. She breathed it in and savoured it, for the factory itself was darkish and the machinery whirred and clanked loudly, but yet it had the smell of newly cut grass, but more fragrant. Almost a 'tea' smell.

She had already heard phrases like 'first flush' and 'oxidation' and supposed she was to learn in time what it all meant. Drying the twisted leaves followed…then several women were engaged in sorting and grading them to different types of tea after which tasting had to take place.

Duncan Arkins was an accomplished taster. She watched the process; a row of small freshly-brewed cups of tea with different colours and strengths awaited him on a table and he went from one to the next, swirling the liquid about his palate before spitting it into a bin on wheels that a labourer moved along to keep pace with him, frowning a little at one, nodding in satisfaction at another, muttering once the words: 'middle palate.'

The next room held the leaves, now looking like real tea leaves, in hillocks on the floor, and several men were packing them into tightly-bound packets for shipment that very evening, by night train to Calcutta, where their destiny was to be poured into the silvery blue bags bearing the caption 'Localsh Quality Tea' and the logo which was a Camellia Sinensis leaf.

CHAPTER 9 *The Piano*

She walked back to her house on her own, slowly savouring all she had seen from the car two days before. She had overcome her horror of meeting a snake, but she remembered the bossy nurse's admonition to Alec that one had to watch one's step. So she did. She did not know what to do after she returned; but decided to try the piano. She had several music books and brought them all out and put them into the piano stool. She tried to learn a Strauss waltz, but the piano was out of tune, which made her efforts a succession of discordant chords with long pauses between each. She was almost sure she heard Rosa and Preti giggle from the the 'bottle-room' – rather like a butler's pantry, it was where the cleaning and polishing were done. She gave up and began a letter to Grace instead. But she was interrupted by the sound of a vehicle and went to the verandah to see a white car halt, and the day *chokidar*

Mohammed – the man who had opened the gate yesterday - open its back door to allow the passenger to alight.

A young Indian woman in a brightly-coloured sari was coming to visit, and she stopped and stared in amazement when she saw Frances. Her dark eyes were like saucers.

'*But you are not Vera!*' she cried. 'You – where is Mrs. Whittier?' her eyes darted behind Frances to the verandah door in expectation.

'I am Mrs. Whittier,' Frances said, smiling. 'My name is Frances Whittier.'

'Wife of Alexander, no. You must be his sister, yes? You said *Miss* Whittier - ?'

'*Mrs*. Whittier. I am Alexander Whittier's wife.'

The woman seemed stunned, then she covered her mouth in embarrassed laughter at her mistake, and apologised profusely, after which she introduced herself as Mrs. Laksmi Dutta, from the neighbouring Farah tea estate. She had an energetic, lively air, and, the mistaken identity over, talked to Frances as if she had known her all her life. Her English was perfect. She brought cakes and sweets and a wedding gift, a set of six placemats, white with embroidered green elephants with their trunks reaching up to the tops of high palm trees. They were exquisite. Frances was very grateful, even if they had been meant originally for Vera. She warmed quickly to her visitor, all the more so when she found out that Lakshmi, though Hindu, had attended a Catholic school run by Irish nuns. She knew a great deal about Catholicism and told Frances that there was Mass on Sundays in Sundarpur Mission Chapel. Lakshmi was very chatty, and looked around quite unabashedly at the verandah and then walked into the lounge, and remarked that if she needed any help with furnishings, she knew the best shops in Sundarpur and would make sure she got a fair price. She left after half-an-hour, refusing tea, but drinking a glass of lemon water, and extracted a promise from Frances that she would go to see her. Nath knew the way to her house, and she got into the car saying that she should put Caladryl on her mosquito bites. And rub the inside of a banana peel on new bites.

What did it matter, Frances thought, mindlessly scratching her bites now that she had been reminded of them, as she watched the white car leave the driveway, if the two old bats in Bungalows One and Two didn't like her? She had only been here two days, and she had two friends already – Lydia and Lakshmi.

When Alec returned for dinner, she told him of her visitor. He knew the Duttas. The Farah Tea Estate had been sold to an Indian company soon after Independence. Mr. Dutta was a junior manager. They were nice people, and it was very good of her to call upon Mrs. Whittier, and seemed amused when Frances said that she was taken aback to see her. His mind then went to other matters more interesting to him – now that he was back, the Finches were taking off on a short leave, to Shillong, the following morning.

'It's because of Lydia,' Frances told him. 'She isn't feeling well.'

'Well you are a little ferret, aren't you! Not here two days, and you know more than me about the matter! In that case, Mike would probably come back alone in a fortnight, leaving her and the child there.'

'She'll be there alone!' said Frances.

'No, not really. She has cousins. Mark married into a tribe of Stuarts, all in Tea or some other venture. She'll be well-taken care of.'

Frances was a little dismayed though, at the thought of having to do without Lydia for some time. She had looked forward to their going shopping together, and discussing

Gone With The Wind, and who was going to answer the millions of questions she had about setting up house here in Assam?

CHAPTER 10 *Sundarpur*

The following day Lakshmi came to see her again in her white car. Would she like to go to town?

She was thrilled at the invitation, and got her hat and her handbag, and within five minutes was taking the road to Sundarpur. Frances mentioned that she would like to look at some curtain material, and Lakshmi said that she knew the best place. They entered the most colourful street Frances had ever seen, a street splashed with arrays of vividly dyed fabrics visible through its open shopfronts, almost mesmerizing to the eye. They alighted outside one and as soon as they were seen by the proprietor were bidden to be seated on a long, broad bench, and Frances followed Lakshmi's example and drew her feet up and tucked them underneath her. The proprietor, having ascertained what Frances wished to see, rapped orders to a nimble youth who climbed a step-ladder to take bolts of cloth from the shelves and tumbled them open upon the bench in front of her.

Frances, seeing the splendid collection before her, felt almost dizzy with choice. Her European eye went to a rather subdued material - a pale blue with lemon daisies. No! Wishy-washy! Surely like something Marjorie Jamieson would put up, she thought, unkindly. The more vibrant shades caught her fancy – she settled upon a kingfisher blue background with a very ornamental purple hibiscus pattern. This would be for the lounge. For her bedroom she chose crimson climbing roses – again very ornamental – on a white background, with twirling green stems. Luckily she had studied Domestic Economy at school and she'd already measured the windows with the help of Anwar, and knew how much she would need to buy.

After Frances had chosen, Lakshmi began her work. She haggled and bargained until she was satisfied with the price, and Frances carefully counted out the rupees – she was as yet unfamiliar with the currency – and they left the shop with her purchases.

'Would you like to see some clothes?' asked Lakshmi, eagerly. 'A sari?'

'Oh, no!' Frances laughed. 'Saris are lovely but I wouldn't have the foggiest notion how to wear one! All that winding looks very complicated.'

'*Shalwar kameez* then!' They were back in the car now, and drove two streets away to a large upstairs shop. The ladies serving there were well-known to Lakshmi, and Frances found out that a *shalwar kameez* was a long tunic, with wide trousers underneath narrowing toward the ankle. The outfit was worn with a long scarf. She excitedly tried

113

on a few and looking at herself in the mirror, felt she looked very well indeed. She chose a silky green with white embroidery. As she sat in the chair, one of the ladies opened a tiny tin of red paint and placed a dot on her forehead.

'Now you are truly Indian!' they said, smiling. 'But you will need some bracelets…'

'I think I should be getting home,' Frances said good-humouredly, a little embarrassed at all the attention. She changed into her own clothes and purchased the *shalwar-kameez*. She left the 'deep' on her forehead, wanting Alec to see it.

Lakshmi insisted on taking her to a tea-shop first; it was very simple but had a friendly atmosphere. They drank tea and ate little sweet squares of honey and coconut, and Frances chatted to her of her family in London and related as to how she had met Alec.

'But can you tell me about Vera?' she asked her with curiousity.

But Lakshmi was vague. 'I met her once only, at our company picnic. We all invite the other estates to the New Year picnic. Vera was with the Localsh party. She wore a white dress with a big red silk rose at the shoulder. It was rather tight and a bit shocking. And a red hat, gloves and shoes. Somebody told me that she was the girl Alec was going to marry.'

Frances wasn't sure Lakshmi was telling her all, but she didn't press her. By her reaction in seeing her and not Vera, Lakshmi had implied that there had been more to the acquaintance than she was letting on. But Vera was in the past, Alec hadn't liked her enough to marry her, and Frances was Mrs. Whittier. The reason for Mrs. Jamieson's cool welcome for her was obvious.

She would leave it alone.

They reached the bungalow. It was a little late, but Alec wasn't home yet.

She felt exhilarated at this adventure into Indian life, and when Lakshmi asked her and Alec to dinner the following week, she accepted with happiness and gratitude.

CHAPTER 11 The Melody

She had her bath, being careful to avoid washing off the 'deep'. She was dying to show her purchases to Alec, and looked forward eagerly to the sound of his car.

She laid the fabric out on the dining table for him to admire and stood before him, so that he could admire the fashion accessory between her eyebrows.

'What is this?' he asked, in astonishment, eyeing the table.

'Curtain material!' she said proudly.

'Well done, girl!'

'Do you like it?'

'Yes, it looks all right to me, I mean, that's a woman's department, the curtains and furnishings etc. You didn't go on your own, I hope, you couldn't, in any case, without a car. And you would've been fleeced on your own, poor *nuton memsahib*. Who brought you? Marj? Edith?'

'Mrs. Dutta – Lakshmi.'

His expression changed to one of concern.

'You went with Mrs. Dutta! Come on, Fan, you didn't.'

'Well, I did! She made sure I got a very good price, too!'

'I wouldn't care if you have been cheated, but I wouldn't want you going about with Mrs. Dutta!' His eyes narrowed. 'She put 'deep' on you!'

'Yes, isn't it pretty? I feel very naturalised now.'

'You shouldn't have let her.'

'Actually it was the ladies in the shop.'

'What shop? The curtain shop?'

'Oh no, I bought this as well.' She whipped the *shalwar-kameez* from the chair where she had laid it and held it up against her.

'Where are you going to wear that?'

'Oh, I don't know…I'm sure I will get an opportunity!'

Alec went quiet. He frowned. He picked up some of the curtain material and flung it down again.

'It's very - Indian-looking. And as for your clothes - you are supposed to choose British – things – from a catalogue. That's what the women do.'

'You thought the material was nice until I told you Mrs. Dutta was with me when I bought it.' she said rather wonderingly. 'My parents had two Indian friends, a lawyer and a doctor. They used to visit the house. They always brought sweets for me, and flowers for Mum. It's not like I'm unfamiliar with Indian people.'

'Yes, I am sure they were very decent and respectable men! I have nothing against the Indians, by the way, we are in their country now, but you are new here, Fan, and you should mix with the Europeans here, at least until you get to know the native people. Their culture is very different.'

'You said the Duttas were friends of yours!' Frances was puzzled.

'We know them, we meet socially of course, but why could you not have asked Marjorie or Edith to go with you?'

She paused, and looked down. She felt thoroughly deflated.

'They don't like me,' she said defensively.

He digested this information.

'That might be my fault,' he conceded. His annoyance had subsided. 'But you should have asked me what to do about going to the bazaar. I could have asked one of the other European women, from the other tea estates, to go with you. What was your hurry? We'll meet more people at the Planters Club on Saturday, and you will be sure to make new friends there. I don't blame you for not liking *Cabbage* and *Pince-nez*. They are stodgy old puddings.'

Frances had to smile at the nicknames, unkind as they were.

There was silence for a few moments. Frances began to gather up the material.

'Time for my bath,' he said, as he left the room.

'Alec, wait!' she called after him, biting her lip.

'Mrs. Dutta asked us to dinner next Tuesday. I accepted.'

'Oh no,' he groaned. 'You shouldn't have done that, Fan. You're over your head, here.

They always want something from us, the Indians. Well we can cancel.'

'Why should we cancel? I would like to go.'

'Well, we are not going.'

'Why not? She was kind enough to ask us and it would be very rude to cancel!'

'She only asked you out of curiousity. She knows the – the situation. She wants to find out things, so she can talk.'

He pursed his lips and strode from the room.

Frances felt the tears break through her eyes.

She looked in dejection at the curtains. Neither the ornamental hibiscus nor the climbing roses seemed as attractive now. She would forever associate them with the first disagreement of their married life, and she wasn't sure she wanted to put them up after all.

She sat at the piano and opened the lid, turning her back on curtains and *shalwar-*

kameez, which had also caused consternation.

The piano was a *Collard&Collard* upright, its plain panelling dulled with age, with yellowed keys and a mellow tone. Its four brass-toed legs stood sturdily in pots of kerosene to discourage ants.

There was a melody her grandmother used to play, she never knew its name, but it stole into her mind now. Grandmother used to be fond of playing it for months after Grandfather died unexpectedly, in his sleep. It was rather simple. A little sad and sweet at the same time. She softly picked out the notes, one by one.

She could hear Alec coming out of the bathroom, so she called for dinner, a chicken casserole. She had obtained a list of what Joseph could cook.

They ate in silence. Frances felt a bit gloomy.

'I think we need to get the piano tuned,' she said brightly, trying to change the mood.

'What for? Neither of us play.'

'I like to tinker about on it. And visitors might play.'

'I don't know anybody who plays. And I don't know if we could even get a tuner. I never heard of one. Will you tell Anwar to hurry dessert? With Finch going away, I have to go back to the Factory.'

Frances made to get up, but Alec said, 'no, we don't get up. Just call his name. What's for dessert? Not rice pudding, I should tell you, I don't like rice pudding.'

That night Frances awoke with a fever and a very upset stomach. She had to run to the bathroom several times. Alec woke.

'You ate something bad,' he said. 'Did you eat or drink anything when you were out?'

She nodded with misery. 'Tea and a little sweet thing in the bazaar. But the water and milk were boiled up together for the tea; I saw him do it.'

Alec sat up and put his arm about her shoulders.

'The cup might have been dirty. Or the sweet thing as you call it. Poor Frances! But never mind, it happens every newcomer. You have to get these tummy bugs, and after a while you get less and less of them. You build up immunity. Poor miserable Frances. Drink a lot of water.' He kissed her, lay down and was asleep again in a moment. She went out to the dining room where Anwar always left a jug of water for them. She drank it all over the next few hours, lying on the couch in between visits to the bathroom. She ate nothing the following day, but drank as much water as she could. She felt much better towards evening.

It may have been a co-incidence, or not, but that afternoon, the day after she had gone to Sundarpur, Mrs. Jamieson and Mrs. Arkins paid her a call and were extremely kind and gracious. She rather felt that word had gotten to them that Mrs. Whittier had gone shopping with Mrs. Dutta, and they could not be seen to snub her.

Mrs. Arkins posed a pointed question about curtains, almost apologising for taking hers with her when she had vacated the house. 'But I was so fond of them. My sister sent them to me, from *Harrods*, you know. But do you have some material?'

'I haven't made up my mind about the curtains,' Frances answered a little stiffly. She didn't want to tell them she had material, though she was certain they knew already, because they would expect to see it and pass judgement, and how could you compare *Chandra's of Sundarpur* to *Harrods of London*?

'If you need anything at all, just ask us,' was Edith Arkins' parting sweet-talk. 'We have lived here for decades. We know everything there is to know. And thank you for the tea and biscuits. Joseph can make very tasty biscuits. I see you didn't eat any yourself, and they are so tasty. Aren't they, Marj?'

'Yes, indeed they are, and Frances will grow to appreciate them in time, won't you, Frances?'

Frances already knew the lemon biscuits were delicious, but her stomach was not up to taking food yet, and she was determined that as well as finding out that she had purchased Sundarpur curtains from the bazaar, these two women were not going to learn that she had gotten a nasty tummy upset there as well.

CHAPTER 12 Planters Club

She was over her stomach upset in two days and eating again. On Saturday evening they drove to the Planters Club, and Alec was correct – there was a good mix of Europeans there, but not as many, as Mrs. Jamieson woefully declared, as before Independence. Oh, the company they had then! Oh, how the place buzzed with life! There were Indian men there as well, she wondered if *Boro Mem* resented that they had had to allow them in.

Frances could see with what obvious satisfaction Alec introduced her to the other British people first at the Planters Club in Sundarpur. Her eyes sought out any woman about her own age, any possible friend. There was a cheery girl named Polly Lathrop, who was married to a planter in another estate owned by Localsh Company. Rajaphur was at least fifteen miles on the other side of Sundarpur, making it thirty from Localsh. The Lathrops attended the Club every Saturday, so Frances was hopeful. Polly was a giggler with a big, bright smile. She smoked all the time, and downed whiskies like the men.

'You are a lucky one, aren't you?' she said to Frances. 'We all get moved about, except for Alec Whittier. And Duncan Arkins of course. But that's because Edith Arkins has a sister married to a coffee planter in

127

Rhodesia who keeps the Jamiesons in the best coffee. No *Instant* for them! But how does Alec do it? He's been in the same estate for all the time he has been here. I'm on my third move. Do you know how many estates Localsh Company has?

Frances had to shake her head.

'Oh, five. Dotted here and there from Rajaphur all the way up to Darjeeling, near the Himalayas, you know. *Yours* is the biggest though. Jamieson superintends them all but likes his mansion in Sundarpur. I had to spend two years up in Darjeeling, it was beautiful to look at, but I was freezing of course. But I want you to find out for me how my Roger can stop getting moved around. If it takes a big fat bribe to Mr. Billingsworth – the big boss you know – in Calcutta – I would do it. I've got this gold necklace, you know.' She laughed loudly, patting her neck. 'Some *baksheesh*, you know, yes? It wouldn't surprise me at all if Billingsworth was open for business. Did you meet him, no? We know him from another Company. He's rather devious. Just so you know.'

She was tipsy, Frances thought. It was news to her that Localsh had five branches. And news too that her husband was able to dodge being moved from the one he obviously liked best.

'We thought you'd be *Vera*,' Polly said then, briefly pointing her cigarette towards Frances.

Oh, not again.

'You aren't the first to say so. Vera appears to have been on everybody's mind! What *was* she like?' Frances asked, her curiousity kindled.

'Oh, she was all right. Tall, dark-haired, quite a personality, dressed very well. A hard look in her eye, though. I wouldn't cross her. Wild. Rather sophisticated. *And fond of a drink.*' she whispered then, draining her glass. Frances smiled.

'Was she – beautiful?'

'The men thought so. I actually heard her compared to Joan Bennett. Men are so foolish, that if any woman flatters them, they get a swelled head. We didn't like her much. She flirted with everybody's husband. We rather dreaded her coming back actually, and we were ever so glad it was you, and now that we see you, we approve of you even more.'

Frances wasn't sure to make of this. *Now that we see you?* She supposed that she was no threat to anybody's husband!

There was a dance, and Alec and Frances found themselves ushered onto the floor to lead off. They received a warm applause as they began.

'They approve of marriage,' Alec said. 'They make such a fuss over everybody who takes the plunge. Let's give them something to look at, Fan!' He swung her backward almost all the way to the floor.

'Alec, what are you doing?' she laughed. 'I don't know this dance!'

'It's all right, you don't have to do anything, just let me lead you – well you could just dance a bit exotically. Throw yourself into it. We can do a kind of tango. Let yourself go.'

'What here, in the middle of this crowd?'

'Don't be so stodgy – we *are* married. Come on, Frances, put a bit more effort into it. It's supposed to be naughty. Show 'em a bit of leg.' He swung her up and around and down again the other side.

She was sure the tops of her stockings were showing. 'No, I can't. They are all looking at us. Stop, Alec.'

'Oh all right.' He swung her back into her two-step as other couples took the floor.

After the dancing, they went to a table.

'Well, what do you think?' he asked her eagerly. 'Aren't they a funny lot?' He indicated the dancing couples.

'I've only spoken to Polly and a few more people, the Lanes and the Ropers seem quite nice, and someone called Masterson a *box-wallah*, which he told me was a businessman.' she whispered. 'But they seem quite friendly.'

'Polly! Oh goodness, don't believe anything *she* tells you. Come on, I'll introduce you to some other people. Oh, brilliant. Here's old Grainger. Excuse me a minute, Fan. I have to see this old bounder. Haven't seen him for a year I am sure. Grange!' he hailed him loudly and disappeared. Frances was on her own for at least twenty minutes until Tom and another bachelor, from Rajaphur, came and sat down beside her, chatting to keep her company. It was nice of them, but it made Alec look neglectful, so she made an excuse and left to find him. He was at the farthest end of the bar, talking to Grainger.

They were at last introduced, but immediately the men took up their conversation again, about getting up two teams for football.

CHAPTER 13 On the Wind

The Duttas had, before the weekend (and happily before the Whittiers wrote to cancel) extended their invitation to all the Europeans of the Sundarpur Localsh Tea Estate to come to dinner on Tuesday, and Frances felt that Mrs. Jamieson and Mrs. Arkins knew who was to blame for this. *She* was happy and excited. She was going to an Indian house, and wondered what it would be like. Tuesday came; they had a very pleasant evening, even if they did sit at a table identical to any in an English home, and drank Alec's '39 Burgundy. They were greeted very warmly by Lakshmi and her husband Ashok, and Frances savoured the Indian ambience in their spacious house, with carved ornamental chairs and cabinets

in dark wood, the room softly-lit, and exotic
scents. Frances learned from Lakshmi that
they were frangipani and jasmine. There
were other guests as well, officials of the
Farah company, and their wives. They were
served platters of chicken biriyani, a tasty
dish usually served at festivals. Frances'
mouth burned after a few mouthfuls and
Alec, seeing this, told her to eat a *chappati,*
in small bites, this being better to soothe the
fire within than gulps of water. Yogurt,
when it was served, was like manna from
heaven, and later, she was able to drink tea.
This of course was Farah tea, leading to a
great deal of banter between the rival
companies.

After the meal, feeling happy and full, she
asked Lakshmi if she might walk in the
direction of the wind chimes. They delighted
her. She was directed to the verandah.

She came up behind two figures already
there, her host Mr. Dutta and Mr. Jamieson,

smoking and chatting together as they looked out on the fairy-lit lawns.

'Where did Whittier find her?'

'Picked her up in London when he was on leave. An orphan. I hope they can be happy, but I have misgivings about it. She isn't his type at all.'

'Ah, you wanted him to marry your wife's sister! I know all about that.'

'Did you? I suppose everybody knows that for miles around. Yes, that would have been ideal. But until my wife hears from Vera, who is not a good correspondent - we won't know the real story. Marjorie isn't over it yet, the shock was dreadful, and we only heard about – *his choice* - a bare few hours before they were upon us. We were so sure Vera was on her way that Marj even had the house all ready. Curtains up, everything. She went and took them down immediately, and whisked some other nice things away. She even had a party planned at our Bungalow.

Fairy lights in the trees, champagne, music - food. Then – nothing. She cried for the whole evening.'

He paused, and Ashoke said nothing. Mr. Jamieson exhaled a long plume of tobacco smoke.

'Well, marry in haste, repent at leisure. It happens to planters a lot, I'm afraid.'

Frances withdrew quietly. She felt the grave blow to her heart. How had Vera – and Marj – misunderstood so much? How had Alec given everyone the impression that he was to marry Vera?

Marry in haste, repent at leisure! Oh no, Mr. Jamieson was quite mistaken about her and Alec.

That night, as they got ready for bed, it came into her head to ask him if he loved her. She had asked the question without even thinking of the consequences of the response if it wasn't a wholehearted 'yes'. He looked at her in an odd sort of way, before saying:

'Well, what do you think? Didn't I marry you?' But it wasn't really a question at all, he got into bed and went to sleep immediately.

Perhaps, she thought, as she lay in the darkness, if he doesn't love me terribly now, he will grow to love me in time. She got out of bed and went to the lounge. The moonlight streamed in through the curtainless windows, the windows that were bare because she was not Vera. She sat at the piano and played the melody again, that nameless melody, her grandmother's melody – quietly - with one finger. It chimed softly through the house.

'Want to go to Mass this morning?' Alec sounded quite chirpy the following day. 'I'll drive you in. If you want to fast, skip breakfast and we can get a bite to eat at the Club before coming home. Oh, better tell Anwar – no lunch today.'

She was happy again. She hoped he would attend Mass with her, but he told her flatly that he had no intention of going in this Sunday or any Sunday, or converting, and she was not ever to try. He believed in God, of course, and put *C* of *E* on all the forms, but it never went any further than that. He never attended services when the vicar came down from Silchar. He was going to the Club, and would collect her afterwards. If she tried to convert him, he would not drive her to Mass at all.

Suitably chastened but happy to be able to attend Mass, she had to content herself for praying for him and thanking God that he was willing to drive her in. Mass was in Latin of course. As always she followed it in English in her missal. The sermon was in Bengali, but the priest said a few words in English for the benefit of the foreigners present. He had a delightful Irish brogue which reminded her very much of her father.

Frances looked for more white faces in the congregation. Several nuns, a middle-aged couple, two young men whom she recognised from the Planter's Club.

She met the priest afterwards, Father Fitzgerald. As well as a large parish, he had a school and a clinic, run by Italian sisters. He welcomed her to the parish, and said he would come up and visit them someday, which she was very happy about. The other couple she saw approached, as curious about her as she was about them, she supposed! They were Polish, and their English was not good, but she understood they were from a tea-plantation some forty miles off. She wondered what had brought them to India, and decided they were lucky if they had spent the war here instead of in their home country.

CHAPTER 14 'Not your house'

The rains ceased completely, the bushes were completely picked of 'two leaves and a bud', and the planters were busy getting ready for the next plucking season.

The factory needed an overhaul, the engines serviced; the tea bushes needed to be drastically pruned; thousands of seedlings were to be grown in nurseries. Bungalows Three, Four and Five - *the chummery* - had their thatch roofs repaired. This was necessary every year. The bungalows were given fresh coats of paint.

Frances' days began to follow a routine. She had a very happy time at home during the day. The servants were always friendly and warm. Even Joseph, after she had announced that they were going to get a fridge. This was very much to his liking, even if it was to be kept in the 'bottle' room. She heard that Joseph was telling everybody in the bazaar that he was going to have a fridge, and that it would run on kerosene, or *kerashin*, as everybody called it. Frances very willingly took all the credit for the new acquisition.

The servants took a liking to their new, awkward *memsahib*, and helped her enormously in her first shaky weeks, when she'd been learning about the different way of life, the different ways of doing things and of course, the language spoken. They understood the British mind.

Soon the Sundarpur branch of Localsh Tea were told to expect a visit from Mr. Billingsworth himself, all the way from Calcutta. He was to stay with the Jamiesons and Alec told Frances that the bungalows would take turns in hosting dinner for him, inviting the other Europeans.

Here was a challenge indeed! But she learned the true worth of Anwar. He was unfazed, and said he would manage everything. There was no need at all for *memsahib* to worry.

Frances did not like it when Mrs. Jamieson sent for Anwar one day, and he reappeared with the lady herself in tow, and with a rolled up set of curtains ready to hang, and an odd-job man named Kiku who worked on the estate. The *Boro Memsahib* charged up the verandah steps, let herself into the lounge, banging the screen doors behind her, and unrolled the curtains on the dining-table. Frances looked on, dumbfounded.

They were from *Timothy White's* in Calcutta, she barked, and they had to put their best side out for Mr. Billingsworth, and he could not possibly come to a house without proper furnishings. Why had Frances not put up her curtains yet? Any curtains would be better than none! She lectured her as she bustled about Frances' home, giving orders to Anwar and Kiku as they quickly hung them on the rails.

Vera's curtains.

'I wish you wouldn't do that, Mrs. Jamieson,' she said, half-fearful, half-indignant. 'It's my house, and I should decide!'

'But it is not your house, my dear.' The older woman was speaking rapidly and with great emotion. 'I do not have a house, and you do not have a house. These houses that

Localsh have provided for our residences must be adequately cared for and furnished! Mr. Jamieson is most anxious that we all appear to best advantage. After all, our livelihoods are at stake. There are thousands of people employed by Localsh. You might think of that, Frances.'

Localsh could close for the want of lounge curtains in one of the bungalows? She bit the words back. Mrs. Jamieson looked as if she were about to have a stroke. Frances felt like a schoolgirl.

'What did you do with the material you got in the bazaar?' the older woman barked.

'They are in the bedrooms.'

Frances had reached a compromise about the hibiscus and roses that she had loved and then disliked. She had sewn them into curtains for the spare rooms. They would not be wasted, and she would not have to look at them, a permanent reminder of her first quarrel with Alec.

'Well, that was a good sensible thing to do I suppose. I hate waste. Kiku, don't take all day! I want you to come up to *my house – amar basay* – and fix a lamp there! Come on, come on!'

And she bustled out the door. Frances flung herself into a chair. What an old bag! *Vera's curtains.* Ugh! She stared at them. Peach with white pin stripes. *Boring.*

Alec arrived home after a time. In case he would not notice immediately, she met him and drew him over to the windows.

'By golly, where did they come from? Have you been shopping again?'

'No, I am not responsible for those.'

'They are not bad, actually, wherever they came from. I suppose *Cabbage* or *Pince Nez* had some lying around, is that it?'

He strode through to the bedroom, pulling at the buttons of his shirt. She followed him and stood at the door.

'It was Mrs. Jamieson. And – I don't want them.'

'You don't want them? Oh come on Frances, what's wrong with them? Not colourful enough?'

'Well, they aren't but that's not my objection to them. The thing is, Alec, they were not intended for *me*. They were already in this house until the day we arrived. When Mrs. Jamieson realised that it wasn't her sister who had married you, she came down and took them away.'

It seemed to Frances that he froze. He looked at her in an odd way.

'You say that they were for - ?'

'Vera.'

'Then I do not want them either.' His voice was quiet and angry, his words slow, as if he put a full-stop between each. He buttoned up his shirt again and strode out of the bedroom. 'Anwar!'

The bearer appeared.

'See those curtains, Anwar? *Memsahib* does not like them. Take them down this minute.'

'But *Boro Mem* said –'

'Don't mind *Boro Mem*! Frances, where are those curtains you got at the bazaar?'

'In the bedrooms.'

'We'll put them up. Anwar, curtains in bedrooms go up here, all right?'

'I thought you didn't like -' Frances began.

'I do like them. I love them.' Without waiting for Anwar to call someone to help him take down the curtains, he grasped a chair, hopped up on it and began to unhook the pegs.

'*Boro Mem* is driving everybody mad,' he remarked hotly. 'She will be without servants before Billingsworth gets here. They are all ready to pack up and leave in Bungalow One. Here.' He flung a curtain down and she caught it.

She was very glad the curtains had come down, but not so happy that he had taken them down not because she did not like them – but because he harboured such a dislike for Vera that he even couldn't bear to be reminded of her.

CHAPTER 15 *Director Sahib*

The VIP arrived early one afternoon, and went straight to the Factory where it was assumed he would most wish to be, but he only spent ten minutes there before he was driven up to Bungalow One for a long rest. There he remained until late the following morning, when he was fetched to go and inspect the Factory again, and do a tour of the Gardens end-to-end in the Jeep. He had worked on the Sundarpur estate himself as a lad fresh out from Aberdeen, before he went to work at another Company, and now that he was back, he never intended to leave Localsh Tea again, and would direct its fortunes from Calcutta until he retired.

There was a grand dinner for him that evening in Bungalow One. Alec had been consulted about the wines by Mrs. Jamieson, who spent quite a long time wondering which one would be best to serve the Managing Director in whose hands all of their fates would lie, while Alec uttered helpful suggestions.

'A red Burgundy, what else? A port for after dinner, but I suppose he is a whiskey man. What about a Reisling at dinner?'

'German! Not German!'

'The war is over, Mrs. Jamieson.'

'But his son fought, you know, he mightn't like a German wine. Can't you make it two French wines? No Italian either. His other son served under Montgomery. He might not like to drink an Italian wine.'

'They changed sides.'

'Who?'

'The Italians. They became Allies.'

'Oh, never mind! I want French wines only. Those Italians jump on the grapes with their bare feet. I saw it on *Pathé News* when I was Home. It would put anybody off drinking *their* wine.'

'White Burgundy, then, but I can't guarantee the French don't jump on the grapes in their bare feet also. I have heard though, that they thrash about in the vats of grape juice to assist in fermentation – it sounds like a lark.'

Frances smothered a giggle.

'I have never heard of the French doing that, it sounds disgusting,' said Mrs. Jamieson. 'But haven't you got any *Dubonni*? It's very popular, Vera thinks it's the best.' Mrs. Jamieson stopped suddenly, a shadow crossed her brow and she pursed her lips. Frances looked down.

'No, I do not have *Dubonnet*,' Alec said after a long pause, his tone a little tense.

Frances wondered if Mrs. Jamieson had had a letter from Vera, and burned to know the contents, but there was no use even wondering about that. *The real story*, as Mr. Jamieson had put it at the Dutta's bungalow.

The dinner party was exceptional. Roast beef and Yorkshire Pudding was the main course, with boiled potatoes, and courgette stuffed with aromatic rice and peppers, followed by bananas fried in rum with a topping of real Devon cream out of a tin.

Alec was in his element, as was usual with him in company. As could be expected with him, he brought the subject around to what wine one should drink with what.

'Pairing is very important,' he was saying 'It has to complement the food. Now with Mrs. Jamieson here, I couldn't get her to say whether we were having beef, or chicken, or goat, or fish, and therefore could not make up my mind until she had made up hers.'

'Now Mr. Whittier, I did tell you last week we were going to have a cow butchered. But you weren't listening, I'm sure.'

'Indeed I was all ears, Mrs. Jamieson. But that doesn't mean you would be successful in obtaining the meat, for instance it might have been bone-thin, and you might have gone for a few of Kareem's fat goats instead. You could have presented me with a dilemma, for I would not know what to serve with goat meat.'

His hostess glowered.

'There was no question of that,' she said primly. 'As if one could eat Yorkshire pudding with goat meat. Do have some more, Mr. Billingsworth.'

'Roast beef and Yorkshire pudding, just like at Home.' chimed Mrs. Arkins.

'It's an excellent choice of wine,' Billingsworth said, knowing nothing about the subject, but twirling the glass in his hand as he had seen his bank manager in London do when they had lunch together once. 'Didn't expect such fine banqueting this far away from civilisation.' He turned towards

Alec. 'What is its vintage?' He emphasized the last word knowingly.

Alec then began to relate the woes of French vineyards under the Occupation, the raided *châteaux* and poor harvests to boot, but it was quite lost on him who would, in actual fact, have been happier with a Bulldog Ale with his Roast Beef and Yorkshire Pudding.

'I am sorry we have no roast potatoes,' Mrs. Jamieson said. 'I could not make Cook understand what I meant by them, and I had no time to teach him or stand over him giving instructions. Oh! Back in the old days, they were taught everything. We had a cook then who could put a Christmas Dinner on the table and you could not tell if you were in England or in India. It's not the same now at all.'

'Your roast beef is tops, Madam,' Mr. Billingsworth said. 'Such succulence, and taste, I wonder what the animal was fed.'

Frances felt a little mirthful during this exchange, but in reality she felt a little nervous – her turn was to be the day after next. For one thing, she did not know what to do for a salt and pepper set, because they did not have one. For guests to have to help themselves from little heaps spilled onto plain saucers would hardly do. And what would Mrs. Jamieson say about her curtains having been taken down?

The morning after next, Anwar led her out to the chicken pen to choose the birds for her table. Frances, raised in the city (they had moved no further than Stevenage during the Blitz) felt a little queasy at the thought of having to kill these unsuspecting, happy birds for food, and when Joseph appeared brandishing an axe, she chose two and very quickly made an escape before the evil deed was carried out, feeling horribly guilty.

That evening, she surveyed the table before the guests were to arrive. She had a long white tablecloth which had come from

Alec's ancestral home, and Anwar had somewhere procured a pretty crimson square for the center, with delicate embroidery and scalloped edges. The table was very well laid. The silver butter knives were very similar to Mrs. Arkins' fish knives. How odd!

'Anwar!' she said suddenly remembering. 'We have nothing to put the salt and pepper in!'

'No need to worry, *memsahib*. I know where there is a cruet set, which will be very suitable.'

The guests arrived, Alec poured sherry (he disdained the planters' fondness for whiskey, though he offered it in a half-hearted way) and everybody was in good humour. The Jamiesons, the Arkins', Mike Finch (Lydia was still in Shillong), and Tom Robertson. Mr. Billingsworth was gentlemanly towards his young hostess.

She saw Mrs. Jamieson's eyes wander to the windows before surreptitiously drawing Mrs. Arkins' attention to the sight. The two women conferred for a hurried few minutes, and Frances could well guess what was said.

When they sat down to table, she was horrified to see what was unmistakably Mrs. Jamieson's silver cruet set on the table, and it was then she recognised Mrs. Arkins' silver fish knives, which they had used only the evening before in her home, doing duty as the butter knives. What kind of trouble had Anwar got her into? She stole a look at the two women, but they didn't appear to have noticed.

The Whittier bungalow served baked chicken with an onion saffron sauce, roast potatoes (Joseph's suggestion) and large tomatoes stuffed with rice and peppers. Alec picked a '45 Burgundy (the first 1945 he had opened since he arrived) and a Reisling, and offered everybody a choice. Nobody knew the merits of one over another, but all pretended to, and everyone chose what their neighbour had not, and both bottles emptied at an equal rate.

The roast potatoes drew happy compliments from their honoured guest, and Tom Robertson dug his fork into the platter more than three times to help himself to more. The dessert was a baked apple tart with raisins with cinnamon custard, and they all enjoyed a cup of Localsh tea. Happily one of their wedding presents had been a china tea service and Frances and Aunt Margaret had packed it very carefully so that every piece survived the voyage.

As they sat on the verandah Mrs. Jamieson contrived to get near Frances, and in the sweetest tone asked her:

'My dear, what happened the curtains I went to the trouble of putting up for you?'

'I like those better,' was all Frances said. 'Do you want yours back?'

'I have no use for them,' Mrs. Jamieson said, vexed. 'Really, I do think you could have left them up! If you didn't like them, you should have said so at the time! After all the trouble I went to! And, if you don't mind my saying so, and I pray you won't take it the wrong way, but the onion sauce was rather too much with the chicken, it made the fowl tasteless, one should seek to enhance the taste of the meat, not overpower it.' She departed in high dudgeon to sit beside Mrs. Arkins, who gave her a comforting look.

'I say, Whittier, I'd like a word with you tomorrow morning,' Frances heard Billingsworth say in a low tone to Alec, as the guests were about to take their leave. 'Ten o'clock. All right?'

After the guests had departed, Frances felt a surge of both relief and exultation. She flopped onto a sofa, stretched herself, and exhaled deeply.

'It went all right, didn't it?' she asked eagerly, jumping up again.

'Why yes, of course.' Alec answered. He left the verandah, and she saw him pick out a book from the bookcase.

She followed him.

'Was everything all right? Really? I never had guests before, not really. Not important ones. That was the first time I ever had a dinner party.'

'It went fine, you did very well.' he said, looking at his book; a wine book, of course. 'Tom is having hilsa and prawn curry. I'm trying to decide if a Rosé would be best; can't say I like prawns, so let's try to make up for it with a good wine at least – what shade of Rosé - '

'Did you like the onion sauce?'

'Yes, everything was tops.'

'Mrs. J wanted to know where the curtains were.'

He did not speak, he just turned pages in the dim electric light.

'I told her I didn't like them.'

'That was a good enough reason.'

'I offered to return them. She seemed very vexed about it. But she doesn't want them.'

'Hmmm.' He was reading.

'Alec?'

'Yes?'

'Don't you want to talk about the evening?'

'Why?'

'Because it was the first dinner party we gave, and it was all rather exciting, at least I thought so!'

'What do you want to say?' he slammed the book shut and returned it to the shelf. But he was irritated.

'Well?' he looked at her impatiently. 'I told you, you did very well. Like an old pro.'

159

But Frances' heart had sunk a little. Her triumph dissolved into a disappointed mood. What was the point of forcing somebody to talk when they would prefer to do something else?

'Never mind,' she said, huffily. 'You don't want to talk.'

He sighed. 'I'm tired, Frances, I'm going to bed.'

Alec went to their room and shut the door.

Frances returned to the verandah. She felt hurt and rather alone. She wanted a cup of tea, but even if she knew her way around the kitchen she would never go there at night. The servants were gone to bed. She drank the last of Alec's wine which he had left. Though he loved the beverage, he never drank very much of it, and was of the opinion that those who drank too much were missing the entire point of the epicurism experience.

Her mood dropped further and her thoughts took a gloomy turn. Not six months ago, she had been a busy girl at a very busy school, and though she was never one of the more popular girls, she had a few solid and steady friendships. Grace, Mildred and Kathleen went everywhere together, helped each other, lent everything to each other, did each other favours, and supported each other. Joys, sorrows, frustrations were shared. When Kathleen had a letter from home saying her dog had died, it was everybody's loss. Mildred's brother got married one summer and she came back with a photo album; they pored over it for days with delight. Grace fell in love during the Christmas Holidays but the boy never wrote; they consoled her in her disappointment and spoke among themselves about what a rotter he was. Even after they had left school, Grace, who was in London, called to her home often to keep Frances company while she was looking after her mother, and ran several errands for Mrs. Sullivan. At school and even beyond, Frances hadn't known what it was to have a joy or a sorrow unshared.

But only Aunt Margaret and Grace had written to her.

She missed them now. Aunt Margaret was a fond aunt, avidly interested in her niece's wellbeing. Cousin Jane, a very simple, sweet girl, older than Frances but forever childlike due to brain damage at her birth, could not write. Her other cousins, grown men now, had flown the nest. Boy cousins don't write, though.

Oh, Mum! The thought of her mother was far too much. She missed her terribly. To think she'd never see her again! It was too much. She cried a little, but very quietly, because she didn't want Das the *chokidar* to hear her. She tried to pull herself together. It was ridiculous – but Alastair Jamieson's words haunted her. *'Marry in haste, repent at leisure.'*

Was Alec happy?

CHAPTER 16 *'Envious of Whittier'*

She woke with a headache, and felt the melancholy and doubts of the night before come upon her again. She was in no mood to talk to Alec at breakfast; not that he wanted to, as he was still mulling the shade of Rosé to bring to Tom's, and again bemoaning the prospect of prawns. After he had left, Frances questioned Anwar about the table the night before. He replied that it was the custom for one house to borrow from other houses; they did it all the time, and the cruet set and fish knives had been returned that morning to *Banglats* One and Two, all washed, clean and shining. Was not *memsahib* pleased? Yes, she was very pleased, and he had done extremely well. But the red square of cloth – whose was that? He smiled happily. That, he said, was

163

all *hers*. The servants had decided to present their new memsahib with something as a welcome gift to India. He had arranged it all, had it woven, scalloped, and Preti had embroidered it in her spare time. Did she like it? he asked eagerly.

Frances was very touched, and almost in tears, she thanked him. '*Khub shundor*' She had learned a few phrases and that was one of them. Very beautiful. Out of their paltry wages (she knew the servants were paid only a little more than the going rate) they had done this for her. She felt comforted. She made sure to thank them individually that day, and wanted to do something for them, but she did not know what. She examined the tablecloth again, and decided that it would be one of her most precious possessions, given that she had received it on a day when she been feeling isolated and lonely, and from people who could ill-afford such a gift. She thanked God for their kindness on a day when she needed a little lift of her spirits.

At lunchtime her mood was still rather quiet, and she waited for Alec to tell her what Mr. Billingsworth wanted to speak to him about, but he said nothing, and she would not ask, and they ate in silence. She told him about the tablecloth the servants had bought for her, and he said that it was very decent of them, but she should be on her guard, because they would expect something in return, and take advantage, ask for advances on their pay, or loans.

Did you have to spoil it? She asked him silently, sadly.

The type of fish served was very popular in the region, and Mr. Billingsworth said: 'Ah, hilsa fish,' but in such a way that nobody could interpret whether he was pleased to see it, or the opposite. Tom's prawns were a bit tasteless, but nobody expected much from a bachelor, who was as clueless as instructing a cook as he would be at cooking. But Tom was not even a good host, and forgot to offer Mrs. Jamieson a pre-dinner drink, until he was prompted to do so by Frances, who didn't want him to be the target of her ill-will. He thanked her *sotto-voce* later for doing so when she helped him hand around tea on the verandah.

'I don't want to find myself transferred tomorrow morning. Oh by the way, we are all so envious of Whittier!'

'Of – of Alec?' she looked at him curiously.

'Oh, yes –' he moved away hastily, realizing she didn't know anything.

Frances thought of nothing else for the rest of the evening, and not even the alarming news that the dreaded horror the *'tea-bag'* was in danger of launching a mass invasion of England held her attention. It could ruin the country; a greater threat to England had not been seen since Hitler. Alec was in great form, and his deprecating view about the American invention very well received by all. There was very lively argument, with the older ladies and Alec declaring it would never take off at Home, and Tom and Mike pessimistically in disagreement. Mr. Billingsworth mulled about the changes in production that would follow should the tea-drinking world be converted to the tea-bag.

'I heard they are envious of you,' Frances remarked to Alec as they drove the short distance home. Walking was not recommended, a tiger had been spotted in the area some weeks before. Nobody wanted to be caught out walking in the dark and see two amber eyes before them between the tall silhouettes of tree-trunks. It was a thrilling sight from one's house but an experience to be avoided anywhere outside.

'What? Who said? Envious of me, are they?' he chuckled. 'I'll say they are!'

'Well, aren't you going to tell me what everybody appears to know?' she cried.

'Of course, calm down. You were in a mood at lunchtime, so I didn't say anything.'

She allowed this to pass.

'And I hadn't decided what to do.'

'But what is it?' she tried to keep her voice from becoming shrill.

'Billingsworth realises that I am under-utilised here. He wants to exploit my *supreme education and polished position* as he put it' – here Alec laughed, '- for the good of the Company. Localsh want to expand our Markets in Asia and he asked me to work part of the year in Sales. There's nobody else at present who can do this; he has concluded that Arkins has lost the ability to use coherent speech, and Finch and Robertson are not *–brushed-up* - again, his words. Upon his tour he has observed the planters in the other gardens closely and none of them come up to the standard which he feels would *behooven a Purveyor of Tea*. It would involve some travel.'

168

'To where?' They had turned in their gate, opened for them by Das.

'First, to Headquarters in Calcutta. Then to Singapore, Hong Kong, and other places where there are British people and where we are trying to establish markets.'

'What did you tell him?'

'I accepted of course, what would you expect me to do? All expenses paid. I leave on my first trip very soon.'

'You are taking me, yes?'

He turned off the engine.

'Frances, that's impossible. No, don't say anything, don't start. Wives don't go on business trips. Did Mrs. Billingsworth accompany her husband here? No. Sorry, Frances - you can't come.'

'For how long will you be away?'

'Calcutta one week; straight to Hong Kong, and then return via Singapore. I will be away for three weeks. After that I return, I will be here for Christmas. I insisted upon that.'

She couldn't stand it.

'It's so lonely here, Alec! I have no company! I can't bear the thought of you being away! This is – not what I imagined. I mean, I like India and everything, but I don't want to be alone. I feel alone.'

'Oh, this is all my own doing,' Alec then muttered to himself, tapping his fingers on the steering-wheel.

'What? What did you say?'

'Nothing, look – Frances, old girl. I don't want you to be unhappy. I feel responsible for you and your happiness here. But taking you with me is out of the question. That's it. Don't argue with me; it's Company policy. But you don't have to stay here while I am away. You can go to Shillong - join Lydia Finch there. In fact, Mike was saying that she's quite fed-up, and you would like it, it would do you good. It's beautiful there, like jolly old England. Don't say no. I've made up my mind. Besides, I don't want Bachelor Tom falling for you if you stay here alone. Billingsworth wants me to leave as soon as I can. In three days, with him, actually. So you pack a few things and I'll assign Nath to drive you. You will stay in the Pinewood Hotel, and if Lydia's cousins invite you to stay with them, you must accept. You will like it there. There's a smashing cathedral, a Catholic one. The stained glass is wonderful. All right? Say yes, Frances, and make me happy.'

Das had been waiting by the driver's door to open it for him, and when Alec gave him the signal, the door opened and he got out, and as Das hurried to her side, he strode up the verandah steps.

Frances had not consented, but she rather knew that Alec had his mind made up.

CHAPTER 17 *Shillong*

Shillong was colder than Sundarpur, and she was glad of Mrs. Jamieson's curt advice to bring her warmest clothes. Nath had driven her all the way and had dutifully delivered her to the Pinewood Hotel.

This part of Assam was indeed like England. Cool, green and fresh. The Pinewood had an English look. But she barely appreciated its fine lawns and flowerbeds. She went straight to her room and ordered tea, because she was shivering. Her heart was heavy.

Alec had been very loving over the last few days. Considerate of her every need, full of advice and counsel. But she could not fail to see that he was not suffering from this parting.

'Don't begrudge me, Fan. Haven't you ever wondered why I'm the only planter here with a title? I'm not being a snob, but I should not really be in Tea. I belong – well

172

in wine I think – *viniculture* - and if the War hadn't come, you'd be running *Château Delarbrey* instead of Bungalow Three. I had everything planned. In fact, I haven't completely given up the plans I had. I am completely bored in Tea, and I hope we will break out of it. You will support me, won't you? I'm going to need to put by a tidy sum, and this is an opportunity. We're in this together. Understand?' He kissed the tip of her nose.

She calmed. Of course, a man loved to be promoted in his career - that was only natural. Her father had been very proud to become headmaster. And it was true that he was bored. Of all the tasks allotted to him, he hated Paydays the most. Every Saturday he sat at a table with a large sack of cash in front of him, and several hundred workers filed past. There were disputes - over hours worked by part-timers, over deductions made for coming to work late or going home early, which were soundly protested. He and the Garden Supervisor had to make sure all the accounts were correct. Payday took all day.

 But why did she feel he could hardly wait to see her off? When she was being driven away from the house, he had stood on the verandah and waved. She waved back, then looked away and looked back hardly a moment later when she'd reached the gate, and he had already gone back into the house. She knew he was up to his eyes getting ready for his own trip, but she thought he could have seen her out the gate.

It was noisy here with rickshaw bells and car horns. Mike had written a letter to Lydia to say that Frances was on her way. She wondered if Lydia had got the news yet.

She had a meal in the dining-room, but she felt too miserable to eat much. She wondered what Alec was doing now. Was he missing her as she was missing him? She was not at all sure that was the case. As she made her way across the foyer to return to her room, she heard her name called by the receptionist. He smiled and handed her a bouquet of flowers with a note.

Her heart leaped. Alec! How lovely of him! But the donor was not Alec – it was Lydia, saying that she hoped she had a good journey and that she would send a taxi over for her on the morrow, at eleven o'clock. Frances was hardly comforted and too disappointed to appreciate the kind welcome from the woman she had only met a few times in Sundarpur.

They were at an elevation of 5,000 feet, and the evening was much colder than she could have imagined for India. How quickly she had adapted to the heat of India's plains! She found an extra blanket and snuggled herself in it, and fell asleep.

The car arrived at eleven sharp, and Frances was driven only ten minutes away to a busy street, and the driver tooted his horn at a gate in a high wall. This was opened by a *chokidar*, and they drove into a neat courtyard. Several homes looked out on this, and she saw a European child wave to her from a balcony as she got out of the car. It was little Lucy, who ran downstairs, took her by the hand and led her into the now-opened front door on the ground level, to a darkish set of rooms separated by archways with beaded curtains, very Indian in style. But the room they entered was like a different country. It had a portrait of the King and Queen and a St. Andrews Cross and framed paintings of castles on craggy cliffs on one wall. There was a sofa and easy chairs upholstered in Victorian chintz; a table covered in white damask. The room seemed cluttered with ornaments – a clock in the shape of Big Ben; a large china golden retriever; silver candlesticks. All reminders of Home.

Lydia was lying on the sofa. An older woman and a younger were in the room, one knitting what was most likely a scarf, the other – the older - darning socks. It seemed to Frances that she had stepped back to Britain.

'Oh I am so glad to see you!' was Lydia's cry. 'Not that they aren't good to me here, they are wonderful - but I want all the news, for Mike, like most men, can't put two words together on a page. I was told of Billingsworth's visit but all he could say was that he had arrived, and left, and found everything all right. Imagine! No description of anything else, where he ate, what anybody put on the table for him, the talk, anything! I am so glad to see you, Frances! Come here, give me a kiss.'

Frances was warmed inside by this welcome, and gladly bent to kiss the sick woman on the couch.

'How are you?' she asked her anxiously.

'Oh, I am all right as long as I can rest. It would be very boring to be in Sundarpur and having to stay in bed most of the day. The climate here is perfect for expectant mothers, and as you can see, baby is growing! I miss Mike dreadfully, but there's no point in even thinking about it.'

'I want a sister,' chimed Lucy.

'We will be happy with whatever God sends,' her mother said. 'Will you go and ask Ayah for tea? There's a good girl. I want you to meet Mary my cousin, and her daughter Lorna. Mary's husband is away at the moment, and her boys are at school at Home, so we are all women here, Frances! All women! I hope you will all be great friends!'

'You're welcome to move out of that Hotel and move in here,' Mary said, getting up and coming over to shake hands. 'We have a spare room with a view out the window of Our Lady Help of Christians Cathedral in Bosco Square. You're Catholic, aren't you? You'll like that, then.'

Frances shook hands with her and Lorna, and felt her heart melt a little more. She too found herself hoping to be friends with all of them, for in the book she was reading at present, *Northanger Abbey*, Jane Austen had said: *'Friendship is certainly the finest balm for disappointed love'*.

And she was feeling disappointed.

CHAPTER 18 A Lesson

Frances moved into the Stuarts, and offered to pay her way, which they accepted. She could see that there was not much money; for one thing, the family shared a courtyard and other outdoor spaces with many families. She wondered what had happened but supposed that Independence had altered a lot for Europeans who found themselves in a new India, an India that might not indulge privilege as the Raj had. The older *sahibs* and *memsahibs* had not yet accepted the change.

Lydia had not been joking when she said she wanted news – she feasted on it; wanting to know every detail of the food served, the wine Alec picked out – and why - the desserts, everything, what everybody had to say about everything. She wanted to know about the servants, whether Nath's wife had her baby yet, and if Frances knew if Ahmed, her cook, had found out the cause of his little girls' limp? Had Mrs. Arkins heard from the school her boys were at, there was talk of their moving to another building in the same town. How was Mrs. Jamieson's mood? Did she have any servants left?

Frances proceeded a little cautiously at first in her talking of the two older ladies. It didn't feel right to gossip, and she wasn't sure where Lydia stood with them. But one or two outbursts from the latter showed her that she thought them rather narrow and petty.

'I suppose you were heartbroken leaving Alec,' Lydia remarked on her second day. 'You two are still newlyweds. I thought you had a rather dejected look when you came in the other day.'

Frances acknowledged this and thought that perhaps Lydia had guessed that things were not all they should be, so, feeling bitterly unhappy in case she was betraying Alec, she told her some of what was on her heart.

'You mustn't expect a man to be your friend as a woman is,' Lydia counselled her. 'They are different. They don't like to chat with their wives. Oh, they will chat to other peoples' wives – very annoying isn't it? Can you please hand me that cushion? The tapestry with the brown stag. Thanks. It took me a full two years to get used to Mike's odd habits. The early days in a marriage can be a challenge. Alec has a treasure in you. I saw that immediately.'

It was what Aunt Margaret had said.

'We're going out,' called Mary from the door. 'We want to get some shopping done.'

'Frances, I want to say how happy I was that you offered Mary something for room and board,' Lydia began a few moments later when the other women were out of earshot. 'Things are difficult for them. The Company her husband was working for shut down after Independence, and he goes about filling in wherever he can. They moved from a beautiful house outside town, to in here. The expense of keeping their two boys in school takes nearly everything.'

'Why can't they move back Home? Then they could go to a day school, couldn't they?'

'They have nothing to go back to. He won't find work at his age. It's awfully sad, but educating their sons will hopefully lead to better times. Then they can go Home and retire to a small house in the country. That's why they are holding on to all – this.' She indicated the cluttered room.

'And what of Lorna?'

'She left school last June like you. She's thinking of going Home to work. She could apply for the Civil Service, or become a telephone operator or do a secretarial course or something. But where would she live? In a grotty little flat? They don't have the money to set her up, and her father wants her to be here with her mother while he is away. But if she waits too long, she will be too old to apply for the Civil Service. She knits to earn money. Shocking, I suppose, but I have to say I admire them for being so plucky about everything. Don't mention a word to anybody in Sundarpur, will you?'

Frances promised that she would not.

Later that day she went to see the Cathedral. It was indeed lovely inside, and after praying her rosary she wandered about it. There were a few other people there. The following day was Sunday, so she went to Mass. She saw many Eurasians and a few other Europeans. A couple singing heartily from a hymn-book. A few little children with their mothers. Even a few with their ayahs. There was a tall man with thick coppery-brown hair falling over his forehead.

When she was coming out, she almost tripped on the steps, but the man happened to be behind her, and caught her by the arm in a firm grip.

'Steady now,' he said, smiling shyly.

'Oh, thank you, I can't tell what happened – I need to look better at where I'm going,' she said lightly, and walked on.

When she got back she described the Europeans, and though Mary and Lorna could readily place nearly all of them, they had no idea who the young man was, even though Frances was sure his accent was Scottish or Irish.

The weeks flew after the first, and though she missed Alec every single hour of the day, she found herself enjoying Shillong. She loved the bazaars, the local sights she was taken to see, experiencing Indian life closer than she had before, the new friends she had made, and most of all her chats with Lydia. They celebrated St. Andrews Day in the Club with all the other Europeans, Scots or not - a party was a party. They had a lively ceilidh, and ate baked haggis and skirlie, shortbread and fruit tarts. She met many interesting people, danced to exhaustion, and had as good a time as could be had without Alec.

A few days later, to her delight, the doctor told Lydia that she might go home. A car was sent for them both and they travelled back together, with Lucy and of course the ayah, Basana. They were a happy party. Frances was in a far different mood from the one she had been on the outward journey, and she couldn't wait to see Alec again.

But she had also learned something that she hoped she would not forget. She had enjoyed herself when she had been sure she could not. She realised that she could opt to be entertained by new sights and experiences, and be outward rather than inward looking. Or she could indulge her gloom and fail to appreciate the novelties and enjoyment offered around her. She was determined on the former attitude, if Alec had to go away again. She would at least try.

CHAPTER 19 *Christmas*

He was waiting for her, a bottle of Dom Perignon set out on the verandah and little boxed gifts upon the table. He held his arms out wide in greeting, swung her around, kissed her and was as happy as he had been during their courtship, and she could not have been more ecstatic.

'Did I not tell you it was the right thing to do?' he said, after he had heard her excited reports on her stay in Shillong. 'You would have been totally miserable here. Wouldn't you? Wasn't I right? Yes or no?'

She had to acknowledge that he was right. Then he told her of his time in Calcutta, Hong Kong and Singapore with great gusto. He was elated; he'd won contracts, and met very important people, and had to admit that he had enjoyed the experience more than he'd even thought he would.

She hadn't known then that Alec was keeping an important detail from her about his trip, and he only mentioned by-the-way that after the New Year, Billingsworth wanted him to go to Honkers again. Hong Kong. And as he was over in the vicinity, he would drop in on Singapore as well and follow up on the contacts he had established there.

Frances wasn't very upset this time; she remembered her resolve, and besides, Lydia was back. She hoped that by then, she would be expecting a baby as well. It would be so wonderful to have small babies at the same time!

Christmas and New Year's Eve were very social times for the Sundarpur Europeans. The Planters Club became the focus for all the celebrations. Christmas Dinner was held there, with much merriment and partying.

Santa Claus, in the person of Dr. Lane, brought gifts to the little children. There were no children over seven and the parents of those in England or Scotland or Wales had to keep their chins up and bear the absence as best they could. Their children had to go to relatives or friends in Britain for the holidays. If there were none, they had to stay at the school. If the mothers shed tears, they were shed in private.

There was dancing; Tom had to muster up the courage to ask Mrs. Jamieson out on the floor. He had been dreading this ever since Alec had informed him that it was expected and that there was no way out of this courtesy unless he broke his leg. Tom was a dreadful dancer and he was fearful he would tread on her. He made sure to dance with her early in the evening so he could enjoy the remainder of it, but Alec told him that Mrs. Arkins would be very offended not to be offered a dance with him as well, so he did that as soon as he could and could finally sit back and drink with the other bachelors, which is what he wanted to do.

New Years' Eve was also a great party, and they had a ceilidh. Alec was very impressed with Frances' competence with the complicated *Dashing White Sargeant*. He hardly knew it; with much laughter, she half-led, half-pushed him around.

By now Frances had met most of the other Europeans in Sundarpur and beyond, but inevitably there were some new faces, a few reclusive types, or those too far away to get to Sundarpur except for a major event. She'd met the Polish couple – the Wójciks – again. Mrs. Wójcik had had a brother a priest who had openly defied the Nazis. He had died in Dachau, where most of the outspoken priests were taken. The Wójciks had fled and come to India as refugees. Fr. Fitzgerald had known Fr. Nowaki in Rome, and he had helped them to become settled. Frances found them very interesting to talk to, and invited them to come and stay a few days

189

with them whenever they wished, which they said they would be delighted to do.

Frances and Alec, taking a respite from the floor, were sitting with the Sundarpur party when they were approached by a man Frances did not recognise as being a regular Club attendee. His bright green party hat had slipped over one eye and he seemed unsteady on his feet as he lunged towards their table.

'Hey, there you are, Whittier! Haven't seen you for an age. I thought you were in prison for passing off milk as white wine.'

'Spence! I heard of a tiger who makes awful jokes and thought he had swallowed you.'

The lame ripostes got over with, Alec invited Spence to join them for a drink.

'Maybe later!' He peered at Frances. 'Is this not the Tango dancer? Unforgettable turn, Madam; truly unforgettable.' He bowed.

At first, Frances thought he was making fun of her non-performance of a few months ago, but the awkward pause that followed, even from Alec, made her look around. Everybody looked askance at the speaker, who, not realizing he had said anything wrong, grasped Frances' left hand and seeing a ring on the third finger, remarked:

'Congratulations to both of you!' He moved away, into the crowd.

Mrs. Jamieson chose this moment to make her announcement. She coughed in a very important way.

'You all might like to know that I have heard from my sister Vera for Christmas,' she said. 'She sends her best wishes to all of you. And now for some excellent news - she is getting married.'

'Congratulations to Vera,' Alec was the first to say. 'We shall all drink a toast.' He raised his glass. 'To Vera - and her intended?'

'His name is Liversidge,' announced Mrs. Jamieson. 'Peregrine Liversidge. He's a barrister. His father is Judge Liversidge. Peregrine – they call him Perry - went to Eton and he works for the Crown. In an office near the Old Bailey. If he is anything like his father, he has a brilliant future ahead of him; I could not be happier.'

Everyone politely pretended to have heard of Judge Liversidge, and Mrs. Jamieson looked very pleased.

CHAPTER 20 *Alone*

The Cold Weather months went by. Sundarpur and the surrounding area were as dry as the desert. Thick dust penetrated every nook and cranny of the house. Streams dried up, making paths where there had been none.

In spite of her resolution to be happy, Frances' heart knew its own dry season also.

Alec travelled again in February, this time for five weeks. He returned for her birthday on the 23rd of March and had a party for her at the Club. In April, Lydia moved again to Shillong to the Mission Hospital and had a baby boy there in May. Frances hoped every month to see a sign of a baby on the way for Alec and herself, but again and again her hopes were dashed.

Mr. Billingsworth wanted Alec to transfer to Calcutta, but he, who disliked that city more than any other, contrived to stay where he was. His absences would be more frequent; he was required to go to Calcutta at least for a week every month, and every so often undertake a longer journey also, a round trip from Calcutta to other capitals in Asia.

Frances took his absences bravely, but sadly. She could bear his going, if he would be a little bit sorrier to leave her. It hurt her that he departed her side with so little trouble or sadness. He never said he would miss her, and never looked back at the gate to see her standing at the top of the steps.

When he returned, he was always in wonderful form, full of stories, triumphs, arguments in which he had prevailed, jokes he had pulled on colleagues at Head Office, outsmarting competitors in the cities he travelled to. He always brought her an expensive piece of jewellery.

But over the course of a few days, he would become morose, and he seemed to grow increasingly silent and almost absent to her.

'What do you do in your spare time?' she asked him upon his return from yet another trip to Hong Kong and Singapore.

'There isn't much time off. In the evenings, we have meetings, or business dinners. I take influential people out to dinner so that I can win a contract from them.'

'So what do you do during the day, then?'

'Goodness, is this an inquisition? I have lunch (usually a business lunch), then it's back to my hotel room and write up reports and research how I can best sell Localsh tea to these prospects. It's no picnic, I can assure you.'

'Won't you be due some leave this summer? I was thinking, maybe I could join you on a trip to – Singapore or somewhere, and you could take your leave directly after concluding the business, and we could have a good time travelling as tourists.'

He was silent.

'That wouldn't work at all. I have so much to do post-trips, an abysmal lot of paperwork. I do it in the office here after I get back. But I have an idea, when my Annual Leave comes, we'll go to Darjeeling. You'll love it there. Everybody does.'

'Oh, the vicar is coming to Bungalow One next Saturday to conduct a Service.' she told him.

'Will you go?'

'You know I'm not allowed to attend a Protestant service without a dispensation such as what I got for Mum's funeral! But I can go up to Bungalow One – there's a lunch afterwards - and sit in another room while the Service is going on.'

'I think I'll go up too,' he said. 'You must be having some sort of good influence on me, Fan! Usually I just put my feet up here and read whatever is lying around.'

They went up to Bungalow One the following Saturday. Frances sat outside on the verandah while the Service was being conducted inside. She could hear it. The Church of England Liturgy followed the Catholic Mass very closely, but the Protestants didn't believe in the Real Presence of Jesus in the bread and wine. Perhaps one day the Churches would heal and reunite as they had been before. She hoped so. She knew that both of her grandmothers had been aghast and in opposition to a mixed marriage. But her mother and father had been very happy and it wasn't an obstacle to her and Alec's marriage either. If there was an obstacle to their happiness, it wasn't that. It was something else, and she was at a loss as to what that might be.

CHAPTER 21 *The Rains*

Frances thought she would die from the prickly heat caused by the increasingly hot and humid pre-monsoon temperatures. Her back felt like a pincushion. The days were searingly hot now; tempers flared among the staff; the house staff, the gardeners, drivers; factory workers - all had short tempers. Even Frances snapped at times, and then felt very sorry. '*Hot-Head*' Anwar explained to her. 'We all have *Hot-Head*.'

Then one dark night thunderclouds tumbled in and the monsoon began abruptly with a series of lightning flashes, booming thunderclaps and hammering rain. Sitting suddenly up in bed, Frances heard the windows crash open and a cool wind sweep all around the room. Alec was away. She got out of bed and struggled to shut them but was lashed by driving rain that seemed to be coming almost horizontally from outside. She had to admit defeat and allow the storm to do exactly what it wished. She sat curled up in a corner chair, frightened yet fascinated as the lightning lit up the room making the white walls and bedlinens look ghostly. When the storm abated, she at last shut the windows and all fell quiet again.

At last, cool, soothing rain poured down on the land and the people. Black umbrellas, used for shade in the sun, now sheltered the users from downpours. Everybody welcomed the monsoon, even when it brought with it muddy walks and slippery paths. After a few days of torrential rain, what had been arid paths were now brown bodies of water, ankle-deep. The weather wasn't going to stop her going out for walks. There were no wellingtons of course, she sloshed through them in her sandals. She got a leech in her leg and fearfully went to Dr. Babu on the Estate to have it removed. But she found her usual nervousness of doctors and clinics was not as marked as before, even though the Estate Hospital held stronger and more odours than any in London. She didn't know why she felt more at ease, but she was pleased. Dr. Babu told her how to remove the leech herself the next time. Never pull it. Light a match, hold it to the leech and it will come out by itself. Frances balked at having to do such a thing, but bravely carried out his instructions the next time it happened, and happen it did, often enough, and soon she could do it without hardly a thought. She also encountered her first large snake on a jungle path. She stood perfectly still, and it slithered away into the undergrowth. After a few moments she walked on past the place where it had been, and congratulated herself on being still alive, for she was beginning to acquire a sense of humour about Assam's many and unexpected inconveniences and dangers. She felt even more pleased with herself when she looked it up later and found out it may well have been a cobra.

All of Nature looked green and fresh and sparkling! The tea bushes, drastically cropped, began to surge upwards again. Rice grew green and tall in the paddy fields and rippled in the wind. It was a glorious sight. Flowering trees and plants burst into bloom. But she had nobody to share her marvel with, and that made her feel rather more alone.

The Finches were due a long leave, and they planned to go to England in the early summer to get Lucy acclimatized before the start of her first school term in September. Lydia grew very miserable at the thought of leaving her little girl after her in England; and how dreadful that her daughter would miss her brother's childhood! She would never, ever forget her own mother leaving her in a boarding school when she was only six. There had to be a way around it; there had to be!

'I wish I had your connections,' she said gloomily to Frances one day as she sat on Frances' verandah with the baby on her lap.

In between storms the weather was getting hotter and hotter. An electric fan whirred on the ceiling. The canna had bloomed with red flowers. Tall ferns flourished in the corners, while creepers spilled their foliage and flowers up, down and around anything they could find.

'My connections?' Frances was puzzled.

'Oh, you know what I mean - Alec's.'

'Oh you mean his brother,' Frances said. 'To be honest, I had forgotten all about them! I've never met them and we never hear from them.'

'Really?' Lydia was amazed.

'All the same,' she went on, 'if Alec wanted to move back to England, I'm sure Lord Delarbrey would be able to find him a situation.'

'Alec doesn't want to move back to England,' Frances said. She was embroidering a pillow-case. She had learned how to embroider from Preti, who was in a class of her own. She had paid her extra for the lessons.

'Alec is always able to do whatever he wants,' Lydia said then, with a little flash of jealousy.

Frances felt a little uncomfortable. She had noticed that a combination of charm and assertiveness usually got Alec what he wanted, with Mr. Jamieson, with Mr. Billingsworth, with her. Everyone.

'He's never even had to transfer!' Lydia burst out.

'I do not know why that is, to be honest,' Frances admitted, pushing her needle into the lawn fabric to complete the leaf of a banyan tree.

'I know why Mr. Jamieson gives him his own way.' Lydia offered.

'I don't,' Frances said quietly.

'I rather thought you didn't. Shall I tell you?'

Frances thought that if it concerned her own husband, she ought to know of it.

'Alec got Jamieson out of a scrape. Quite a bad one. Involving a woman. A garden girl.'

'Oh my goodness,' Frances felt this was gossip, but she still felt that it did concern her if it concerned Alec.

'You know the Eurasian girls working in the office? They are the daughters of planters, but not from this estate of course. That would be too close for comfort. On this estate, Jamieson had a son by a native woman. It was before he married Marj. He was very fond of the boy. He called him

Andrew. But as happens with all planters who have affairs with native women, they eventually marry a European woman, and then they pay off the native woman, and give her enough money to raise the child, or children if there is more than one. Well Mr. Jamieson had his son educated and he was by all accounts a fine young man, intelligent, popular, handsome. He had a good job in Silchar and a good future ahead of him. He was about twenty-two when War broke out and he wanted to fight the Japanese in Malaya. He was killed in action.'

'Oh how horrible. His poor mother. And Jamieson?'

'He was dreadfully cut up about it. He took Alec into his confidence and asked him to take care of the funeral and everything, on the QT of course. Jamieson wasn't in any position to do it. He had to go on as normal. As if nothing had happened to upset or disturb him. He asked Alec to meet the

mother and pay her some more money –
quite a lot – because she had never married
and was completely dependent on Andrew
for her old age. He had to do the right thing
by her.'

'What a shame he didn't do the right thing
by her twenty-two years before.' Frances bit
off the thread.

'Oh no, Frances. How naïve of you! He
would have been ostracised, you know, by
all Europeans.'

Frances shook her head. 'It's all so tragic.
Did Marj ever find out?'

'I doubt it very much. But if she did, what
could she do about it?'

'So now you know why your husband is
highly favoured,' said Lydia in a teasing,
merry tone after another minute. 'He can
spend half the year on the estate, and it looks
like the other half off on tours to exotic
cities – oh Frances, I am sorry – it's no fun
for you, I know!'

'No, it isn't,' Frances said. 'Even when he is here, Lydia, he hardly – sees me.' She put down her work. 'I just feel he – sometimes I wonder if he – regrets marrying me. We did it in rather a hurry! I was bowled over by him – I still am. But I'm not at all sure if he feels the same way about me, really.'

'Oh no, don't be silly!' Lydia soothed her. 'Men are like that. They all have trouble showing their feelings. But what am I going to do about Lucy? My heart is torn apart, Frances, I almost feel I should go and live in England, but I can't leave Mike by himself, and I don't want to leave Lucy by herself.'

Frances brooded for a while after Lydia had gone home to her own bungalow. The truth was that she and Alec had little in common, little to talk about. They never really chatted together, he seemed uninterested in much of she had to say, unless the subject had something to do with him, or whether she had some gossip about their neighbours. But they had no shared interests. She liked reading and discussing what she read, he had no interest in reading unless it was one of his wine books. They had a record player and she liked listening to all kinds of music; but the only music he liked was Jazz and Swing. Luckily, as an only child she had learned early in life how to amuse herself, and with Lydia's friendship she was not lonely for a female friend, but she still longed for some cosy companionship in marriage. She wondered how long it took, in a marriage, to get to '*two hearts beating as one.*'

But Alec always came to life in company. He loved to entertain, and their house was a lively one when they had their neighbours to dinner. When the cases of wine ran out he had more imported, or brought it back with him from his travels. Frances wanted to know if it was legal to bring it all in, he had said that whether it was or not, *baksheesh* would ensure it would get past customs.

Alec bribed everywhere. It was the done thing.

They had at last asked the Duttas and other people from Farah Tea to their bungalow. Frances was growing confident in her *memsahib* life. As Alec predicted, Lakshmi asked questions – but everybody asked questions. Everybody wanted to know how she and Alec met. She never mentioned Vera – neither did anybody else, after the first surprise. In truth, Frances hardly thought of the soon-to-be Mrs. Peregrine Liversidge at all.

Frances loved to go over all the events of the evening after the guests had gone home, but she had to accept that Alec did not share her enthusiasm for post-party observations.

After all of his animation and joking with the guests, he would lapse into silence, mix both of them a drink, and go out on the verandah for a short while. She always joined him – it became a little tradition she fondly imagined to be cosy and just *theirs* -

but she had generally to be content with just his physical presence. Her attempts at discussing the evening were in vain. *'Wasn't Mrs. Arkins very happy this evening? The new school building her boys are in has central heating.'* Just a grunt. Men, of course, were not very interested in family matters. So she would try something like: *'Didn't Mr. Jamieson tell a good story about Mr. Churchill?'* To that he would say; *'Yes, old Boro Sahib can tell 'em. Better turn in, Fan, I don't know about you, but I'm fagged.'* And he would finish his drink, stub out his cigarette, leave her on the verandah, and often he would already be asleep when she slipped into the bedroom.

She found India filling the void left by Alec! As the months progressed, she was coming to love Assam more and more. She was open to loving all it offered her, and Assam loved her; apart from the usual tummy bugs everybody got, and the dust in ones eyes and the prickly heat, and frogs coming up the toilets and other annoyances, this part of the world treated her very well. She never suffered from the cold! Assam's heat rushed about her everywhere, creating an enveloping warmth about her person, and she was caressed by it as she went about her day. Unlike most Europeans, the heat had not in general disturbed her. She wore summer dresses all year long; the visiting tailor, sitting on her verandah, could make a dress from a picture in a catalogue. She loved living in India, even if Assam had a dark side. The weather could change, clouds roll in in a matter of moments, and dispense thunder, lightning and sheets of drenching rain that would soak you in a minute if you were caught out in it. But having lashed the landscape so ferociously that the ground underfoot became a river of mud, Assam would reveal the sun in its glory again and make up for soaking you by drying you off in minutes, so that after a quarter of an hour you had forgotten that you had gotten drenched at all. It was totally unlike the cold rain in England, which never allowed you to forget you were chilled and wet until you reached the shelter of home and a vigourous towelling-off.

The life of a memsahib could be a leisurely one, and that she did not want. She was in the prime of her life and had great energy. She allowed herself only two hours to read every day. She read Jane Austen's six novels, finding the characters friendly and funny, like real people. They were good company.

Mrs. Jamieson tried to interest her in golf after Mrs. Arkins stopped playing due to a pain in her back, but she found the game slow and long and the wife of the Superintendent rather much to bear – though her manner had softened. Frances presumed that since Vera had gotten over Alec, and met and become engaged to someone else, Mrs. Jamieson's heart was more at ease.

Frances used her energies to tackle the vegetable garden. She had no idea what to

211

grow! The head *mali*, Shankar, was a great guide. He'd put many *memsahibs* through his knobbly old hands and directed her with great wisdom. His knowledge was very wide, and he was quite pleased to see that *memsahib* was unafraid to get her hands dirty in the soil. She found that she, a city girl born and bred, enjoyed gardening – she was good at it, and rejoiced to see her little shoots and plants coming up.

When Alec was away on his second trip, Mrs. Jamieson had thoughtfully asked her how she was to go to Mass on Sunday. Frances thought that this would be a great opportunity to learn to drive the Humber, but everybody, even Lydia, was aghast. What if she broke down on the road, with jungle on all sides? What if the ever-feared *dacoits* heard of her lone journeys, and they lay in wait? Frances was forced to give up the quest. She discovered that the drivers on the estate were willing to earn some extra money by driving her there and back, and they would, of course, use the Humber, which they were rather pleased about driving. While she was at Mass they could go to the bazaar and have *chai* and gossip.

Many of the Anglo-Indians – or Eurasians as they were also called - were Catholic as well, and they had long accompanied them to Sundarpur. Alec had found himself chauffeur to four ladies in all. Frances had felt a little reserved with them – they had been born outside marriage after all – but in time, she came to realise that such an attitude on her part was wrong. If God didn't regard them as inferior – and obviously He didn't - what right had she to think it? So in Alec's absence, Frances often asked them to the house, but noticed that only Lydia of the other *memsahibs* liked to see this. For them, it wasn't because of religion as much as the Eurasians being reminders of the weaknesses of their men. Frances ignored their disapproval. She noticed that she was getting bolder and not at all as fearful of what people thought.

Frances learned Bridge and had to make four more often that she liked with the other *memsahibs*. Cards bored her, and the talk was all the same – Mrs. Jamieson was still in mourning for the Raj – everything was better then – when she'd come out in 1922, there had been twenty families in the area they could see. Oh, the parties! Oh, the tennis! Oh, the servants! So faithful, not like *now*. After Independence in '47 they had tried going Home, but Tea was all Mr. Jamieson knew, so they returned. Oh, the changes, with all the dear Officers gone! Oh, the very few people they knew now! And the new laws, of the new Indian Government! Frances listened to the laments over and over, and could have recited them all herself.

The Wójciks came on a visit when Alec was at home. They had almost unbelievable stories to tell and spoke frankly and matter-of-factly about what they had seen, about their own escape, about all they had lost, but they always expressed gratitude for what had been salvaged from the War - their lives, their health, even a few photos. Alec and Frances were dumbstruck by their experiences. They had known of the brutalities by the Nazis towards the Jews but had not known of the crimes towards the others who had opposed them. In India, they had had the Japanese to contend with, and that had been difficult, as refugees streamed from Malaya.

CHAPTER 22 A Secret

After every trip abroad, Alec asked her how she had been treated by the Jamiesons, and he was satisfied to hear that Mrs. Jamieson was being more gracious to her.

'She had trouble getting used to me,' was Frances' explanation.

She understood much better the deep disappointment that *Boro Mem* had endured in preparing for her sister to come and live as her near neighbour and then to find out, quite suddenly and painfully, that it was not so. She must have been so certain of the marriage! Vera should have cabled her or somehow got a message. Or Alec should have cabled that he had married and given the name of his wife. Then she would have been spared the shock only hours before the intended arrival.

'She's happy,' she said to Alec. 'Her sister got over you and moved on to find happiness.'

He lit a cigarette.

'Miss Vera Padgett' he said a little derisively. 'Everybody thought we were a match, especially as I had a Leave coming up in '49, when I would be expected to meet her and propose. It was a great joke to have surprised everybody by returning to India with a different bride. What a shock you were to them, Fan! But they should have thrown you a proper party just the same. I resented that. It was due to you, as my wife.'

'I wonder why Vera didn't write to her sister to say she wasn't seeing anything of you in England. Then she'd have known not to expect anything. That I do not understand.'

'Maybe she hoped that I would look her up before I went back, at least.'

'Poor Miss Padgett! Vera!'

'Why poor Miss Padgett?' he stared at her. 'She brought it all on herself. Don't feel sorry for her.'

'You must have encouraged her, though. The Tango! Didn't you dance *that dance* with her?'

'She was a good dancer, yes. I can't say I didn't reciprocate a little – I was flattered after all. She dressed well and liked dancing. So yes, I probably led her to believe I felt more than I did. You do know that the

Jamiesons are snobs? You must have noticed. I think they lived in hopes that my older brother would kick the bucket and then I'd be Lord Delarbrey,' he'd remarked with humour. 'And *Boro Mem's* sister would be Lady Delarbrey.'

'Oh, Alec, really!' had been Frances' reproach, though the Jamiesons were a bit snooty. One only had to watch them at the Planters Club, where hierarchy mattered as much or even more than it did in Britain.

'I heard she was like Joan Bennett.'

'Oh, no. She had looks maybe, but it was all make-up. All out of a bottle.'

As Alec seemed to be in a talking mood, she took a breath and told him she knew about what he did for Mr. Jamieson after he had lost his son.

'Who told you?'

'Lydia.'

'Somebody blabbed, then.'

'And if Lydia can know, surely I can know. But I'm not angry you didn't tell me. It was a long time before I arrived, and very delicate.'

'I should have, because it got out. Everything gets out, I suppose.' he sipped his drink. 'We're an abnormal kind of society, aren't we?'

'I suppose it is very different from England. We depend on each other more. I have decided that Mrs. Arkins just follows whatever Mrs. Jamieson thinks and says. But she's all right.'

'I'm happy you have settled in so well, then. I don't feel so bad about leaving you here when I have to be away.'

'Do you miss me, when you are away?'

He paused, as if he had to think about it.

'I get so busy,' he said at last. 'that I rarely think of here when I'm away. But I'm always happy to be home again.'

That would have to satisfy her, she supposed. And she wondered how she could be satisfied with that.

She examined her new bracelet.

'You shouldn't buy me such expensive things,' she said. All the same, she was pleased. He did think of her – he just would not admit it. Why, she couldn't tell.

She slipped it on her wrist. Indian women loved their jewellery. They wore their wealth upon themselves. There seemed to be no such thing as locking it all away in safes. Frances had taken to wearing a lot of bazaar jewellery. It was a lark. She bought brightly coloured bangles and ankle bracelets, and sometimes put gardenia in her hair. She put on her *shalwar kameez* and wore gold-coloured sandals studded with brightly-coloured beads. But this was when Alec was away and she was going about her own house, because the Europeans would think she was '*going jungli*'.

Her engagement ring and seahorse brooch remained locked up, as well as other pieces he had given her. This bracelet too, she was sure, would end up in the safe...

CHAPTER 23 the Tuner

The monsoon didn't stop the trips to the Club, and her friendships there deepened. Polly visited her house, and gave her unasked for advise on how to get pregnant, involving buying some kind of herb from the bazaar, but then she took it all back suddenly, remembering that the herb she recommended was to induce labour, and Frances was to forget everything she'd said.

She had been successful in having the piano tuned! Mrs. Roper from another tea estate had a piano and one Saturday night Frances found out how it was to be done. Mrs. Roper told her that her piano needed to be tuned up as well, so if they would go halves, they could bring the piano tuner from Silchar and he could do the two. They would pay his train fare and accommodation in the village and of course the fee for tuning the instrument. Frances was delighted. Alec was away at the time in Calcutta, and Mr. Roy, having finished his task, left very happily with his fee and handsome *baksheesh*.

After he had left, she sat down with confidence as if having the piano tuned would make her a pianist. Alas, she was as incompetent as ever! But though she could read music a little, she didn't think she made any progress at all, and floundered through the books she had, attempting a piece, discarding it because it was too difficult, and with a sigh, going for another.

She persisted though, with Grandmother's *Melody*. It expressed her mood so aptly – that of *Love, Longing* even - it was her favourite. Perhaps she had it in one of her books – she flipped through them, but what was the use, when she didn't know its name or who composed it? She set the stack of music books aside. Eventually she could play *The Melody* with her right hand, from memory, choosing the easiest key with the least black notes. She felt pleased with herself.

She took walks along the paths of the tea gardens. She wished she could take a basket and pick a row – *two leaves and a bud*. Some of the sari-clad women were three times her age! They were thin, gave her toothless smiles, and worked long hours in their bare feet, filling their baskets. Others were young women, pretty and adorned in bangles that jangled. She would have loved to have taken a basket herself for a day! But she knew she couldn't even think of joining them, not even for an hour, it was one of the things that were just *not done*. Not just because she was European either. India was full of people who did different jobs and would never touch anything else because they would demean themselves by it, and they were shocked at anybody who didn't keep within the boundaries of their class, or caste, if they were Hindu.

So the year went on – Lydia and Mike went Home for a holiday and to Frances' delight, they would be back. They had solved their problem. They had chosen a convent school run by Irish nuns in Kodaikanal, in South India. The education was excellent. Lucy would go there in a few years, and in the meantime, she would be taught at home by her mother.

Mrs. Jamieson was shocked to the core, and argued with her. You had to have your children educated in Britain, if you did not, they would not know their own country, their own heritage, and worse still, they would always speak English with that dreadful giveaway - the *accent*. The boys would never get a good job. The girls would be passed over by potential suitors. Lydia was doing the worst possible thing she could do for Lucy. Lydia argued that times had changed. The world was modernising and everybody was becoming equal. But Mrs. Jamieson, who was supported by Mrs. Arkins, would not budge. Of course there were personal feelings involved; her two daughters and Mrs. Arkins's sons were being educated at Home. Even with a war on, they declared, with British ships in danger of being hit by torpedoes, they had secured passages to send their children to be schooled at Home. It was evidently better to be sunk, Frances wryly reflected, than to acquire the dreaded accent.

Frances quietly took Lydia's part, and was secretly delighted. If she and Alec had children, Lydia had set a precedent. But Lydia and Mrs. Jamieson did not speak for a full week, although they made peace before they left. England was far away, and sometimes, thrown together as they were in Sundarpur, they almost felt like a family. As they were about to put a great distance between them for the next months, they made up their quarrel.

CHAPTER 24 England Leave

*F*rances hung the teatowel on a nail beside the cooker to dry. But her thoughts would not be stopped. She remembered how the years had passed very quickly, until it was time for Alec to have Home Leave.

They'd come to England in 1953, and had stayed for a short time with Lord and Lady Delarbrey in Nottingham. The English branch of the Whittier family lived in one half of an old country house, which had for two hundred years been the family seat. It had once seen the good life with a sizeable tenantry and large house parties. Delarbrey, as the house was called, had once teemed with servants. Now they were reduced to three old people who had been with the family for nearly forty years, two of whom were for the outdoors. Helen did the cooking, and she and the gardener's wife shared the housekeeping.

'We do much better than that, don't we, Frances?' Alec had smirked as he flung himself down on the bed, shoes and all, after a tramp outside in the lanes with the dogs.

'Oh really, Alec. And look, the counterpane's stained! It's hardly fair to that old lady who does the washing, is it. Get up; I'll dab it.'

'Sometimes, you're so good you make me feel ill,' Alec had said, getting up. She felt hurt and said nothing. It was not the first time he had said something of the sort, and she didn't want them to have an argument.

At this stage Frances had quite gotten over her own feelings of inferiority to the social ranks above her own; she had been in charge of a household for several years now, and felt able to laugh at her former self. She'd muddled through and learned from many mistakes involved running her bungalow. She'd dealt with some family matters involving the servants who often came to her for help, and made peace between servants if they quarrelled. She'd had to reprimand. She learned to be firm but never hard. Fair and to not show favouritism. She felt she could hold her own with anybody. She found she got on very well with Helen. But she was sad to see that George and Alec tended to skirmish.

They left Nottingham rather abruptly, the morning after a dinner given in their honour by an old friend of the family, a neighbour who lived in another crumbling old house. Alec had encouraged Frances to dress to the nines and handed over her jewellery, which she didn't even know he had brought. To her embarrassment, Lady Delarbrey was not at all as adorned as she. She felt dreadfully showy. Later, she heard angry voices from downstairs as she lay in bed, waiting for Alec to come up. When he did, he wouldn't tell her what it was about, but it was obvious that he and George had quarreled, and they left the following morning, after a stiff goodbye.

But it had been wonderful to see Aunt Margaret and Cousin Jane again, as well as her friends. Kathleen, Mildred and Grace were married; the first two had babies and Grace was expecting. As Frances had moved into her world in India, they had moved into theirs, of motherhood. It pained her to realise that though she had been married longer than they, she had no child yet.

But Frances would remember this holiday as the beginning of her unhappiness with Alec. The winter before, Aunt Margaret's home had flooded, and it had cost a lot of money to repair the damage, which put her in debt. Frances decided to clear the debt for her. She asked Alec to take some money out of the Bank to give to her. But Alec was unwilling. He seemed surprised that she should ask – it was, he said, an expense they could not really afford. They should be very careful how they spent their money. If they did this once for Aunt Margaret, she would expect it again.

This was startling news to Frances. It was the first time she had heard Alec say they could not afford something. His salary was remitted in pound sterling from India to England and was mounting up. In India, the Company paid for the house, food and transport, and they had little day-to-day expenses, far less than they would have if they lived at the same level in England.

'Why did she not have insurance? That was very lax of her. I don't think she ever liked me, by the way,' he said crossly.

'I want to give her money,' Frances said, with doggedness unusual for her. 'I want five hundred pounds to give to Aunt Margaret. Will you go to the Bank?'

He grudgingly did as he was asked. When he returned, she asked him what the balance was of the money deposited there before she had left England, and he had replied that it was two hundred pounds. She was astounded.

What of his monthly salary? Was that not going into the same account? It appeared that his salary was not going into that account at all, but was in a separate account that had a better return, and it was better not to touch it.

'Where is all my money?' she asked him. 'What happened to my five thousand pounds? And the money from the sale of the house?'

'Oh come on Fan, you want for nothing, and you have nothing to worry about either. You have to trust me. Surely you know it's a regular thing for a bride to bring money with her when she marries, and that her husband may use it as he sees fit. You told me about those sisters in one of those Austen books you're always reading and how much they had each – and how those other women whose father died were unmarriageable and turned out of their house because they had nothing. It might be a hundred and fifty years since then, but it still applies.'

'I didn't even know you were listening to me talk of the Bennets and the Dashwoods!'

'Good gracious, Frances, when I get home in the evening I invariably have to hear the details of whatever you have been reading during the day, before I can even have my bath.'

She was deflated – for a moment she thought he found her amusing, but it turned out she was simply annoying. She stalked out of their hotel room, and went for a walk, and had a little weep her herself in a quiet church.

Was he tired of her? Was his heart elsewhere? Had he met, and fallen in love with another woman on his travels?

And where was her money? Their money?

They visited Wardo and his wife, who had just had their second baby. Alison and Frances chatted in the kitchen as Alison had to prepare the feeds for the next day, while the men were deep in conversation in the sitting room. She did not give Alison a hint of her difficulties with Alec. She did not know her well enough. In any case, there was no need to burden a busy young mother with her troubles.

They spent the last four weeks of their leave in France visiting wineries in Bordeaux. Alec was toying with the idea of becoming a partner in a *château*, the name the French gave to the Estates that produces wine, even though the headquarters of the winery may not be a castle or anything like it. Though Frances enjoyed the novelty of seeing new places and using her school French, Alec mentioned that the French loved vivacious, charming women, and that she should make an effort with the people they met, for he hoped that a certain Monsieur leBeau would take him on. As often happens when a person quietish by nature is told to liven up, she became self-conscious, and her manner became a little more stiff than loose. But it was not her fault that Alec was turned down by Monsieur leBeau. He lacked experience; he lacked background. Wine was a way of life quite unlike Tea. It was a family affair. One was born into it. It was in one's blood. Alec could, of course, borrow money to purchase his own winery and have a stab at it on his own. But it could take generations to become established. He would have to work very hard, for unlike a Tea Estate, there was no army of dirt cheap labour at his disposal. He would have to put in long hours among the vines, and for what return? He would be ninety before he would be able to enjoy any of it. It was a dejected Alexander Whittier who embarked '*The Pride of India*' at Marseilles to return to his manager post in Assam. He was stuck forever in Tea. It was some consolation that he had acquired several cases of good Bordeaux, purchased quite cheaply, for there was still some gratitude for England helping to drive the Germans out, and he had not been slow to remind them of it while he bargained, very charmingly of course. He had also taken extensive notes about the *châteaux* they had visited, and purchased several books about viniculture. Frances felt sorry that his dream of owning a vineyard was gone, but also felt relieved. She had been sure that Alec would not want to put in the hard manual work required, and would have predicted failure. And – they would have had to leave Assam.

As she saw the European coastline grow smaller and smaller, she decided to forget the unpleasantness of their Home Leave. Alec got over his disappointment, courted her anew on board ship, and told her that she looked quite beautiful in the new, smart dresses and hats he had encouraged her to buy. He had also acquired several linen suits in white or sand, and looked the picture of urbanity as they strolled the decks every evening after dinner.

A few days out from shore he apologised for his ill humour at Home. 'Delarbrey, though my old home, seems to bring out the worst in me. My brother inherited all the property.

There wasn't much in the bank to leave. My late father was very unfair to me. But I suppose I am glad I don't have to keep up that old place, it is costing George a fortune. I'm not so badly off, after all, and I'm sorry you should have been in the middle of our disputes.'

There is something about silvery moonlight kissing the waves and starry nights to rekindle the flame of love, and the voyage passed very pleasantly after that night.

CHAPTER 25 *Glad to be Home*

Frances was very happy to step ashore at Calcutta, and as they made their way to Assam, she luxuriated in the sights and sounds that had grown so dear to her. Nearing the end of their journey, the jungle of trees and plants along the road from Sundarpur looked like old friends. Soon the car was drawing up at the old familiar entrance, the gate clanged in the usual way, and they were welcomed by the *chokidar* there. Thankfully Nath turned in the gate of Bungalow Three, and she felt relieved that no change, promotion or demotion had sent them to another, less desired one.

Anwar and the other servants came out to greet them, as they had the first time, and she felt a rush of great affection for them all. Preti thought she was too pale. England was not a good place, when people returned with faces like ghosts! The servants' children flung themselves upon her with posies of garden flowers and by now very proficient in their language, (Hindi was spoken on the Tea Estates; Bengali in Sundarpur), she asked them how they were and if they did not like sweets? For she had several packets of bon-bons and jelly babies in her luggage.

That afternoon, after a bath and a sleep, she examined everything in the house and outside, noting the bounding new growth while they had been away. Mother Nature had, in the course of several monsoons, given them a garden pond in a dip in the lawn at the front, and this year, the pond was home to carpets of leaves sitting flat upon the surface like green dinner plates, while fresh young white lilies rose from the water. She wondered if the beauty of the pond was worth the risk of the new colonies of mosquitoes that would result. Surely it was far enough from the house not to bother them overmuch! Yes, it would stay.

Alec went down to the factory and Frances was soon joined by Lydia and her little boy Michael, who was now three. They went to the verandah and Frances ordered tea, for even though the day was very hot, tea was surprisingly refreshing. There was a warm exchange of news over that and a plate of Walkers Shortbread, and of course Frances produced a bar of Cadbury's for Michael, who made short, if messy work of it. Lucy had begun school in Kodai and appeared to be settling in. She already had several friends, of whom Lydia had had the satisfaction of telling Mrs. Jamieson were also *fully European*. Bachelor Tom had left for a promotion in Darjeeling. They had a party for him at the Club and he had become a little drunk and sang for them, and in doing so, had positively stunned them. They'd had a *Caruso* in their midst and never knew it. They had rounded on him because he had never told them he could sing until he was leaving. He sang *'Santa Lucia'* – Frances could hardly imagine the brawny Tom singing *'Santa Lucia'*. Mrs. Jamieson declared she was going to hang a sign around his neck so he wouldn't do the same thing to the Darjeeling people as he did to them. It was all in good humour of course, but what a canny lad he was all the same!

'Oh, I'm so sorry I missed that!' Frances said ruefully. 'That must have been an enjoyable night indeed!'

There were a few candidates in the running for his job. It was Calcutta's job to choose the man who would come to Sundarpur.

Calcutta could be relied upon to take their time, and for the moment the machinery in the factory was humming, and they hoped it would not break down, as Tom was the only person who had intimate knowledge of every part of it.

The Arkins' had had an anxious time about their youngest son, John, but Frances knew about his burst appendix. She had been given parcels by both Mrs. Jamieson and Mrs. Arkins to post for their children. Instead of posting them, she had delivered them, and had happened to be able to visit young John in hospital, who was ecstatic at receiving presents from his mother and father while he lay in his hospital bed.

'I'm so glad you are back, Frances! This place hasn't been the same without you!'

Frances sighed happily and sipped her tea, casting her eyes about at her favourite place in the whole world. She was pleased with what her senses presented to her. The verandah had an easy comfort. She thought of it as an 'outside room', combining comfort to relax, and a touch of elegance to entertain guests. Their breakfast-cum-lunch table was covered by a white damask cloth; a vase of bright flowers always adorned it. The walls were white, the rest of the furniture, two sofas, chairs and occasional tables, were white cane with cushions embroidered with red rhododendron and green parakeets. She kept a few books on a small round carved table; here and there a shelf or stand held English porcelain ornaments from her old home in London, and a fine bronzed elephant adorned one corner. Everything was beloved and familiar, like one's old friends.

The fan whirred, gently wafting the lacy asparagus ferns to and fro. An abundance of greenery made the verandah cooler to the eye. With loud chirping, one tik-tik suddenly chased another up the wall. Michael smiled at her with a chocolate mouth and chin and said: 'Dank you for the chaclat, Auntie Fanci.'

The women laughed.

'It's so good to be home,' she said. England had been the foreign place. This was Home now.

They ate dinner that night at Jamiesons, and Frances was surprised to be greeted with effusive warmth by Mrs. Jamieson and Mrs. Arkins. The first kissed her on the cheek, and told her that it had been so kind of her to visit her girls. June had written to her, and said that they had been taken out for high tea in a restaurant, and she had never enjoyed anything ever so much, and had apple tart and real cream. 'It was a pleasure,' said Frances. June, the youngest, was a sweet and grateful 12-year old, but she had not taken too much to the older, Fiona. She was hoity-toity and bossy and Frances could see the makings of a *Boro Memsahib* in her.

Mrs. Arkins was just as effusive in her gratitude. How was John looking? And Bertie, had she met Bertie? Frances had met him also, and taken him out for tea. Frances didn't really know how to relate to a fifteen-year old boy, so she just asked him about his school sports and about his Latin and English masters, etc, but soon gave up. He was very shy and dedicated himself to wolfing down potted chicken sandwiches, tinned peaches and cream and drinking a bottle of lemonade. If only Alec had come, Bertie would have related better to him than to her.

She had been angry with Alec for not coming to the boys' school. He had been about to, up to the day before, then he had received a message informing him about a wine merchant staying at the Connaught who had cases of vintage at excellent prices, and as she had already phoned the school to say they were coming to take the boys out to tea, she couldn't cancel. It made it worse to discover that one of them had been in hospital, for they would have been at ease if they'd had each other's company. She did not relate any of that to the Arkins', but they might have wondered why Alec hadn't put himself out. Duncan and Edith, as she was now told to call them, were very grateful that she had taken the time and trouble. As it happened, Alec had not availed of the opportunity to buy any wine, he had gone there and discovered it was rather a swindle.

CHAPTER 26 *the Newcomer*

The new man was chosen. He was an engineer, an experienced planter who had excellent references from another Company in Ceylon. He was to begin after the monsoon ended. Calcutta had never met him, he was chosen on his experience and references but they were confident they had chosen well.

They tried to find out as much about him as they could. He was a bachelor, that much was established. He was Scots from Inverness, and as to his appearance, they would have to wait patiently until he arrived, which was to be as soon as Calcutta was ready. His name was Hugh Anderson.

He moved into the *chummery* late in November and Mrs. Jamieson decided to hold a welcome party for him that very night.

The first thing that everybody noticed about him is that he was tall, pleasant-looking if not exactly handsome, and rather quiet. His thick coppery hair swept onto his forehead in a wave, and he had deep green eyes. He had a measured, quiet way of speaking, and his accent had a soft Scottish burr.

All were introduced. Frances felt that his eyes lingered on her for a moment longer than on anybody else, but she dismissed it as her imagination. He was offered a shot of whiskey – a *chota peg* – from Mr. Jamieson and accepted without delay, confirming him as a whiskey man to Alec, a man who would probably always choose it over sherry.

'I hope you don't have any talent you will hide from us, Hugh,' Mrs. Jamieson charged during dinner. 'I shall never forgive Tom Robertson. He could sing. We had *Kenneth McKellar* here and he hid his light under a bushel until the night before he want away. Do you sing?'

'No, Mrs. Jamieson,' Hugh replied. He looked a little shy of Mrs. Jamieson.

'Well, if you can't sing, is there anything you can do?'

Hugh looked uncomfortable. 'I tinkle the keys,' he mumbled.

'The piano? There's a piano at the Club, so we will have the pleasure of hearing you. And there's a piano in Bungalow Three.'

Hugh cast his eyes about the table to see whose was Bungalow Three, whereupon

Mrs. Jamieson indicated that it was Alec and Frances.

'Oh, do come up and play it whenever you like,' Alec said cheerily. 'We don't play. Frances picks out tunes with one hand. That's as far as we go. Do you know any Glenn Miller? *American Patrol*? *Chattanooga*?'

'Not well, but *In the Mood,* yes.'

'Better still!' Alec declared.

'You should never have admitted to being able to play the piano, Hugh, because you will find that you always have to play at every dance we get up at the Club, instead of having the chance of dancing yourself.' Mrs. Arkins said.

'Oh, Edith! We're not in *Persuasion*, where poor Anne Elliot had to play so that the giddy Musgrove sisters could dance with Captain Wentworth!' Lydia chortled. Frances had lent the set of Austen novels around, and they were all familiar with the characters. Lydia in particular shared Frances' love of the stylish comedic novels. 'I assure you we have a record player, and plenty of dance records. There's the Andrews Sisters, Duke Ellington – oh, many records left over from people who have retired and gone Home.'

'I shall be able to dance so,' Hugh said, rather unhappily, Frances thought. He might prefer to hide behind the piano. The poor man probably had no idea who Anne Elliot was and thought that Captain Wentworth was from the time of the Raj.

'Oh! Those were the great days. We had Billy Cotton and his Orchestra, but I'm sorry to say it got badly scratched. But we still have a reasonable Jack Hylton. And Irving Berlin! Oh! We used to have such wonderful dance parties! It's all gone now.'

'All gone, Marj?' asked her husband with a twinkle in his eye. 'I could have sworn I heard *Button Up Your Overcoat* recently. In fact, you and I did a happy little fox-trot around the floor. It must have been a dream.'

'Oh, I meant that those good days are gone! Really, you misunderstand me half the time, and on purpose as well.'

Her husband winked at Frances and Lydia. Hugh, across from Mr. Jamieson would have seen it. Frances looked down at her plate.

'It's a great wonder we are still here at all, in India.' Edith remarked with gloom. She always echoed Mrs. Jamieson. 'I was sure the Indians would throw us all out. I should not like to go Home. It's gone to the bad. I believe it's impossible to get servants now, so what is the point of going Home? We are too used to it here, Marj.'

Mr. Duncan as usual said little. Frances was sure she had only heard him speak half-a-dozen times, and then only during Bridge when his wife and Mrs. Jamieson got into prolonged chats. That irritated him and he could get quite verbose and indignant but they only laughed at him as they reluctantly resumed the game. He seemed to have no interests beyond cards and whiskey.

Frances wondered what on earth Hugh thought of the company he would be required to keep for the next several years. She very much wanted to know if he played any of the popular classics on the piano, but refrained from asking. She felt sorry for him, being under the spotlight from the moment he had set foot in Bungalow One. However, now that the conversation had changed to that of the servant crisis at Home, she felt Hugh could relax for a time, as the two older ladies could be depended upon to get twenty minutes out of that particular grief.

'Where have you travelled besides Ceylon and Calcutta?' Mike asked, shutting his ears to the exorbitant wages paid by a chain of vulgar shops named *Woolworths* to young girls straight out of school.

'I've been to Rajasthan and Singapore on holidays. And one year, I went up to Darjeeling. I returned via Shillong and spent a few days there. That was – '49. Around this time of the year – a bit on the chilly side, but very pleasant.'

Frances remembered suddenly. Was Hugh the man she had seen in the Cathedral - the man who had stopped her from falling, and said 'Steady there' or 'Steady on' or something like that?

'Why, weren't we there at that time, Frances?' Lydia said. 'But I was unwell, and didn't go out much.'

'Yes, I was there too, for about four weeks.' Frances confirmed to Hugh, smiling, and was sure she saw recognition on his part as well. She remembered clearly now.

One evening a few weeks after Hugh arrived, he came to see Alec, but Alec was late coming back from the office.

Frances poured him a *chota peg* and asked him about his family in Scotland – he was the second-youngest of five, and his father had been a teacher, like hers. This led to her talking about herself; her father had been almost at retirement age when he had married her mother who was many years younger. 'They never expected to have a child,' she had chuckled, 'My impending arrival was a total shock. And then, my parents just couldn't be bothered getting into the whole 'let's train up this child properly' frame of mind, and discipline? They were more like grandparents; very laissez-faire, I should have grown up a spoiled brat! Luckily, four years of boarding school rubbed some corners off.'

Hugh innocently asked if she missed them, and she said: 'They died too young – my father when I was fourteen, my mother – just before I married.'

Hugh startled – he had meant about the distance between India and England, and had had no idea that they were both dead. He went a little quiet, after mumbling 'I'm sorry,' in a rather confused way.

She wanted to put him at ease. 'I think we met in Shillong,' she smiled. 'I think it was you who saved me from a tumble down the Cathedral steps. Does an incident like that come to your mind?'

'I thought it was you,' he said. He blushed a little.

They spoke of Shillong for a while, its situation, sights and all that struck them about it. He had stayed at the Pinewood. They spoke of the Cathedral. She found out that he was from a mixed marriage, as she was. His mother had been O'Donnell from

County Donegal, who had moved to Glasgow as a young woman.

She asked him how he was settling in, and if he had picked up any useful phrases in the local language? He had shaken his head ruefully. He had to have a working knowledge of Bengali, Hindi or Assamese; it was a priority, and in a year would have to take an exam to get a bonus.

Alec arrived then, and asked him to stay to dinner. After that Hugh asked, rather modestly, if he could try the piano. Under his practiced hands, harmony and joy at last sprang forth from the instrument. He was indeed a good musician. He complained that he hadn't played for some months, and he played some pieces from memory, and after a little stumbling and apologising, got some Scottish tunes perfectly down. Frances was delighted with the sound of live piano music in the house. Alec asked for '*In the Mood*' which he made a good fist of. Frances then asked him about some popular classical pieces and he knew Beethoven's *'Moonlight Sonata'* and Elgar's *Enigma Variations*. Hugh liked the piano's tone. It had a sweet, mellow sound. It was very old, of course. Perfect for traditional airs, parlour songs. He played a medley of Thomas Moore, which delighted Frances, who was taken back in time to her Granny Sullivan's cottage in County Kerry, with its turf fire and warm slices of soda bread spread with butter. She had been there twice before the War, and on their last night they always had a sing-song with a neighbour playing the fiddle.

Alec got a little bored by the music after a while, and took up last month's *Country Life* magazine that had come in that morning, while Hugh and Frances talked of music and pianos in general, while Hugh tried out different pieces to hear how they sounded.

He came to visit often after that, but never came when Alec was away. Frances hardly noticed. She rarely thought about him, except as her husband's assistant and a bachelor who should be fed, and wondering vaguely if he would go to England or Scotland to find a wife. She was sure she would be great friends with Hugh's bride, who was at this moment just spectral in shape and form. Surely he wouldn't have to be with Localsh Tea for ten years – not when he had already had done seven or eight in Ceylon. He must have a bit put by. He couldn't have a Home Leave for four years though. She and Lydia speculated with eagerness about it, but decided with reluctance that they would have to wait for their new friend.

CHAPTER 28 A Parting

In November Alec left for a trip to Calcutta, Hong Kong and Singapore. Two days after he departed, when Rosa was dusting the ornaments in the verandah, she gave a long sigh.

'Oh, *memsahib*!'

Frances was arranging fresh flowers in the vase.

'*Kia hua*, Rosa?' she asked her. *What is the matter?*

'Oh, *memsahib*, you will be so alone!' she sighed as Frances' porcelain received the swish-swish of the feather-duster.

'Alone, what do you mean?'

'You and *Memsahib* Finch, you are such good friends!'

'And why will I be so alone?' A dreadful suspicion came to mind.

'Oh, you must know, *memsahib*! How do you not know? *Sahib* Finch, he is transferred. To Darjeeling. So far away.' She sighed again.

'Where did you hear that, Rosa?'

'Everybody knows that, *memsahib*!'

It was not at all unusual for staff to get news of births, deaths and transfers before the people most concerned even heard, so Frances had to bide her time, resisting the temptation to run to Bungalow Four to verify it. She hoped that the servants had got it wrong, but Anwar was throwing glum looks in her direction and she feared it was true after all.

She and Lydia were due to play tennis that morning, but she did not come, instead sending a message that she had some urgent business and would appreciate the morning to herself.

Frances grew uneasy.

Lydia did not visit with the news, and Frances wondered if she should go to her. It was entirely possible that she was too upset to talk about this. Frances plucked up her courage and walked the short distance down the road to Bungalow Four.

'Apparently my husband can be shoved from pillar to post,' Lydia said without turning around after Frances walked into the lounge. She was halfway up a stepladder taking down pictures from the walls and flinging them onto a table, one on top of another. Frances expected to hear glass crack. 'I just thought – we just thought – it was someone else's turn to be moved,' she added with a little spite.

Frances shut her eyes and half-turned away.

'That's right, turn away and go. Some people are special people,' Lydia went on bitterly, crashing another picture down on the pile.

'Lydia, I don't know what to say. I'm really sorry. This is horrible news for me as well. I'm going to miss you terribly.'

Another crash, and this time the unmistakable sound of glass breaking. Perhaps it was that which caused Lydia to pause and collect herself. She came down from the ladder.

'I'm sorry. I know it isn't your fault.' She said. 'Omar! Can you bring some tea?'

'If you're busy, I can just go away - '

'No, it's all right, I need to take a break. And lemon water!' she shouted in the direction of the back of the house.

'But this is a promotion,' Frances said.

'No, it isn't. You haven't been told anything, have you? They're cutting out a job here. This new man is so super-efficient at what he does, that he has time to take on more. They want to cut costs, so they are going to give Hugh half of what Mike does, and Alec the other half. So Mike has to move, and to Darjeeling. Because Tom Robertson has left. He has moved to another company, he hated it up there. If anything, it's a demotion for Mike.'

'That's terrible. I am so sorry this happened.'

'It's all right. You don't have any control over your – husband.'

'Alec? I'm sure Alec had nothing to do with this! These decisions are made in Calcutta!' Frances was aghast.

'Recommendations are made here. Alec and Jamieson must have talked at length of it, and not in the factory offices - did you know about this?' Lydia asked suddenly. 'You didn't have an inkling?'

Frances recalled Alec going up to Bungalow One a few nights in a row, but hadn't thought much about it.

'No, absolutely not.'

'I don't know whether to believe you or not. I shall hate Darjeeling. It will be too cold there. Our ayah isn't coming with us. We'll have to start all over again. Michael will cry his eyes out.'

Frances forebore to say that she thought that they had allowed Michael to become far too attached to Basana.

'Why are you saying you think I might have known?'

'Oh, I don't think you knew, on second thoughts. You're an Innocent. We all know that. Thanks Omar, please set the tea there.'

She poured out two cups. Her hands were shaking.

'And it's that much farther away from Lucy,' she said. 'Lucky you, no children.'

Frances winced. This last remark stabbed her heart. Lydia knew how much she wanted children. This was too much. She took a few sips in a very unhappy silence.

'I must be going,' she said rather coldly, without finishing. 'Let me know if I can do anything.'

Lydia gave a bitter laugh.

'Mike found out that Billingsworth, Jamieson and Alec are into something, something not quite legitimate. I wonder why, Frances – I wonder why Mike is being moved, really.'

'What on earth do you mean?' Frances was alarmed.

Lydia had hopped up on the steps again.

'Ask Alec,' she said mysteriously. 'Oh, he's away, isn't he? Good timing. I'm afraid I'm going to be very busy for the rest of the week.'

Frances walked heavily up to her bungalow. She felt very troubled, and tears came to her eyes. What was Lydia implying? That Mike had suspicions of Alec? That was utterly ridiculous. Lydia had all but made a serious sort of allegation against her husband. Frances was distraught. She should never speak to her again. Many wives would not.

She burned to ask Alec. But he wouldn't be home for three weeks! She carried her burden alone. Though relations with Mrs. Jamieson (she would never be Marj) and Edith were much improved, this was not a subject that could be broached with either. Lydia's words constantly replayed themselves in her head.

Three days later, Lydia walked up to her home and with a great deal of remorse, asked her forgiveness for being so horrible.

'I took my feelings out on you,' she said. 'I shouldn't have. I am very, very sorry. Please forgive me.'

Frances forgave her. It was what she wanted more than anything in the world, but she knew it could never be the same – never truly the same – again. She asked Lydia about the truth of what she had alleged, but Lydia refused to be drawn, saying only that she had been angry and said things she hadn't meant.

'I've lost my best friend,' Frances thought ruefully. 'And she probably won't write.'

Within two weeks, the Finches had packed up and left. There had been a farewell at the Club. They put on a brave face and made the best of things. It had been smiles all round, and they convinced everybody that they had always had a secret wish to spend a few years in Darjeeling, with splendid views of the Himalayas.

Their bungalow lay bare and empty, and was likely to continue so. Frances felt extremely lonely and unhappy. She couldn't believe that Alec had something to do with Mike being transferred. Alec knew she had only one bosom friend, Lydia. He could not have recommended this transfer!

CHAPTER 29 A Quarrel

Alec returned in his usual great form, with a pair of teardrop-shaped gold earrings for her. They were studded with tiny rubies.

'24-carat,' he said, pleased, as he opened the box with a flourish. Alec always mentioned carats.

'They are certainly beautiful, but you shouldn't spend all that money,' Frances protested, taking the box from him and peering inside. She really meant this.

'I'm very well paid at the moment. So don't worry. Anyway, it's an investment. That's what the Indians do, you know? They don't have money in the bank, they buy jewellery.'

The Indian women wore their wealth, but that was not a British thing to do. Certainly not at any tea estate function. She had nowhere to wear pricey jewellery except the Club, and if she did, she felt self-conscious about it. She had some tasteful, inexpensive pieces which she kept out to wear on a regular basis. Valuable pieces might be brought out at Christmas or St. Andrew's Day, but not on Saturday nights.

'I'll put it in the safe,' he said, holding his hand out for the box after she had looked at them.

'To join the gold necklace from Hong Kong and the watch from Singapore? And the brooches and the Akoya pearls? I simply don't understand where the money is coming from, Alec, for all this.'

'Don't worry your pretty head,' he said, taking the box and patting her hand. 'Let me simply say that Localsh business is booming.'

He poured himself a glass of sherry and exhaled. The fan whirred and he loosened his shirt.

'You're a little thin,' Frances said.

'The food was horrible. I hardly ate. You have this place looking nice,' he remarked. 'It's good to be home again. Hong Kong is a very sticky, noisy place, and I didn't know how anybody could live there. My hotel was on the street. Singapore still looks bombed out. Anything happen here?' he asked her casually.

'The Finches have left.'

'What, already? I knew it was in the offing, but I didn't expect them to be gone by the time I had come back. Was there a Farewell for them at the Club?'

'Yes, quite a lot of people turned up. They were very popular.'

'It's a new start for them. I hope they took it in that spirit.'

'No, I'm afraid not. They put on a good face, but Lydia was simply awful about it.'

'Was she?' Alec said, sounding rather surprised. 'Surely she knew when she signed on with Mike that she'd have to up stakes now and then.'

'She said some dreadful things to me about it.'

'Did she really? Well, I hope she is over it by now, and settling in. Darjeeling is magnificent. She'll like it.'

'She seemed to blame you for it all, she implied dreadful things about you.'

'About me?' he frowned. 'That seems rather unfair. What sorts of things?'

'She seems to think the transfer was your doing. She said that Billingsworth, you and Mr. Jamieson are up to some funny business and Mike found out. Why would she say something like that?'

Alec wasn't as indignant as she thought he would be. He simply raised his eyebrows and said:

'Spite, I suppose.'

He went on after a moment.

'I know there's resentment that I can stay put, but it's an unusual circumstance. I've resisted a transfer to Calcutta. I will not live in that or any horrible, crowded, smoky, infested city. Quite possibly Lydia is simply jealous. I'm senior to Mike anyway, so it's not as if *we* could have gone to Darjeeling.'

'Alec – I have to ask you.'

He frowned. 'What is it?'

'Couldn't the post in Darjeeling have been filled by someone else – someone from another plantation, Rajahpur perhaps? Lydia told me it was not a promotion. Is that true?'

'Quite true. But Mike was in a rut.'

'He surely did not request the move?'

'No, not at all. I'm sure it was the last thing he wanted. But as I said, he was in a rut. When someone stays too long in one place, doing the same thing over and over, they can get stagnant and sloppy. I noticed it. I reported it, and recommended the move. We all felt it would be better for him to get a move on.'

'Another thing Lydia said was that you were going to take over some of Mike's current responsibilities, and the position that Mike held may be eliminated.'

'Oh, not me.' Alec declared. 'I'm not taking on extra. I have more than enough. Marketing and Sales are a handful in themselves, without having to supervise production and all the rest of it. I have so many reports to write up it takes me a week to do so after every trip, and then it's off on another trip four weeks after that.'

'Also, Lydia seemed to think Hugh had encroached on Mike's territory.'

'Lydia seems to be lashing out at everybody. That's incorrect. Anderson is efficient, though. Old *Boro Sahib* thinks he can take on more. That would be good news for me.'

'I'm very sorry to see Lydia go. My only good friend, really.'

'Is that a reproach?'

'Did you even think of me when you recommended Mike for a move?'

'No. Not at all.'

Alec was silent. He tapped his fingers against the glass and frowned into it.

'Artificially sweetened, I'll say.'

'So it didn't occur to you that this move would affect me.' she said wonderingly.

'Localsh can't afford to take the feelings of wives and families into account when making decisions that affect the Company.'

'Couldn't *Boro Sahib* have had a word with Mike about his work, and waited a bit. They're farther away from Lucy than if they were here.'

'What if Lucy was in England? How do you think Marj and Edith feel about their children? It seems Lydia gave you some sort of a quarrel. I hope you stood up for me, when she said she thought I had something to do with it.'

'Of course I did!'

'It seems you entertained some suspicions about me, though.'

Frances sighed.

'If you would only tell me more of what's going on, then I wouldn't feel I'm put in a spot. I never knew that Mike was 'in a rut' as you say. Lydia always seemed to be *au-fait* with everything going on in the estate; I know nothing and I sometimes feel stupid.'

'I am sorry it caused you so much trouble, Frances.'

'I do feel that you should tell me more about what's going on!' she persisted.

'What a homecoming! What kind of home is it, when a man comes back from a long, tiring trip, and his wife picks a quarrel with him? Damn well not a good one! I'm going for my bath, and then I'm going to kip until dinner-time, and I hope that by then you will behave with more affection towards your husband. And you don't seem in the least grateful for the gift I brought to you!' He got up, pocketed the box, and went into the lounge, slamming the screen door.

Frances jumped up and followed him.

'Of course I'm grateful! Alec!' But he had passed into the bedroom and slammed that door as well.

Frances was left feeling empty, foolish and sad. In the wrong. She'd been looking forward so much to his coming home, as she always was, for many days now. She'd ordered his favourite dinner, and dressed up and taken extra trouble with her hair. But he would probably not speak to her for the evening. The homecoming was spoiled – completely spoiled!

She'd play the piano for a while, it always made her feel better. But instead of picking out the notes, she laid her head on her arms on the piano keys and shed tears.

CHAPTER 30 'On Her Majesty's Service'

Alec was cheerful enough by lunchtime the following day, and ate heartily. He seemed to have forgotten that they had ever quarreled. Frances' feelings were different. She harboured some hurt. She brooded.

Mrs. Jamieson sent for her in the late afternoon.

'Do come up. I thought you would be lonely, and would like a game of cards,' she wrote.

Frances' heart sank. She hated cards. Evidently Mrs. Jamieson had recalled this by the time she arrived, for there was no sign of the deck, but a Scrabble board was set out on her verandah table.

'Where's Edith?'

'She's at home, lying down with a headache. And I thought I would take this brief opportunity to see you, Frances, because there's something I want to say to you. I know you must be lonely now that Lydia has left, you are she were more or less of an age, and were very chummy. I don't think you should write to her, if you were thinking of doing that.'

'Why on earth should I not write to her?' Frances asked fiercely.

'Shhh!' Mrs. Jamieson threw her eyes towards the interior of the house. 'Pick your tile to begin.'

'G'

'Well, I have R, so you begin.'

Frances scrabbled for her tiles and set them out on the tray. GERONTI

Mrs. Jamieson leaned in toward her.

'I must tell you, Frances,' she said in a low tone, 'that our husbands – yours and mine – are involved in work of a very sensitive nature – listen carefully, because it's not something I shall ever speak of again. It might help you to understand – certain things.' Mrs. Jamieson's eyes were popping out of her head. Frances was astonished.

'Can't you make anything?' her hostess said then in a very loud voice.

Frances rearranged her letters and quickly put out the word 'TONE'

'Is that all you can do?' again a loud voice as she scribbled down the score.

Frances reflected that she could have done a little better if she hadn't been pushed to make her move. But she had hardly thought about her letters anyway. She drew her replacement tiles. GRIEEZE

Mrs. Jamieson leaned toward her again.

'It's because we are located so close to the East Pakistan border.'

Frances looked at her in more astonishment.

'You see how we can be of service to His Majesty,' she whispered. 'I mean, Her Majesty,' correcting herself.

She put letters out to make TABLE using the T of TONE.

'Ah, TABLE!' she cried loudly.

'Very good,' murmured Frances.

'I don't expect Alec to have discussed it with you, but I suspect that on his trips to – various places, he passes information.'

Frances blinked, hardly seeing her letters.

'Come on, play, play,' Mrs. Jamieson whispered, as if they were being watched by a hundred eyes.

'BREEZE'

'Well that is very clever of you! The Z and all! On a double word!' She counted up the score rapidly and scribbled it down.

'You're ahead,' she said with gloom. Then she leaned in again.

'Mike Finch was becoming a little too curious about the affair. My husband and yours had to act.'

'Did Mr. Jamieson tell you this?' Frances asked, disbelieving and aggrieved at the same time.

'Oh Frances, not at all. But isn't it all obvious? Alec comes up here and they are closeted together for an hour at a time, just the two of them. I have to take myself off into the adjoining room. But occasionally, I catch a little of the conversation. They speak very low, but I distinctly hear the words 'agent' and 'currency' and 'free exchange market,' words I don't really understand, but put it all together, and it makes perfect sense. *Espionage!* Don't tell anybody! Are you going to play?' This last in a loud voice.

'It's your turn, Mrs. Jamieson.'

'Oh. There we are.' She shelled some letters out on the board and arranged them to make BAT.

'What of Mr. Billingsworth?'

'He must be a part of it, because he sends Alec away, on *sales trips*. That's the cover. And he doesn't insist he move to Calcutta. It would defeat the entire operation to move him away from the border. Don't you see? What else could it be?'

'What of the Arkins'?'

'Nothing. They know nothing. I am convinced of that.'

'And Hugh Anderson?'

'Nothing.'

'It may simply be business terms they are using.' Frances mused.

'No, they are not talking about Localsh Tea. I overheard something else, '*smuggling*'. They are investigating some very shady doings between Pakistan and India, some movement of goods or – something - and considering that we ruled them up to recently, it's in His – Her Majesty's interest to know exactly what is going on. And with your husband's high connection, why would he not have been tasked with this assignment?'

'I see,' said Frances, not seeing at all.

'Oh, I forgot to enter my score. Oh, never mind. Let's have a cup of tea instead of playing Scrabble. Indeed I have no mind for it at all.' She swept up the board and tiles from the table and put them all back in the box.

Frances left Bungalow One some time later both highly amused and rather worried.

CHAPTER 31 Dark Night

'Mrs. Jamieson thinks you are a spy,' she said to Alec that evening as they took their seats on the verandah.

He looked astonished, and if he *were* a secret agent on Her Majesty's Service, Frances thought, he could not have acted the emotion of pure amazement, any better.

She told him about her afternoon. He burst out laughing.

'What a hoot! A few words here and there. This is the funniest thing ever. And my connection to Lord Delarbrey makes it all so credible!' He was laughing so much the tears were almost streaming down his cheeks. She had rarely seen him so amused.

'*Boro Mem* has too much time on her hands.' Frances said.

'Now you didn't believe her, did you?' he wiped his eyes with his white handkerchief.

'Oh no, not at all.'

'That's my good girl.' He laughed for some time more, while she took up her work – a cushion cover she was embroidering. There was just enough light to finish the gold pineapple. She laughed with him, while he repeated various parts of what Mrs. Jamieson had said, chuckling, until he could laugh no more.

'I say, you are looking lovely tonight, all sweet and domesticated. The light is catching your hair. Come here, Frances.'

She put down her work and came over to him. He pulled her close.

Later that night she asked him the question that had been on her mind. 'But what *were* you talking about with Mr. Jamieson?'

He was smoking and staring into space. The room was dark.

'Well? Are you not going to tell me…?' She ruffled his hair.

'I suppose I might. Provided you won't take on, all right?'

'All right.'

'*Old Boro Sahib* and I have a little something going on. A sort of side-business. You see, Singapore is what you call a very porous border. You can bring almost anything in that you like, and take almost anything out. Do you understand?'

'Well, yes…'

'Now Honkers – or Hong Kong, if you prefer, is awash in precious metals and Chinese businessmen who trade in them. Understand so far?'

'I think so.' But Frances was beginning to dread what she may be going to hear.

'I'm chummy with this man in Honkers named – well, never mind his name. He's Chinese and he gets gold on the black market. I met him on my first trip there, and he told me about something I could do to earn some money. I could carry a little something for him from Honkers to Singapore. I didn't want to get involved in anything fishy, so I said no, but when I was telling *Old Boro Sahib* about it, making a joke of the whole thing, it just seemed to me that I could possibly do it. I don't know how we decided it – to go ahead – and then *Old Boro Sahib* mentioned it to Billingsworth one time when he was in Calcutta – they go all the way back to their schooldays, you know - and Billingsworth thought it would be a jolly thing to try, if I was willing, that is. And I thought I'd do it, just once. And it worked. It was so easy, actually.'

'What worked?' Frances' heart trembled, and she knew her voice was a little shrill.

'Smuggling. This Chinese fellow in Honkers gives me some gold, worth about £80,000 and I bring it over to Singy in my briefcase, and pass it to some other Chinese fellow over there. I get a jolly good cut out of it. I keep half, because I take the most risk, and the others get the other half between them. Our Retirement Funds. Our three-storey house in Sussex, by the sea. Good, isn't it?'

'You have to be joking about this, Alec.'

'No, not at all. Not a joke.'

'I don't like it.' Frances slid away from him.

'Dammit!' Alec swore, and Frances knew he was angry with himself.

She pulled on her dressing gown and went to the verandah and sat there. He followed her.

'What if you get caught?' she practically shouted to him, forgetting Das outside, keeping watch.

'Now calm down, Fan. There's no fear of that. Customs are very lax, and I keep some cash handy – US Dollars – to hand over to any customs fellow who wants to open my briefcase. That causes them to change their minds. They all take bribes. It wouldn't be worth their while to turn anybody in. In fact, these Malayan and Chinese gangs have a very long reach, and they would be terrified of crossing them. Better to take a bribe, let a fellow through, and that's the end of that. Everybody's happy.'

'I'm not happy!'

'Well I was an utter fool to tell you, then.' He paced up and down. The moonlight cast shadows everywhere, and Frances thought the verandah looked eerie. Alec was a thin silhouette, moving about restlessly between the tall vines.

'I heartily wish I hadn't told you. Are you going to tell *Boro Mem*?'

'Of course not. She can live in her make-believe world of espionage. She's proud of her husband being of service to Her Majesty. Why spoil that? Billingsworth had no right to – to suggest you try it. He's using you! And Jamieson as well!'

He paced up and down silently for a few minutes more. Then she spoke again.

'Alec, it's not just the fear of you getting caught, you tell me that it isn't likely, but I'm not convinced of it. But what you're doing is wrong. It's not honest.'

He swore again. He rarely used the words used now and she winced. He paced the length of the verandah once more and stopped in front of her chair.

'I don't need a moral lecture. Everything is different here than at Home. There, I wouldn't dream of doing such a thing. Here, it's the way the East operates. But keep your morals and high principles to yourself.

You're spoiling it. How do you think we're going to retire? Answer me that!'

'How does everybody else retire? Like the Arkins', or Finches…'

'Without this, all we could afford would be a small house somewhere unremarkable, with a clerk on one side and a grocer on the other. No, thank you. I will buy a decent house for us, in Hove or Brighton. Georgian or Victorian, with a good lawn in front, and a big back-garden. I didn't come from a small house. You saw Delarbrey.'

She stared at him, trying to see his face. She wondered how much money he had earned in this illicit way, when a thought struck her.

'Is that how you are able to afford the jewellery you bring back to me? I don't want anymore of it!'

He swore again, and raised his hand in the air. The blow did not come. His hand was still raised.

'Leave me!' he said, as if in some inner agony.

She cried out in shock, jumped up from the chair and ran back to their bedroom, and he did not join her, he went to one of the spare rooms.

CHAPTER 32 Melody in Tea

The following morning, Alec apologized rather coldly for his anger of the night before. 'I am aware I may have acted in a manner that frightened you. Indeed, it frightened myself. It will never happen again, I promise you.' He said, without looking at her.

She had spent the night in various periods of praying, weeping and numbness. Alec was engaged in a very dangerous activity, mixing with ruthless people who would have no scruples if he missed his footing. He was engaged in criminal activities. What if he got caught and convicted? She could never be easy about these trips again. And to think that he had almost struck her in anger!

This was a suffering she had never envisaged. It tore her heart, and was almost more than she felt she could bear. She tossed and turned, and when she fell into a doze, she woke up crying.

And she was sure all the servants knew that they had quarreled, by now. She hoped that Das hadn't had enough English to understand and relate everything to everybody else.

'I will try to forget about it, and we shall try to begin again,' she whispered. She desperately wanted to be happy with Alec. She still loved him.

'That's generous of you,' he said, still not looking at her, as he got up and prepared to go to the office. 'I will not be back for lunch today. I would however appreciate if you sent somebody down with some tiffin.'

She assented quietly.

All day long, her head ached.

Alec returned from the office for dinner.

His mood had softened a little. He was now able to face her. He apologised again. He didn't know what came over him, she was right of course, to warn him against himself, and he should have taken it in that spirit. His anger had been unwarranted, out of proportion.

'I just want us to be happy, Alec.' she said quietly. 'I want us to be friends, and happy. We don't need a lot of money to be happy. Apply for a transfer to another company. We'll get away from here. Please promise me that you'll give up this smuggling.'

'A new position is out of the question,' he said in a brusque, offended tone. 'Now that I have a taste for travel, I don't want to give it up. I'll end up like Arkins, buried in Tea. Oh, I hope you don't mind - I've invited a guest for dinner. Hugh Anderson.'

She was very glad of it. Though Hugh was quiet, having a third person relieved the tension at the table, and provided general conversation. Alec was always genial in company, and this was no exception. When he found out that Hugh had dined several times in Bungalow One, he teased him that he was being groomed to become part of the family, a prospect for 'the fair Fiona', a suggestion that caused Hugh to look comically distracted, before he realised it was a joke.

'So I would urge you to come and dine with us more often,' Alec said. 'He will always be welcome, won't he, Frances?'

'Of course,' Frances said, wondering if Alec was dreading only her company at mealtimes in the future. The thought depressed her.

'Whatever the Jamison's intentions towards you with regard to marriage, Anderson, one thing is perfectly certain. It will be expected of you to take *Boro Mem* out on the floor at the Christmas party for a waltz.'

'I thought I was to play the piano for the dancing,' Hugh said quickly.

'Not at all, we'll put on records. No excuse. Ah, dessert.'

Alec looked down at his plate.

'We had chicken curry with rice for dinner, and now we have creamed rice for dessert. You know I don't like this dessert, Frances.'

He glanced up at Frances momentarily, and she knew that in that moment, that Hugh glanced at her as well. And Hugh saw the tears come into her eyes, and the tremble that had suddenly taken hold of her hand. She was cross with herself for being so sensitive! But the small reproach had jolted her feelings which were very off-balance today.

The fact was that this morning, feeling so dreadful, she had not opened the go-down but told Anwar to decide the menu himself and speak to Joseph. He could cook something from whatever was out in the kitchen. There had apparently been a great deal of rice out.

Hugh ate all of his dessert. Alec pushed the plate away and took some fruit.

When they were retiring to the verandah, Hugh asked if he might play the piano first.

'Oh, by all means, go ahead,' Alec waved him to it as he proceeded.

Frances had risen from her chair. She looked forward to hearing Hugh play. He played well and was able to get the best out of the old piano, as if they were old friends. She hoped he would play something soothing, peaceful.

He began the first chords. They drifted into her consciousness like an old familiar friend – surely it was – it was *The Melody*. Her grandmother's *Melody*!

He played with expression. The piano cradled the precious arrangement of notes and pauses, themselves part of the music. Frances shut her eyes and allowed *The Melody* to wash over her. It gently filled the room as it grew dark and what was left of the sunlight streamed in ribbons of light through the rattan blinds. She was rapt. The last notes died down.

It was over too soon and there was silence except for the usual outside noises.

After Hugh had finished, he went to the verandah. She remained where she was. She did not dare follow or ask what it was he had just played. She had lost her voice. Her heart was full, and she thought she was going to burst into a torrent of tears. Hugh drank his *chota peg* quickly and took his leave, saying that he needed to go back to the factory to check a piece of machinery that had been giving trouble earlier.

'*Stop thinking, Frances!' she reminded herself again, sternly, as her fingernail rent her flimsy stockings as she was putting them on. 'That was sheer carelessness!' She rummaged in the rickety chest of drawers for her second pair. But damaged stocking nothwithstanding, hers was a weakened exhortation. She was annoyed that the wireless was pushing 'Gymnopédie' farther back from her consciousness. She remembered the last two years in Sundarpur, and how it had all fallen apart in the end.*

As Alec was continually inviting him, Hugh came to dinner very often after that. His own bungalow suffered neglect, no memsahib was there to see to the small details that kept a home in perfect order. Hugh often had to go back to the factory at night, and sometimes he spent very little time in his bungalow. It cannot have been a very comfortable place.

Alec felt sorry for him, for the sociable Alec, eating alone was a great penance, and Alec always had an excuse as to why he should dine with them - a bottle of Bordeaux that he had been told had miraculously survived two World Wars in a Parisian cellar, or one successfully concealed from the *weinfürher*, the man charged with acquiring the best wine for Germany. One might as well not eat at all, as eat alone. St Benedict had reserved that punishment for the most serious infractions in his monastery. Father Fitzgerald had told him that. He visited them every now and then and he and Alec got on very well, for *Fitzy*, as he dubbed him, though devoted to his work with a gusto that Alec could never understand, was a clever, jovial man who had the happy knack of relating to everybody. Best of all, he was not a whiskey man, but liked a good Burgundy.

Hugh was hardly a talkative dinner guest, but Alec had a way of drawing people out.

'How did you get into Tea?'

'I had a letter from my uncle in Brazil.'

'You had a letter from your uncle in Brazil, so you sail for India. He'll hardly be able to find you *here*. You are quite safe.'

'Och! I wasn't escaping him. My uncle wanted me to come over and work in his plantation.'

'He grows tea?' asked Frances.

'Och no, coffee is what he grows.'

'He's in Coffee then. So you didn't want to go to Brazil,' Alec prompted.

'No, indeed not. It seemed like the ends of the earth. India was much closer. So I settled for India. And Tea.'

After dinner Hugh usually treated them to a few tunes – but he never played *The Melody* again - and then together they watched Assam fold itself up for the night as the heady scents, fanned by hot breezes, wafted their way. The birds, hens, goats, drums and children fell silent, the millions of fireflies glowed, and sometime later he would take his leave, carrying a torch to guide his steps to his bungalow, for Hugh didn't own a car.

Hugh had, of course, been introduced at the Club. He was very likeable. He was pleasant to everybody, and had the good opinion of everyone, and obliged with playing tunes on the piano that people requested. They often had an impromptu sing-song. Hugh was beginning to lose his shyness, and was developing a good rapport with many of the other planters.

But Frances' spirits were dropping steadily, and she often began to feel low and unhappy. Alec was withdrawing from her. Breakfast was hurried – he was in no mood to talk. Lunch was the same, he often absorbed himself in some reading. Dinner – if they were alone, he withdrew into himself even more. When they sat together, he pored over his wine books, and a new magazine or book arrived regularly from England, or the

United States, or from as far away as South Africa. He seemed to have entered another world. She asked him if all was well, and he replied that he did not need to be disturbed. He was writing a book…or rather, researching for a book he intended to write. He would begin the writing soon. But he hated writing, putting sentences together on paper was a great bore…he would put that off until the very last minute. Sometimes he sat up very late.

She lay awake in the bed wondering when he would come in, hearing the mosquitoes buzzing angrily outside the net, wondering why he no longer talked to, or held her. The jackals howled. She began to experience a frightening loneliness. She kept the best side out for their friends.

CHAPTER 34 Gymnopédie No.1

Alec chose one evening when Hugh was dining with them to inform Frances that he would leave on a business trip the following Monday. It looked bad, she knew, that he required a third party to be present when telling her. She said nothing, just bit her lip.

The subject was not pursued. Frances asked no questions, and Hugh kept his counsel. Frances thought that a bit odd. Would it not be natural to ask Alec more about his travel plans? *Where are you off to this time, Alec?* But he did not ask.

Hugh knew something.

He went to the piano again after they had finished eating. He played Debussy's *Claire de Lune*, and then to Frances' quiet delight, began *The Melody* again.

After a moment, Frances spoke.

'What is the name of that piece?' she asked.

He began it again.

'*Gymnopédie.*'

'*Gymnopédie.* Who is the composer?'

'Erik Satie. French, lived in Paris. He died about thirty years ago, co-incidentally, the very day I was born. July 1st, 1925.'

'I have often heard that piece, but I never knew who composed it. It's beautiful. Stirring.'

'Satie was something of an eccentric. After his death, they went through his things, and found a composition stuffed behind his piano. He had been missing it for years, and had told friends he'd left on a bus. His rooms were in a terrible state, he never bothered to have them cleaned, wouldn't let anybody in. Except stray dogs – he took them in. But for all his mucky ways he was a pleasant and sociable chap and dressed very well. In velvet coats. I am not exactly sure which one they found behind the piano, but it wasn't this one though. This piece, *Gymnopédie no. 1* was early in his career – his later works were experimental and I can't say I take to them. They are as odd as he was himself.'

302

She wondered with quiet amusement if this was the longest speech Hugh had ever made. It must certainly be the longest he had made since he had joined Localsh.

'It's gentle. I wonder if he loved Nature, and was sitting by a lake when he was inspired. Or – maybe sitting in Monet's garden!'

'Not so – he said that his inspiration for this was a Grecian urn.'

'A Grecian urn!'

'An urn with engravings or paintings – something like that – of a group of Spartans doing exercises.'

'The music doesn't suggest anything like that to me!' Frances had cried out, frowning.

'Nor to anybody else, it seems.' Hugh began the piece again. 'But then, one never knew with Erik Satie. He liked to put people off the scent, and wrote some of his later music as a satire of other composers.'

Alec snorted. 'Composers bury themselves for years and emerge with one raucous two-hour din that they call a Rhapsody that one has to pay twenty-five pounds for a ticket to hear at Covent Garden. And afterwards everybody is afraid to say they hated it.'

'It's tranquil – but I sense an underlying *frisson* - what it suggests to me is – *longing*.' Frances said thoughtfully. 'You must have an opinion, Alec. Alec? You must like this!'

Alec made no reply, but left them for the verandah. The screen door banged.

Hugh was still playing.

'*Longing*?' he asked her.

'Yes, *longing, and loss*, perhaps. *Longing for what was lost*. What does it suggest to you?' she asked, after a pause.

Hugh cocked his head to one side.

'The passage of Time. Life itself, perhaps, days closing into nights, nights disappearing into the next day, and all repeated, over and over and over.'

'How funny! Two very different things!'

Hugh did not answer, but played on, and there was silence except for the melody. Frances tried to see the *time* in the piece that Hugh spoke of; but she still thought it represented *loss and longing*.

As Hugh played on, Frances became aware of a new feeling, a current of feeling between her and Hugh – unmistakable – unwelcome! Unwelcome! She and Hugh and *Gymnopédie* were alone. She knew she ought to join Alec, but felt equally impelled to stay where she was and absorb the music.

'My grandmother used to play it. I brought out almost all of her books. Perhaps that piece is in there. I must look. Did Satie write it for piano, particularly?' She spoke in a bit of a rush.

'He did,' Hugh played on. 'Debussy, who loved it – arranged it for orchestra. I have heard that arrangement – they use a wind instrument – oboe I think – for this part -' he repeated a particularly stirring section.

'An oboe,' Frances mused. 'Yes, I can hear it in oboe…it would, I think, give it some melancholy, or a plaintive mood.'

'You asked me, Frances, so I shall tell you what that composition suggests to me,' called Alec from the verandah. 'I have had some familiarity with it before, and it suggests to me a Blankness, a Void. An endless Void. That Satie fellow has tricked us with it. He has made fools of us all. Damned mosquito!' They heard a slap. 'Are you coming out or not?' His mood was again angry, and Frances' pleasure in the moment disappeared.

She moved away hastily and joined him on the verandah and took up her glass. Alec didn't look at her; she put her arm on his – he moved his arm away. Hugh had ceased playing after the outburst, he came out, sat with his drink, and after a very short time said 'goodnight.' Not abruptly – in a leisurely fashion, after making a remark about a storm gathering. He should get back to his *banglat* before it broke. She saw him going down the path towards their gate. What would he think about tonight? Would he think about her? No, please, that would be – unwelcome.

Alec's eyes appeared to follow Hugh's figure, a moving point of light as he shone his torch before him in the blackness as he strode away. They heard his voice wish Das goodnight, and the squeaking of the gate as it opened and then shut behind him.

'You said yes to me, too soon,' he said flatly.

'Alec, what on earth do you mean?' she cried out, then was afraid that her voice had carried over the garden wall to where the point of light bobbed along the road.

'You didn't know any other men, you couldn't, you were young,' he said. 'Your mother had just died; I think perhaps you were susceptible -'

'Alec, you are dreadfully wrong,' she said. 'I fell in love with you. And I'm still in love with you.' She meant it. Her marriage was sacred.

He sighed deeply, as if her words had been almost unwelcome. He was silent for a time, then put out his hand to take hers.

'I don't deserve you, Frances. This might seem like a funny thing for a husband to say, but if you ever wanted – another – and I'm not much of a husband – I would say I shouldn't really mind all that much.'

She gasped. Tears stormed her eyes.

'Why do you say that? Alec?'

'It won't get any better.'

'You are talking nonsense!' she cried, in great distress, forgetting her voice could carry.

He had gotten up from his chair. 'I'm tired. I'm off to bed,' he said and went into the house.

The storm broke. It shook and thundered and lashed the bungalow for twenty minutes and then all was quiet again except for a rapid drip-drip of water from the verandah roof. Frances sat the storm out, her feelings as turbulent as the weather.

CHAPTER 35 Hartal!

She tried to avoid Hugh, or at least she tried to avoid being alone with him, and she saw he was doing the same. She saw that he waited until Alec was home before he came to the house. Once he made a mistake, but she saw him coming up the path, and she told Anwar that she was taking a short nap before dinner, and disappeared into her room. She heard Anwar tell Hugh that *memsahib* was sleeping, and not three minutes had passed before she heard the piano. He played the usual airs, then paused

- he played *Gymnopédie* – rather slowly and with more feeling - and she felt that he knew precisely that she was awake and listening to him. She felt angry. Alec arrived soon after; but Frances was still angry with Hugh and hardly looked at him or spoke to him for the evening.

Alec departed for another trip in May. Some communist agitators perhaps used this opportunity to come among the workers again, but whether they did or not, trouble began to brew at Localsh tea estate.

There was one afternoon a month when the workers were allowed to voice their grievances to management, and *Boro Sahib*, like a squire of yore over his tenants, would sit on a chair in the factory yard and listen to everybody before making his judgements. These meetings could get very loud and emotional as people supported each other and tried to make their voices heard. It took a strong, cool man to keep order, and *Boro Sahib* was good enough at this, but Alec excelled. Without Alec, these grievances were not resolved with the same skill, or perhaps it was truer to say that the workers were not placated with the same skill, as anything promised rarely came to be, but Alec had the knack of making it sound as if changes would happen tomorrow. Once, the promise of new goalposts in their football field, and paid time off to train with a view to beating the Farah Team, ever their rivals, had been enough to defuse anger. Without his particular skill at changing the mood of the crowd from angry to peaceful and sometimes charmed, the workers were often left bitter and dissatisfied.

Frances had come to feel sympathy for the workers. They were poor. They lived in hovels, all thrown together in the labourers village called the Lines. It was true that they had a school, but most children had to drop out very early and go to work in the factory or plucking tea. One of the Italian nuns had told her that many tea-garden women

311

suffered from hookworm, a parasite that entered through the feet and made them anaemic. This anaemia put them at considerable risk from loss of blood during childbirth. If they could wear sandals, the worm could not attach itself to the soles of their feet and work their way up to the intestine, where it would cause internal bleeding. Frances was appalled that the women could not afford sandals. She had asked Alec about it, but he had been annoyed and told her to stay out of estate affairs; *memsahibs* didn't get involved. All the workers got a bonus twice a year, why didn't they buy themselves sandals? Frances replied that she had noticed that their children always had new clothes at those times. Alec argued that if the women were ill, all they had to do was to report sick and go to the Estate doctor.

Frances couldn't help comparing the local people to the peasants in medieval times that she had learned about in school. The workers depended completely upon the goodwill of their managers for everything. She felt guilty with her luxuries when those poor women hadn't even sandals. It did not sit well with her, but as a *memsahib* she could not do anything about it; she knew her place and had to keep it.

No matter how bad the circumstances of the people however, she knew that communists would exploit rather than genuinely improve conditions. Her parents loathed communism.

As an only child among grownups, and without a nanny, Frances had often played quietly with her dolls or coloured a book at her mother's feet while her parents and their guests chatted about national and world affairs. She stayed as quiet as a mouse so that they would forget her bedtime - indeed she had no fixed bedtime. Her father was very much a supporter of Catholic social teaching, which asserted the rights of workers, treating them in the way God wished – with dignity and justice.

Communism and Fascism enslaved people, her father used to say. He used to assert that Hitler and Stalin were two sides of the same coin –godless tyrants, both.

Completely forgetting the child in the room, the adults talked about the dreadful things Stalin was rumoured to have done – the Great Purge, (which she didn't really understand but knew it was bad) and starving his own people, which meaning she understood perfectly. Occasionally her mother would remember she was there, and protest – 'Frank, the *child*.' But her father would soon forget again.

Not that anybody felt that India was in any danger of falling to communism. But areas of India erupted into unrest now and then.

This time they caused a strike, and the tea bushes stood unplucked for two days as the workers protested loudly outside the factory. Frances could hear them all day. As nightfall came, they dispersed and went home to cook and tend their livestock.

About midnight on the second day, she was awakened by Das shouting outside. There were running steps, banging noises, and more shouting. She smelled burning. She jumped out of bed and pulling on her dressing-gown as she ran, reached the verandah in seconds. A flame was curling around the bottom of the verandah posts, and the wooden steps were blazing. Das was beating the flames vigourously with a large sack.

He succeeded. The flames petered out, though the steps were blackened. The verandah posts were iron, so the fire didn't take. Then Anwar appeared, and Joseph, and the others.

Frances had to face the dreadful thought that somebody wished her harm, or wished Localsh harm. The bungalow could have gone up in flames if Das had not been alert. She thanked him profusely for his prompt attention after he told his story.

He had heard the gate open and saw a man running towards him with a flame, so he had moved out of the way very quickly – the man had thrown the flame on the verandah steps and run off. Das normally sat on a canvas sack on the verandah steps, and that was the only item to hand to beat the flames with. He was not injured. Frances asked Anwar to get him a glass of water, whereupon the task devolved past two more members of staff until it landed upon the *pani-wallah*, the water-bearer, and Frances, exasperated, knew that even at a time like this, the proprieties of rank had to be observed, and that if the water had been for her, Anwar would have gladly fetched it himself.

All was quiet again, and she went back to bed, but not to sleep. Before the hooter sounded, the news had spread that Bungalow Three had been attacked, and she was up and dressed properly to receive her visitors. Mr. Jamieson, Duncan Arkins, and

Hugh, who looked the most alarmed of the three.

'Well you can't stay here on your own, and Marjorie says you had better come to us,' Mr. Jamieson advised.

She thanked him, but refused.

'I'll find out who did this and hand him over to the police. They were too easy on the last ones, that's the trouble. *Baksheesh* was paid to let them off.' *Boro Sahib* went on.

Duncan Arkins shifted from one foot to the other and grunted his wholehearted agreement.

'Are you sure you're all right?' Hugh asked her anxiously. 'Would – will I tell Anwar to make you a cup of tea? Or – or would you like something stronger? Whiskey?'

'No, thank you,' she replied, amused in spite of her circumstances, at the thought of downing a *chota peg* and so early. Indeed, all the men looked grim and ashen, as if they could do with something. They left for the factory before the hooter called the workers in, promising her they would find the culprits.

She spent the day in a kind of stupor, wondering what would have happened if the entire house had gone up, and if she would have found herself trapped. If the thatch had caught fire! She could not concentrate on anything, no book held her attention, she found herself wandering about the rooms checking windows, for it had occurred to her that there were other ways people could harm her other than fire. How could Das watch the entire house? She was in a fever of anxiety.

Hugh came up that night and offered to stay with her. He said he would sit up all night and keep watch with Das. She wouldn't hear of that, but she felt tempted to allow him to come and sleep in a guest room. She would sleep easier with a man in the house. There would not be anything scandalous about it, because in theory, the *chokidar* was a kind of chaperone. But she did not want him to stay, she felt that it would nurture their friendship and she didn't want that. She felt both attracted to and yet uneasy at the thought of sleeping under the same roof as Hugh. It was better that he leave her, so she assured him that she felt perfectly safe, although she hardly allowed herself to sleep, and every cough of Das' woke her. He seemed to cough rather a lot and she supposed he was nervous as well.

Rumours abounded as to who was responsible, and over seventy names were mentioned, including Das' own, so that it was quite impossible to find out who had been responsible.

Frances gave Das a reward for being awake on the job and putting out the fire so quickly. He was very proud and pleased, and sported a crisp new white shirt soon after. His wife had a new sari.

When Alec returned, the entire story was told. By then the trouble had long died down and everybody was back to work. The agitators had disappeared. *Boro Sahib* thought that perhaps they had been run out of the tea estate because the workers had thought them despicable for attempting an attack on a lone woman. The Whittiers had a popularity. They liked Alec's easy manner and banter, and Frances' sweet nature and kindness.

Shortly after dinner on the night Alec came back, he went up to Bungalow One, and with a sinking heart she realised he was delivering Mr. Jamieson's 'cut' from the smuggling. That put her in a very bad mood, but she did not dare to bring it up with him. He saw her mood and there was silence between them for the next few days until she was able to stop feeling distraught in her heart.

After that, the only excitement, the only event to look forward to in their little society was to occur in August, when Fiona Jamieson was expected back from school in England. When she arrived, much was made of how she had grown, how pretty she had become, how sunny and lovely were her new dresses, colourful and crisp, floral patterned, bodices fitted, skirts flounced. And the confident, pert way she carried herself. She was a short girl with a bright complexion and a great deal to say. Her sister June was still in England, with another two years of schooling to go. Fiona, whose parents had sent her a generous sum of money together with a shopping list, had brought masses of magazines with the latest fashions, and several pattern books. The women eagerly pored over them, planning adaptations of jersey and wool to lighter versions of linen, silk or cotton. Everybody loved having a freshly-arrived young person around, with all her liveliness, new perfumes, fashions and news of Home. Meat was off the ration, everybody was getting television sets. There was a fabulous

American singer named Elvis Presley, and she rolled her eyes when nobody had even heard of Bill Haley's *Rock Around the Clock.*

CHAPTER 36 Telegram

The wireless shut off in the middle of a sweeping, romantic instrumental. A door banged - Jenny was on her way upstairs to the bathroom. A glance at the clock told Frances she would have to stop dallying and get a move on or she'd be late. She gave her shoes a quick polish; she made herself ready for work with speed and then set out into the wet streets at the same time as Phyllis, the glamourous girl who left the same time as she did, but whose work was in the opposite direction.

There was one aspect of being in England that she found stimulating – she was always busy. It took her mind off things, and she felt the better for the intense activity each day brought. Sometimes she had no time to think. She walked quickly, weaving her way among the hurrying crowds, side-stepping the puddles. Even on Meadow Street, where she worked, some of the pavement was still rutted from war damage. Her head down, she charged on, as if she could outrun her thoughts.

In September 1955, Alec left on another business trip. She wasn't even sure where he was going, but she managed to take a look at his airline ticket while he was in the bath, and saw that his route was from Sundarpur to Calcutta, and from there to Hong Kong, back to Singapore, and Calcutta again before coming home. It was dreadful she had to do this when he was going away, but though she suspected the same route every time, he would not discuss it with her.

She'd mentioned it to Father Fitzgerald. She felt she had betrayed Alec by telling the priest and cried after she had returned home. But what a relief it was, to be able to tell somebody she knew she could trust with the information.

She had broached the subject again with Alec. To her relief, he did not get angry. He said that he had been thinking about it all, and that he planned to get out of this business soon. But then he became withdrawn and unhappy. They hardly spoke now, except about household matters. She had a constant feeling of being alone, and wished she could return to the days as a newlywed, when she felt loved and cherished. They no longer slept in the same room, which hurt her very deeply.

About three weeks after he left for Calcutta, she was re-reading *Pride and Prejudice.* How she'd love to have four sisters or, at the very least, four close friends to bicker and banter with! She lost herself in it, chuckling over Mr. Bennett's irritation with having to listen to his wife's accounts as to who danced with whom at the Meryton

Assembly, and wishing that Mr. Bingley had *'sprained his ankle in the first dance'*.

She was distracted by the roar of an engine. A jeep was coming from the direction of the factory, so fast that it created a cloud of dust visible from the verandah. She put down her book and went to look. The roar had also attracted the attention of the day *chokidar*, Mahommed, and he was going to the gate to see it. Was there an emergency? The horn blew loudly with a screech of brakes outside her gate and Mahommed, surprised, opened it as quickly as he could before it thundered into the driveway with the *Boro Sahib* at the wheel and made an abrupt stop.

'What's the matter?' she cried as she ran down the steps. Mr. Jamieson heaved himself out of the driver's seat and came to her, his hands trembling, his face ashen, grim.

'Frances – calm yourself - but I just got a telegram from Calcutta. Alec's in hospital, in Singapore.'

Frances cried out.

'Mr. Billingsworth had a phone call from Alexandra Hospital and telegraphed me immediately.'

'What happened? What happened?'

'I don't know – Alec - he - ' he seemed to be almost as agitated as she.

'What else do you know? What exactly did Mr. Billingsworth say? Have you got the telegram?' she said, her temper flaring. She had a dreadful suspicion – it was constantly on her mind that Alec had said one didn't get on the wrong side of the gangs in Hong Kong or in Singapore – something had gone wrong – her fears were coming true. Her stomach seemed to knot itself up.

'Where is it?' she cried louder, while he fumbled in his pocket and produced a piece of paper. She grabbed it from him and read it.

'He's in Intensive Care,' she said. 'Intensive Care! We have to go to Sundarpur and place a call to Alexandra Hospital! You'll drive me, won't you?' running back into the house to grab her handbag.

Later on, Frances could hardly remember the drive to Sundarpur. All she knew was when they got there, the operator was waiting for a long time to get a trunk line to Alexandra Hospital. They had to wait for half-an-hour before the call went through. Frances waited in pure agony. She began to say her rosary quietly to calm herself down, but terror continually broke through her meditations on the Sorrowful Mysteries so she ended up offering God her fear, born out of love for her husband, as a prayer.

When the phone rang in the booth and the operator told her to take it, she darted up from her seat. She trembled when she realised the operator in Alexandra Hospital put her through to the Chaplain's office. The seconds ticked by – it seemed an age before the phone was answered.

'Mrs. Whittier,' said the accented voice. 'This is Father Valois. I am so glad you rang. Yes, your husband is in Intensive Care. He was attacked on the street late last night, and suffered a stab wound to his stomach area. He had an emergency operation and is critically ill, though conscious, and we think you should come as soon as you can.'

The Chaplain knew no more, only that it appeared to have been a robbery, and that the police were not hopeful of finding the culprits. He added, almost reluctantly, that Mr. Whittier had been coming out of a casino called the Dragon Eye.

Her three minutes ended, the line went dead. She related what she had heard to Mr. Jamieson, except for the part about the casino, because she was sure that was a mistake. He must have been passing the casino.

They got back into the jeep to return to Localsh, but not before Frances had insisted on going to the railway station to buy a ticket for the night train.

'I have to go to him,' she said. 'I have to go there tonight.'

'No, you cannot, that you cannot do.' Jamieson was looking at her as if she were mad, his eyes staring.

'What are you saying? That I can't go and see my own husband? Of course I'm going!'

'I – I can't spare anybody to go with you -' he said lamely. 'Bide your time, Frances, I'm sure there is no need for any sudden decisions.'

'Oh, don't be ridiculous, he's in Intensive Care!' Frances surprised herself with her flaring address. She saw Mr. Jamieson obviously taken aback, his fingers gripping the steering wheel as he reluctantly turned the jeep around in the direction of the station.

'You don't have to send anyone with me, I can travel to Singapore on my own, I am capable of that. And - I know what you have been up to,' she charged. 'If it's something to do with this, if Alec has been injured because of something – illegal – that you and Mr. Billingsworth have been putting him up to, I will never forget it!'

'You know!' he said, confounded, his face under his tan whitening. 'But we – I at least - haven't put him up to anything – it was all Billingsworth – Alec was willing to take the risk and he gets the lion's share! Frances, it is of course the most natural thing in the world for you to want to be with your husband, but it might not be safe for you to go to him!' He hooted the horn loudly to get a rickshaw driver to make way.

Frances said again that she was leaving on the night train to Calutta, from where she could catch an Indian Airways flight to Singapore.

'Does – does Marj know – does she know about - ?' Mr. Jamieson was shaking with nerves as he tooted the horn again at two goats crossing the street.

'About the gold bars and the smuggling? No, she does not. She thinks you're a heroic spy for the British Government, with your secret meetings and talk of customs and black markets.'

'I know you get something out of this, but what do *you do* to earn your cut?' she challenged him.

'I do the Paydays for him, haven't you noticed? Damn boring job it is too, all day in the sun. There isn't another plantation in India where *Boro Sahib* pays the Labour.'

Beyond noting that Alec didn't grumble every Friday night, Frances hadn't thought about Paydays. She thought Alec had somehow passed it off to Duncan.

They had reached the railway station, and she jumped out to go to the ticket office.

She was ready. She'd asked Hugh to drive her to the station in Alec's car. He seemed anxious about her travelling, and she, a little impatient, told him that she would be fine. Really, she had lived in Asia for several years now and everybody thought she was still a little girl.

'I'm sorry,' he mumbled.

'I'm sorry too,' she said, immediately contrite. Hugh was unfailingly polite, and didn't deserve any snappiness from anybody.

'I hope Alec will be all right,' he said to her. 'I know he was up to some business which was a bit irregular, Frances. I think you might know of it. Not that it was obvious you did know; I just *thought* you might.'

He stopped, rather confused, afraid he had said too much.

'You thought right.' Frances said. 'And I didn't like it one bit.'

'This irregular business is why I am concerned about *you*.'

'That is kind and I do appreciate it,' Frances said. They threaded their way, stopping and starting, through motorcycle taxis and rickshaws to much hooting and tooting until they at last stopped before the Railway Station. The night train to Calcutta was waiting. Hugh saw her into her carriage, and as was usual, the station manager had berthed her with other women in a carriage that slept four.

He held out his hand to say a sincere goodbye and wished her a safe journey.

Jamieson had arranged for her to be met at Howrah Railway Station in Calcutta by a driver from Localsh Tea, and he brought her straight to Dum Dum Airport. There was no meeting, nor any message, from Mr. Billingsworth. But she assumed that no news was good news, as she climbed the steps up to the airplane.

She was in Singapore within hours. A taxi from Kallang Airport brought her to Alexandra Hospital, and she was soon walking along a shiny corridor towards the Intensive Care Unit, and her heart was filling with dread. Her old revulsion to hospitals came to the fore. Added to that, she knew that Alexandra Hospital had been the site of a horrible massacre during the Japanese Occupation, and she felt that its history was giving it an added air of foreboding and horror. She felt sick to her stomach. Suppose he was – she hardly allowed herself to think of that! She prayed fervently as she pushed open the double doors and was greeted by a nurse who seemed cross that she hadn't knocked to be let in.

'I'm Mrs. Whittier, Alexander Whittier's wife.' To her utter relief, the nurse turned her head and pointed toward a corner of the ward. She tiptoed down, trying not to look at the other patients, whose moribund states filled her with renewed fear.

Alec was lying on his back, his eyes closed. His face was white. His pyjama jacket was open at the front and she could see broad swathes of bandages criss-crossing over a wide area, almost up to his armpits. It must be a large wound! A drip ran into his arm, and was secured by a splint to keep it in the vein. She put out her hand and stroked his forehead. It was clammy.

Every scintilla of love she had for him, the deep infatuation of her youth, came rushing back as tears filled her eyes and streamed down her cheeks. As she gazed at him, it seemed that they had never been estranged. He was the debonair charmer of the 10:54 from Kings Cross to Stevenage, the attentive husband of the voyage who guided her around the dance floor and when ashore through the crowded markets of Marseilles and Port Said, the solicitous husband who had carefully screened her food in her first days in India, the charmer who wanted her by his side, who guided her and advised her and laughed with her, who brought her to Assam and to her beautiful bungalow as its *memsahib*.

'Alec! Oh, Alec!'

He opened his eyes. She smiled through her tears.

'Frances.' He smiled, looking at her with affection.

'I came as soon as I heard, Alec.'

'Good of you. I'm sorry.'

'Don't be.'

He lifted his free hand and took hers. He gave it a gentle squeeze. The nurse brought her a chair.

'I'm very sorry, old girl.' He repeated to her. His voice was very low.

'Don't be, Alec. You just get better quickly, love.'

He shook his head. 'I'm not going to make it through, old girl.'

'Don't say that, Alec, of course you are!'

He shook his head. 'When it happened - I thought I was going to die. I thought of you.'

'Oh Alec!' She buried her face on the pillow beside him.

'It came to me in a rush. I felt the life going out of me. Odd feeling. I saw my life flash in front of my eyes. I knew I had been a bad fellow, and made you unhappy. I felt dreadfully sorry about it. And I knew Frances would worry about where I had gone when I had – *shuffled off this mortal coil.*' He gave a little smile, catching her eye in a little mischief.

She burst into tears.

'I said a prayer. My first in years, I think. I asked God to spare you that.' He paused. 'Then some fellows came along and they ran. Next thing I know, I'm in this bed - '

'Who were they, Alec? The people who attacked you?'

'I don't know them. Thugs.'

He paused for a few minutes for breath. When he spoke, it was with a little renewed energy and purpose as he patted her hand.

'Oh, Fan. There's a good Padre that comes around. A French fellow. I had a chat with him yesterday.' He shut his eyes and smiled a little smile. 'I told him I wanted to come to Rome.'

'What did you say?' Frances' first reaction was utter disbelief as she lifted her head.

'What, shouldn't I have?' He opened one pale blue eye in a little familiar amusement.

'Of course – I didn't mean – I just couldn't believe my ears!'

'*Oh, ye of little faith.*'

'Why? What made you - '

He looked at her.

'You. And *Fitzy*. A humble, good chap. Other people. The Wójciks – what did I do, to help defeat - ? You know what I'm getting at. I've lived for Alexander Whittier only, and I was full of entitlement and bitterness. I felt I'd been given an – extension - to patch things up.'

Alec paused for breath.

'He booked me in today. I made my Confession, too. I don't know if his English was *that* good though.'

'It doesn't matter!'

'Then I made my First Communion. I received Extreme Unction. Holy Viaticum. The Works.'

'Oh Alec, that's so wonderful. And you will get better!'

339

'Stop it, Frances, stop it.' He meant it, she could tell. The brief vision she had of their future life in Sundarpur, a life united in heart and spirit - *two hearts beating as one* – was in danger of fading before it ever took form. Her happiness was tempered by the fear of extreme grief.

'I've been a very bad fellow. You don't even know yet. I can't do anything about – the *chaos*.'

She didn't know what to make of that, and gave a puzzled frown.

'And tell George goodbye.' He paused.

'Frances? Listen. You might hear something. About the last time we were in England. But whatever my faults – I've always been faithful to you. I swear.'

He closed his eyes and a long pause ensued.

'Alec?'

'Oh God, if I could undo things.' His lips barely formed the words.

340

'It's all right, love, don't distress yourself.'
She stroked his hair. '*All shall be well -* ' she
remembered this last saying from a nun at
school, who was fond of quoting it. It was
from the Anchoress Julian of Norwich.

'*All shall be well, and all manner of thing
shall be well.*' she said softly.

'Thank you Frances. I love you, you know?'
She barely caught the words from his lips.
He smiled and closed his eyes.

A short while later, he stirred restlessly, and
said: 'Frances? Marry again. You'll have
children.' He squeezed her hand.

He appeared to drift away from her, his hand
growing limp. She grew panicked, but his
chest heaved up and down. He was sleeping.

The nurses would not allow her to stay all
night, and since Frances still didn't believe
that Alec was going to die, she went to a
nearby hotel. She rang them when she got
there to make sure they knew where she
was, if she were needed.

A shrill ring jarred her from a restless sleep at 4:15am. When she heard the firm voice begin with: *'Mrs. Whittier. This is Alexandra Hospital. I am very sorry to have to inform you...'* she knew her entire world was in smithereens.

CHAPTER 38 Danger

Father Leo, the 'padre' who had received Alec into the Catholic faith, became her greatest support during the next few days. Alec would have to be buried in Singapore. It would be a very quiet affair, and no mourners but herself. What a grief! She had phoned his brother, who had been shocked, but had offered no practical help, and was certainly not about to undertake a long-haul journey to oversee Alec's affairs or help in any way except to offer her his sympathies. She was a little pained, but supposed that his brother was of the opinion that Localsh was there to assist her. And it was a long, long way from England to

Singapore. Nevertheless, she delivered the message from Alec, and she heard the sobs at the other end of the line.

There was no question of bringing Alec back to England.

But where had Alec been staying in Singapore? She would have to find out, because she had to collect his things. He'd had no wallet on him, and the hospital had no address for him. It was only because he had been carrying some documents in an inside pocket which had the Localsh Tea letterhead that the police were able to inform the Hospital who they should contact. The police, Fr. Leo told her, hadn't yet begun their investigation in earnest and had not found out where the murder victim was staying. His hotel key was not in his pocket.

She found a list of hotels and began the task of ringing them all. How dreadful that Alec had not even told her where he was staying! Years ago, he had stayed in Raffles, but had complained that his expense account would not cover him to stay there anymore. She tried several lesser-known hotels. They did not have a guest of that name. Finally she rang Raffles, and they confirmed that he was a guest there. She took a taxi, and with Fr. Leo's help, who asked the police to confirm the circumstances with the manager, she was handed the key to Alec's room. Fr. Leo waited for her in the foyer while she went up.

The sight of all that was familiar to her was heartbreaking. His clothes. Two good suits, perfectly pressed, hanging in the wardrobe. Washbag and shaving gear in the bathroom. A change of shoes, his brown ones, neatly stowed under the suitcase rack. Papers with his writing on them in the drawer beside his bed. His blue pyjamas neatly folded. A packet of Embassy. A strangely silent room without its occupant. It seemed to know he would not be coming back. She saw his briefcase and found there only letters and papers, seemingly Localsh business. She opened the suitcase. She hoped that she would not find anything there that was contraband, but thankfully it held just shirts, ties, underwear and socks. She packed up everything, and realized that she had no use for them at all. What was she to do with them? She had to throw out the washbag and shaving things. The clean clothes she would give to Fr. Leo for the needy.

With dread she realised she would have to pay the bill here, but how to do that? It was one of the most expensive hotels in all of Asia! She did not have that much money. She remembered that she had to convey the bad news to Calcutta. She would ask Mr. Billingsworth to settle the bill. She wondered how on earth she was to think of everything. And the funeral! How had she not thought of that before now? Was there anything else she needed money for? And why did she immediately have to worry about money, after a death?

What a tangle! As she sat in the hotel room waiting for Localsh Tea to return her call, she heard a noise outside the door. Then a loud, demanding knock which she ignored, keeping as still as a mouse. She heard indistinct talking, angry words, even a push against the door. She kept silent, but her heart raced so fast she felt light-headed. They went away, but she was trembling. Thank God Alec had handed the hotel key in at the desk on his way out! It occurred to her that it might have been stolen as well, recognised as Raffles and the criminals would have been able to let themselves in.

The call came at last, and it was Mr. Billingsworth himself on the line. She told him the bad news. He was very shocked, spoke in halting sentences, and when she told him of her dilemma he agreed immediately to wire a sum of money to cover the bill and the funeral expenses. He then coughed and rather nervously told her to be very careful. He asked her twice if

Alec had had his wallet stolen, and if she was sure it was nowhere in the room, or if there was any money in the room, tucked away somewhere. She assured him that she would go through the room again, just in case she had missed something, but she wondered why he was so insistent. He rang back after a while and told her to ask Reception if Alec had handed anything in for safekeeping. He told her too that most of the bill for Raffles would have to come out of his pending salary, for he did not have permission to stay there.

How had Alec expected to pay the bill, if Localsh was not paying? The only possible answer made her despair. But she had at least the assurance from himself, that he had made his peace with God before he died. She would have to remind herself of that. How good Our Saviour was to the repentant sinner! *'I tell you this day you shall be with Me in Paradise.'*

At Reception, she was very relieved that Mr. Whittier had not given them anything to place in safekeeping. No gold bars! Her mind had been over-active. If there had been a transaction, Alec had carried it out before he had been murdered, and most likely had the payment on him, in his wallet, which was now gone. A part of her felt relief. What she would have done with a set of smuggled gold bars, she did not know. Given them to the police, she supposed, in which case some people would have been rather put-out.

The connection with Lord Delarbrey became known in the British community shortly after Alec died, and Frances found that this was to attract some of Singapore's ton. Back at her own hotel, she found a middle-aged woman in a flowery dress and large hat waiting to see her. She introduced herself as Gertrude Browne, the wife of one of the Crown lawyers, and she insisted she move out of the hotel there and then, and into her home. She seemed to be a plain-spoken motherly woman, rather reminding her of Aunt Margaret, so she allowed herself to be looked after. Mrs. Browne took her under her wing. The criminal investigation took on life. The police superintendent was a friend of the Brownes, and that evening he called to the house, a graceful colonial-style mansion only slightly damaged from the Japanese occupation.

'I'm afraid we have very little information, Mrs. Whittier. Your late husband was set upon coming out of the Dragon Eye Casino in Prince Edward St by a gang of thieves, and stabbed and robbed. A few men happened upon the scene, and gave chase, but they got away. I'm afraid that since it was dark, identifying those responsible may be next to impossible.'

'But I don't even understand why my husband was in a casino. He was not a gambler.'

Superintendent Crowe looked upon her gravely and with sympathy. He scratched his ear and paused before his next words.

'I am afraid, Mrs. Whittier, that he was a regular there. Our enquiries found that he had lost heavily that night. He lost about a thousand pounds in Malayan dollars.'

A new blow.

'And,' continued the Superintendent, 'We have reason to believe from our interview that we conducted with the owner of the Dragon Eye, that the robbery may have been because of some outstanding debts. Your husband had been threatened the night before.'

Frances felt the ground go from under feet. Alec? *Debts? How much? How was she going to pay them? What would happen to her if she did not?*

'I would strongly advise you to leave Singapore as soon as the funeral is over. To that end, I will have a car waiting for you at

350

the cemetery to take you straight to the airport.'

'You think I am in danger?'

'Creditors are angry entities, Mrs. Whittier.'

Evidently he didn't think she should stay to pay off these people, whoever they were. She was relieved that there was no legal obligation on her part, or that if so, he felt her personal safety superseded it. He was concerned for her. She felt ill. She was very grateful that Mrs. Browne had spirited her away from her hotel, for even the slightest noise in her hallway would have created anxiety.

After the funeral Mass three days later, Frances felt that she was being watched by a group of men not one hundred feet off, but when they saw that she was surrounded by a small crowd, they withdrew. They must be creditors. What would have happened if she had been alone? The burial was hurried, and Frances had no time to linger by the

graveside before she was beckoned away –
an official car awaited her. Handshakes,
goodbyes, thanks – all were carried out with
hurry and she ascended the steps of the
plane not an hour after the burial. She was
soon airborne. She had a window seat and
watched the water lapping the Singaporean
coast as they soared above it. Somewhere
below Alec Whittier rested, and she was
alone.

CHAPTER 39 *The Billingsworths*

Mr. Billingsworth and his wife met
her at Dum Dum Airport. She was
to stay with them in Calcutta that
night before catching the train back to
Sundarpur. She had demurred, but she didn't
want to stay alone in a hotel. But she wasn't
there for long before she knew that their
motive was hardly kind.

Mrs. Billingsworth was a rather small, dour,
silent woman. Frances didn't feel that her
sympathy was heartfelt. She wondered if she

knew of Alec's smuggling and her husband's involvement. If so, she may be heartily glad to be rid of Alec. Conversely, she may have been 'in on it' and feel cheated now.

It became apparent that Mrs. Billingsworth indeed knew a great deal. As they threaded their way through Calcutta's congested, noisy streets, she asked Frances if Alec had left any 'envelopes' in his briefcase, or lying around his hotel room.

'Oh, no.' she said, grasping her meaning. 'I made sure to collect everything of his that was there.'

'Did you lift the mattress?'

'Oh, no. Why should he put anything under the mattress?'

Mrs. Billingsworth pursed her lips and frowned.

'He may have placed something in the Hotel Safe.'

'No, I asked them to look.'

'They may have looked, but that doesn't mean that there was nothing there. There may have been cash. They may have lied, you know.'

Frances was silent. It was obvious that Mrs Jamieson was expecting their 'cut' out of whatever transaction had been afoot in Singapore.

'Did the police tell you it was quite hopeless? Getting his wallet back?' Mr. Billingsworth interjected.

'Oh, completely! Was there – something that you expected Alec to bring to you?' she asked bluntly.

There was a pause, before Mrs. Billingsworth said:

'I gave him quite a large sum of money to buy jewellery for my son's wife. I am sorry it appears to have been – lost.' She looked suspiciously at Frances.

354

'I am very sorry too,' Frances said. 'But even sorrier that my husband lost his life.'

'Of course, of course!' said Mr. Billingsworth. 'What's a few pounds compared to a human life, and that of a good employee and friend. The best.'

Frances bit her lip.

A long pause ensued. The driver hooted every few minutes at rickshaws and pedestrians to get out of his way.

'You see, we think you left prematurely. They may have looked harder for the thieves, if there was a relative around to pester them, to make a fuss, you know,' the older woman continued.

'I was advised to leave Singapore as soon as possible,' she said.

'Why was that?'

Here, Frances was stuck. She didn't want to tell them that Alec was a gambler, had debts, and that she was the target for the creditors.

Maybe they knew already, but she was not going to mention it.

'The police thought it advisable. I don't know,' she said rather helplessly. Nothing more was said as they wound into a more quiet, affluent area of the city.

She was shown her room and invited downstairs for a drink before her bath and dinner. She sipped a dry and rather dull sherry in their dark front parlour with her host. Her hostess did not appear.

When Frances went up to her room about a half-hour later, it seemed to her that somebody had been in there – but that was hardly unusual, servants in Asia came and went as they pleased. All the same, whoever it was had moved her things around a little. She'd changed her shoes and left her sandals on top of her suitcase, but they were now on the floor. Perhaps a bearer had moved them.

Her door opened softly, an *ayah* – no, she was an *amah* in Malaya - came into the room, went into the bathroom and turned on the taps.

'Bath, *mem*.'

'Oh, thank you' Frances said gratefully.

She left and was back again in a moment or two.

'This for you.' She handed her a white silk dressing-gown. 'My *mem* said to give you. It belong to her,' she said, and disappeared.

'Tell her, thank you.'

Frances undressed, put on the gown and went into the bathroom. While in the bath, she heard the door of her room open, and someone come in. She assumed it was the *amah* again. But she startled when she heard a snapping sound. It sounded just like her handbag closing! If you did not open the handbag wide enough after unclasping, the clasps snapped shut again on one's finger. You had to reopen it, pull your pinched finger out quickly and then it snapped shut again, loudly. It had taken her a while to get used to it when it had been new, and she had pinched her finger more than once until she had learned the knack of quickly opening it wide so that the clasps wouldn't snap together again. It could give quite a painful pinch.

'Who's there?' she asked immediately, reaching for a towel.

She went out, but whoever it was had left the room. She looked into her handbag, concerned that her hosts had a light-fingered servant. But everything was there. Her purse with her money, lipstick, rosary beads, a handkerchief, and other things. But all the clothes she had been wearing that day had been disturbed. Somebody thought she had hidden money on her person.

Dinner was rather silent. They were suspicious of her. She was very wary of them.

She did not sleep very much. The window didn't shut properly and mosquitoes and other insects flew in. She wondered if Alec had ever slept here. She thought it unlikely, as he would have disliked it very much. Alec would have been given a better room, she thought, as he was the goose that laid the golden egg. Or perhaps he always stayed at the Great Eastern. How little she knew of her husband's other life!

Breakfast was another silent affair, in a breakfast room with a small round table. The couple was clearly out of sorts and did not speak. They must have indeed lost a great deal of money, Frances thought bitterly. She found it difficult to feel sorry for them. She would leave today.

When Mrs. Billingsworth reached for the milk jug, Frances distinctly saw a small purple bruise on the tip of her forefinger.

'I would like you to come into my study, Mrs. Whittier, after breakfast.' Mr.

Billingsworth said. 'We have some affairs that have to be gone through.'

After breakfast, she followed him there. He opened a drawer and took out a folder. There were various forms she had to sign, as Alec's next of kin. She obediently did so.

'As I said, Mrs. Whittier, your husband never had the Company's blessing to stay at Raffles. The bill was enormous. And you must know, of course, that Localsh can't be expected to pay his funeral bills. So I am very sorry to tell you, that there is nothing due to you by way of financial help. Indeed, it seems that Alec's estate may owe Localsh Tea some money. There will be a Widow's Pension, and we may deduct monies from that over a period of time to cover all that we had to pay up-front.'

Frances felt dismay, then anger.

'Mr. Billingsworth,' she found her voice. 'I know the scheme which you and Alec and Mr. Jamieson have been involved in.'

'I don't know what you're talking about, Mrs. Whittier.'

'You know. You do know. You were the instigator! Alec told me about it. About the smuggling of gold bars, or bricks or whatever they were, from Hong Kong to Singapore.'

'I don't know what you are talking about,' Mr. Billingsworth did not meet her eye. 'And I am sure Mr. Jamieson would deny such a charge.'

'Oh, no. He has not denied involvement!'

'I never heard of such an arrangement as you describe, I'm sure it's hogwash. Smuggling gold bars! Somebody was having a little fun with you in a very cruel way. I will hear no more about it.' he raised his hand. 'You will kindly never mention this hogwash matter again.'

Frances looked at him with a mixture of anxiety and revulsion.

'If your husband said anything to you of that sort,' he said. 'That he was a smuggler, or something – he must have been pulling your leg. Alec was just a tea planter with a knack for wining and dining and obtaining contracts. That's all. Or at least, that's all that *I* knew.'

'You were expecting your cut, weren't you? You even think I might have appropriated it!' Frances hardly knew where her words were coming from, they were so audacious. Perhaps what she had been through in the last few days had made her lose her fear of everybody and everything. How could her life become any worse than it was now? 'Somebody has been searching my personal belongings. I don't think it was a servant. My handbag.' She said this last with emphasis.

He grew red and mumbled something she couldn't hear, and fumbled about the desk.

Frances hoped that when she walked out of this house that she would never have to see this obnoxious man and his wife again.

'You have four weeks to vacate your Bungalow. Localsh must pay your voyage home. There is no resettlement money owing. There's nothing else to be done here in Calcutta, and you will be anxious to get back to Sundarpur so that you can prepare to remove. I took the liberty of booking you on the Assam Mail tonight.'

Frances had known that she must leave her bungalow and India, but she had not given it much thought, for everything else had pushed it to the back of her mind.

What will become of me? she suddenly thought. *What am I to do?*

I t was a tedious journey. Her thoughts crowded her and she felt unable to form any kind of picture of what was to come next. She felt – frozen. Indecisive. Frightened.

As the train slowed to a halt at Sundarpur Station, she saw a familiar face among the crowds on the platform. It was Hugh, and her heart flooded with gratitude. He saw her as soon as she disembarked and walked towards her, arm extended in a handshake. He clasped her two hands in his so warmly and murmured that he was very sorry for her trouble. At last, she was with friends.

He drove her home to her dark bungalow. Anwar was waiting with a flask of tea, a plate of cold chappatis, a bowl of lentils and a banana. His face was a portrait in sorrow as he made his salaam.

'I am very sorry to hear about *Sahib*. And now, you will be leaving,' he said in a kind of desperation. '*You* will go back to England.'

'I suppose I will,' she said in reply.

Hugh stayed with her for an hour. She told him to help himself to a '*chota peg*'. She told Anwar to go home and beginning with 'Just between ourselves, Hugh,' she related the events to him. She knew she looked exhausted and shaken and frightened and sometimes her story came out disjointed and fatigue made her words slow and halting. But Hugh listened intently, his brow furrowed with a little frown as he tried to make sense of it all. Of the Billingsworths, she said little. She was conscious that Hugh was dependent on Localsh for a living and was unsure if she should poison his mind against them. He already knew, in any case, about the smuggling.

Frances roamed about the house after he had left her. It was eerily empty already.

'As for man, he flowers like the field, the wind blows and he is gone, and his place never sees him again.'

She slept deeply. She was exhausted. She did not wake to the factory hooter. Eventually Anwar pushed open the door and, averting his eyes to another part of the room, told her that it was ten o'clock, and that she had visitors, *Boro Mem* and Miss Fiona, and *Memsahib* Arkins.

Women, thank goodness, she could just pull on her light dressing gown and drag a comb through her hair. She found them sitting in the lounge, as Rosa was washing the floor of the verandah.

They were as sympathetic as they could be, but though she tried to exert herself, she could not help feeling rather detached. A silence born of shock and exhaustion seemed to have come over her. Thankfully they asked a great deal of questions – and she managed to answer them all without saying that Alec had had a gambling habit and that he was probably murdered over a debt. She wanted them to believe that it was a random robbery. Neither did she mention that she may have been in danger and had to leave Singapore as hastily as she could.

She thought Fiona took an odd interest in the room, looking around at it, staring at the piano, looking with little searching eyes at the bookcase.

'Are you taking all those books with you?' she asked abruptly, after her eyes had roved to the bookcase.

'Fiona!' said her mother.

'Oh, I have to ask, Mummy, because I was going to say, that she might as well take all the books away, because really they have had their day. Some of them must be a hundred years old. Who would be bothered with them? If she likes them, she might as well take them.'

'I haven't even thought about any of that yet,' Frances said quietly.

Anwar brought them iced lemon water, and Rosa finished in the verandah and began to swish her duster around the room.

'You're going to miss having servants, when you go back to England.' was Fiona's observation.

'That's what we would all miss,' Mrs. Arkins lamented, setting Mrs. Jamieson off too, and Frances didn't have to talk for twenty minutes. She watched them depart with some gratitude, and went to have a bath and get dressed for lunch. By the time she emerged from her room, the table was set for one in the verandah and a bowl of lentil soup, chappatis and rice were waiting.

I have to sort out his affairs, she thought. *I have to go through his desk here, and at the office. I don't even know where I am to get money to pay the servants, without his salary. Good Lord,* she prayed, *what am I going to do?*

There's the safe. There has to be money in the safe! Or valuables! The jewellery, of course! It should be enough to pay everybody, and keep me going, and settle me in England. Yes – I may do a secretarial course – even go to University, but am I too old? I will have to do something. That is certain.

She spent the afternoon writing to Aunt Margaret. She had not had time to write to her until now. It was a very difficult letter, not just telling her that Alec had died, but because she had to say that she would be in England again in two months, permanently. Somehow it made it all very final for her, in her own head, and she struggled and paused and shed tears over the words.

Father Fitzgerald came up to see her later. She told him what Alec had said. 'We'd been chatting recently,' was his reply. 'He said he was in trouble and he couldn't see any way out of it. I am sorry it ended this way, God rest his soul, but I'm consoled, as you are too, that he made his peace with God.'

The Jamiesons had invited her to dinner so that she wouldn't be alone. Hugh invited himself along too and they drove up in the Humber. She asked him to help her to sort out Alec's affairs. He agreed very readily, and seemed glad to have been asked.

She didn't trust Mr. Jamieson to help her. Was Jamieson, like Mr. Billingsworth, angry that he had been deprived of his cut? He was very, very quiet and she thought that she would give him the benefit of the doubt, and put his silent mood down to shock at Alec's death and perhaps the guilty worry that the smuggling had had something to do with it. She was not about to enlighten him as to the Dragon Eye, though she had a hunch that it would somehow come out. Didn't everything?

CHAPTER 41 *The Chaos*

All the drawers of Alec's desk at the office were locked. The key was easily found hanging on a little hook underneath. The bottom drawer held a small ledger, in which there were several pages of names and a figure written after each one. The first ten pages of entries had been crossed out. The last four pages had not – and Frances read them down. They were all about money. RS - Rupees. Malayan Dollars - Ringitt.

Roy Chaudhury in Sundarpur, RS10,000.
Thakur RS70,000.
Masterson £90.
Kali Gold and Silver RS15,000.
Mr. Wang Diamond River Jewels 10,705 –
Malayan dollars.

She read on. O'Brien - several sums varying from £25 to £88.70 and more. Many more! Who were all these people? Masterson she knew – he was a shifty character; the

boxwallah. He was a friend of Mark
O'Brien, who was a known card shark.
Could these figures be – debts?
4000 to a Mr. Xi in Singapore in British
Borneo Dollars.
A Mr. Xhou in Hong Kong, $150.
Hugh! He had even touched Hugh for cash!
Hugh was owed RS5,000.

The safe had to be forced open. She didn't
know the numbers. She felt a bit humiliated
telling Hugh this, as if Alec had not trusted
her, or thought she was too young or
gullible. Hugh got a crowbar and opened it.
While this was going on, Frances paced up
and down in severe anxiety. What if there
was nothing there? What if he had sold the
jewellery to pay some of the debts she had
seen crossed off in the ledger?

'We have it,' Hugh said as the door clattered
to the ground. Frances sprinted forward.

Thank God! Most of the jewellery seemed to
be there. There was even her engagement

ring and the seahorse diamond brooch that she had not seen since the trip to England.

Frances need not have worried about finding out who the people in the ledger were. News of Alec's death spread quickly and she was soon receiving letters, cables and even personal visits from local creditors to collect the money owed. By now she had found many other letters stashed in the back of the desk. These demands were coming from afar. A debt incurred at The Dragon Eye was mentioned. Some were downright frightening. '*We will watch for you at the ports – we will find you.*' Why had he returned after receiving threats like that?

Frances was distressed to find that some of the jewellery he had brought back for her was as yet unpaid for. She found several angry demands.

She also found it very difficult to empty the house of Alec's things. What was she to do with his wine books and magazines? She could of course leave them for the next occupant; many people did that with books and records, and they became part of the house.

She only had four weeks, and she managed to pay the debts. With little cash available, the jewellery was used for repayments. Her better English-made dresses and Alec's suits and good shirts were acceptable to the Indian creditors. Anwar and the other servants received the remainder, they were very pleased with them. They would not wear them, but English High Street clothes would fetch a nice little sum in the bazaar.

Hugh helped her to deal with the excruciating demands and dealt with the more intimidating of the creditors. He proved himself more than equal to the task and in dealing with the demands showed presence of mind, sound judgement and a combination of shrewdness and diplomacy. Gone was the diffident Hugh and in his place was a firm, decisive man who did not hesitate to come to her aid in every way. She leaned on his quiet, solid strength.

The jewellery would have to be sold. All of it. It would have to be taken to Calcutta to be sold and from there, the money wired to those who were owed it. It was terrifying. Hugh offered to accompany her to Calcutta upon her return journey to England, in order to assist her to accomplish this. In the meantime, they had to attempt to contact the creditors and assure them that the payment would be on its way very soon, for Frances remembered the 'long reach' remark that Alec had made to her. She did not want them to send anybody to Localsh.

She thought of sending some of the jewellery back to *Kali Gold and Silver* in Calcutta and Mr. Wang at *Diamond River Jewellery* in Singapore, but they couldn't work out the logistics of this. There was too much risk of its being stolen. The most sensible thing was to sell and wire the money. Alec's gold watch and cufflinks would have to be added to the pile, as would her engagement ring and seahorse brooch.

As for the Dragon Eye and the man in Hong Kong, Frances didn't know what to do about that. *Oh, Alec, what a mess!* she said inwardly. She remembered then that Alec had told her about *chaos*. This, then, was what he meant.

'It's very decent of you to do all this for me,' she said to Hugh on one of her last days as she packed up her mother's porcelain. 'I don't know what I would have done without you.'

'I'm honoured you trust me with it,' was his reply.

'I do,' she said, smiling. 'I don't know what to do if Alec owed money anywhere else. I'm afraid something else will pop up, after I've left.'

Hugh was consulting the names in the ledger and the demands. 'These are all accounted for now, including the creditors we will pay off after you have sold the jewellery. If there are any outstanding, you can't verify it, can you? So you will have to ignore any new demands. You don't have any record.'

'I hope that covers everybody.' she said, sadly. Alec had had to surrender his life because of non-payment of debts. It was too much to pay. Poor Alec! She prayed for his soul every day, that if he were in Purgatory, he'd get out soon, and into God's presence. *This day you will be with me in Paradise.* Did that mean the good thief went straight to Heaven? She'd continue to pray for Alec just in case. Father Fitzgerald said that souls went to Purgatory so that their hearts would be purified in the Divine Fire of perfect Love. It was a happy state, he said.

Mr. Jamieson came to see her one day when his wife was shopping in Sundarpur. 'I wanted to take this opportunity to speak with you alone,' he said, with a very wretched expression. 'I can't tell you how sorry I am for everything to do with this. I only mentioned this smuggling suggestion to Billingsworth as a joke, and he took the whole thing seriously. He thought it an opportunity. I went along with it because Billingsworth was keen and Alec was more than willing. It was only supposed to be two or three times, to give us a little extra cash. But Alec told me recently that he couldn't get out as easily as that, and Billingsworth said he would have no reason to send him abroad again if he was not smuggling. He only brought in a few contracts. I have no other excuse.'

Frances was inclined to believe him. They talked a little more, and then Billingsworth took his leave, telling her that at least she would have enough money to set herself up in England, because Alec had earned several thousand pounds in this way, and advised her not to feel guilty about using his ill-gotten gains.

If only you knew, Frances said to herself. But she still wasn't going to mention Alec's gambling habit.

In one of the drawers she had found a bank book for the Bank of India. For the last few years Alec had his salary paid directly in there. There was only a small sum in the account. She knew she could expect little or nothing to await her at Home in the Bank of England.

Pushed to the back of a drawer, Frances also found an envelope containing a letter. She had not shown it to Hugh, because it came from Miss Vera Padgett. It had a London address and was dated 30th November 1949

Alexander
I was not going to write this letter, but I don't think I can ever sleep again until I have expressed myself in the matter of your behaviour. I had a letter from Marjorie last Tuesday. It contained the information that

during your home leave recently, you got yourself married.

I can't tell you what I felt, and what I think of you. You are the greatest brute, cad, everything despicable that I can think of.

Marjorie tells me that your bride is just out of the schoolroom. Poor child! I fear for her. I suppose you turned her young head, as you turned mine. If she can make something decent of you, I will take my hat off to Mrs. Whittier.
VP

Frances had not appeared at the Club for weeks, but on her last Saturday, she went there to say goodbye. Polly, who had left the area for three years and come back again, told her that she had news for her – Lydia and Mike were coming back to Sundarpur soon. He'd left Localsh, and been made Manager with another company!

'Don't a lot of men leave Localsh?' she'd said sotto-voce to her. 'I wonder how long he will last?' she said, indicating Hugh. 'He's not like them at all, is he? I keep telling Roger to apply to Findlays. Maybe he will, soon.'

Lakshmi Dutta was there with her husband. 'At least you may marry again,' she said to her. 'A Hindu widow may not. My poor mother was widowed for sixty years. I think, Frances, that you *will* remarry.' She smiled knowingly. Frances told her shortly that no, she was wrong, and that she didn't want to even talk of this at this time. Lakshmi only smiled.

'He loves you,' she said, finding it unnecessary to mention his name. 'Don't pass it by. I have to speak like this now, because we will not meet again. You two must arrange it secretly before you leave, for after you are gone, anything may happen.' Her eyes turned to Fiona, who, seated on a bench at one side of the room, her flowery organdie skirt spread about her, held three or four bachelors to attention with mild mockery and chirpy smiles. Hugh, however, was not among them.

The following Tuesday all was ready. The house was empty. She packed the wine books after all; it had dawned upon her that they might fetch something in a 2nd hand shop, and she needed every penny she could get. She said a sorrowful goodbye to the servants and their families. Bungalow Three was to be shut up for now. They would have to uproot as well and would transfer to other Localsh Tea houses. Joseph was very put-out, and she tried to encourage him. Fluent now in both Hindi and Bengali, she told him that there were other kitchens just as good as this one, but he shook his head, and told her that he did not care about the kitchen, but she was the best *memsahib* he had ever worked for. Rosa and Preti were in tears. Anwar and his wife were unhappy too. She toured her garden for the last time and walked about her verandah, now bare of everything. The vines had been given away, not wanting them to die, she'd foisted some on the Club. She'd given the Humber to Hugh. He liked having wheels, and it seemed only fair, after all he was owed money as well, and he was going above and beyond the call of the duty of friendship for her, and it eased her conscience. He hadn't wanted to take it but she had told him that he would be doing her a favour.

She gave one long, last look at the Bungalow from the gate. The sprawling, friendly house set in a jungle of flowering trees had been her home for nearly seven years. She'd come there as a young bride, full of happiness, optimism, and love for her husband. She was leaving without him. Her time in India had come to an end. One last look – and she got into the car, and her tears came. Extreme grief for Alec, for her home and for her life.

She felt ripped - torn away. As they turned into the trunk road, they left the Localsh Tea Estate behind them as the *chokidars* shut the gates on her back. Its loud and familiar clank-clank echoed in her ears. Hugh drove calmly on, not saying a word. She felt rather than saw his kind looks towards her every few minutes until she stopped crying.

CHAPTER 42 *Something Forgotten*

England did not feel like home now. It felt like a strange iceberg where she had to battle to eat, stay warm, and try to make herself feel at home.

The visit to the Bank of England revealed fifteen pounds and six shillings – enough to scrape together a few necessities and the deposit on a cheap flat. Thank God Hugh had told her to get a death certificate – she would never have thought of it. Gertrude Browne had obtained it and sent it from Singapore. With that, her marriage certificate, and a solicitous manager, she was able to claim the money. The other account – the one Alec had told her would have a good return – had, as she had suspected, virtually nothing in it.

Hugh had seen her off at the wharf. He'd come as far as the gangway, and she couldn't forget the look on his face when they had parted. He seemed – crushed. Frances felt pity for him. She was certainly fond of him. Anything else was now out of the question. Alec wasn't even cold in his grave. She'd hugged Hugh goodbye though. A long, warm hug where her face had been up against his shirt for at least half-a-minute. Anybody watching would have been sure that they were in love. He had clung to her even after she had begun to ease herself away from him.

'You have my address' she said to him tenderly. Hugh loves me, he really does love me, she realised suddenly. This was something she had known for a long time, but she had kept the information hovering at the outside corners of her mind, not really wanting to see it. She had dismissed

385

Lakshmi's declaration. Now she looked at him and her heart sank, both for him and for her. It could never be, now. They would be separated by thousands of miles and her head and heart were filled with memories of Alec, good and bad.

'Frances, I – I' he struggled to say something.

'No, Hugh – it cannot be. It cannot be!' she unwound herself from his arms, gently. She looked back when she reached the top of the gangway, and waved to him. He waved back, in a long, slow wave…he did not want her to leave his sight. She boarded. She went to the deck as they were casting off. He was still there, searching for her face. They waved to each other again as the ship edged away from the wall and the horn sounded. To both, it was a long, mournful toll.

How horrid love was! Vera loved Alec, who didn't love her back. Frances loved Alec, and Alec didn't love Frances, at least not until he was dying. What a sad way to describe a marriage! Now Hugh loved Frances, and Frances could love Hugh, maybe, but the time was all wrong. All wrong.

She was several days on board ship, with time to be still and to reflect, when she remembered with distress that she had forgotten to take her music books out of the piano stool. Her grandmother's music books! The realisation plunged her into another grief, and she couldn't reassure herself that they were 'only books, only things.' Their loss was bitter to her as well. She found the voyage long and horrible, not at all like the others. Many of the passengers were going back to England on leave or for good, and they were merry. Thankfully her cabin mate had friends to spend time with. Frances tended to keep to herself, reading in her cabin or walking the decks alone, as the vessel churned its way through the ocean.

She had stayed with Aunt Margaret for a month, and during that time she burned to get back to India – and even longed for Hugh's company – though she was appalled at that selfish, disloyal thought - and wondered about all kinds of ways it could be done. But no – it was impossible – she was not a teacher, or a doctor, or a nurse, or a secretary, or anything. She could not earn a living there, and she was afraid that Alec may have had even more creditors - she had nothing left to give them - she could never return to Assam.

She'd taken the train to Nottingham and stayed at Delarbrey for a few days. She held little back from George and Helen. They were obviously disturbed and unhappy. She was sorry about that, but it was only right that Alec's brother knew the truth. George revisited the late Thirties when Alec's future was the topic of conversation at the family table – how he had wanted to go into the wine import business – and how their father, who had fought in WW1, had ordered his sons to enlist after war broke out. George dutifully did so, Alec refused, and to save face with their neighbours, rich and poor, nearly all of whose sons seemed to have signed up, Lord Delarbrey had sent Alexander away to India to grow tea.

'He owes George £1,000 for the last – oh – ten years or so,' Helen said at another time, as she peeled potatoes in the cavernous old kitchen, making sure that Frances knew they were in no position to do anything for her, and that perhaps if she could ever see her way to repaying them, that she should. She mentioned that she was thinking of doing a secretarial course, as soon as she had saved up enough, or if she could borrow the money. They said that it was a very good idea and changed the subject.

The necessities of life would not allow her to brood. She had to find work. The secretarial course was now out of the question. She would have to scrimp for years to save money for the fees. She didn't even know shorthand. She had kept the worst of her circumstances from Aunt Margaret.

She'd come down to the City one day, and met Grace, who had left her baby with her mother for the morning in order to come to town. To Grace she had poured out her heart in a shabby genteel tea-house at the corner of Meadow Street and St. Peter Place. Grace was stricken with horror and compassion, but had no ideas beyond suggesting putting an advertisement in the paper to become a Lady's Companion. *'You can't work just any old place, you know, you can't become a shopgirl or work in a factory.'* The thought of being cooped up with a fussy old lady in what would be a large but decaying house had no appeal. However, something good had come of it – the *'Georgiana Tea'* proprietor had overheard part of the conversation and apologising for her long ears, offered Frances a job on the spot. Frances was mystified, but she supposed that it was the way she spoke – Miss

Spencer was one of those genteel ladies who liked to employ girls who spoke well. Years of drilling from her father – which sessions she had not particularly liked, feeling that he was too particular about her pronunciation - had resulted in a job offer that she had not even solicited.

Frances had accepted it. She had been exceedingly relieved and grateful – too much so she'd afterwards thought – but it was like she had been offered a pot of gold. After the impromptu interview, she had immediately looked for accommodation. In a neglected street only ten minutes walk away, she had seen a notice on a door: *'Flat to let. No blacks no indians no irish'*. Disgusted by the notice, she'd looked farther, but had to return when there was nothing else nearby.

The hours were long, her wages poor, the tips not much, but it was a beginning, and Miss Spencer was all right, a bright, snappy, thin woman who was very particular about the plastic tulips on the tables being dusted daily and shone with beeswax.

Soon after she began work at the café, she received a letter from Hugh, readdressed from Aunt Margaret's. It was sincere, even affectionate, *'if there is anything else I can do to be of assistance to you I would be only too glad, please do get in touch'* etc, but Frances was at the time overwhelmed. She awoke every morning with thoughts of her late husband, her heartbreak at losing him, her anger with him for leaving her this way and her guilt at feeling angry with him because he was dead now; her anger at herself; the loss of her beloved bungalow, her verandah and her vines and flowers and almost everything she possessed, and the abrupt transplantation from the happy marigolds and palms to London's cross grey streets. Questions tormented her. How had Alec concealed his gambling habit so well from her? Was she really very stupid? And one of the burning questions – why had he married her, really? Was he attracted by the inheritance he knew must be coming? She had been so naïve – she'd probably blurted out everything – he had that way of getting people to open up to him! But no, he loved her. No, he did not. She also felt the acute humiliation of how everybody in their small circle in Assam must talk of it; by the time she had left, everybody must have known of her husband's debts, for Masterson, Chaudhury and others had driven out from Sundarpur demanding to see her, and secretaries overhear things that they repeat. Everybody must have deplored her dire situation and they must be saying what a *simpleton* Frances Whittier must have been not to have seen something was terribly wrong.

She wrote Hugh a polite little note back, thanking him for everything he had done for her, but said that she was working now, *'everything was looking up and everything would be fine'*. She was a small sea-creature in a cave, curled up in her shell, with no desire to emerge. But Hugh began to occupy her thoughts more than she wanted to admit, and she wondered why she had been so determined to have nothing more to do with him or with anyone of her former friends. A few more people had written – Lydia for instance – a kind, warm letter of sympathy – pleading with her to keep in touch - but she had not replied. What did she have to say to any of them? Was she going to tell them about her café job and her horrid little bedsit? She did not want anybody to have her address. What if they were on Home leave, and came unexpectedly to call? She did not want them to see how she lived. In any case, her needs took all of her spare time – endless paperwork involving her widow's pension; she was knitting a warm scarf, mittens and a hat, on needles borrowed from Phyllis; mending, more mending and making-do – she could not afford anything beyond the bare necessities. She hardly had enough for food and rent for her bedsit, and needed to think about every electrical appliance she used, because she had to feed the meter to keep the electricity on for heat. Even so, her feet were always cold.

Miss Spencer claimed a vague heritage going back to the most famous of the Duchesses of Devonshire, and a portrait of the eighteenth century socialite dominated one wall of the small tea-shop. Underneath this portrait were four tables with green oilcloth in a lattice pattern and the vases of plastic tulips. Two more similar tables were by the window. It was warm though and on this cold morning Frances was glad to get inside, and was within ten minutes busy serving tea and two brown scones to Mr. Hodges, a regular at this time of day, and a couple with an Irish brogue who asked for extra butter.

Business was brisk this chilly morning; at eleven she took her break, sitting down in the screened part of the room where they kept the supplies, savouring her own cup of tea and two malted milk biscuits. She had just arrived back from her break to allow Miss Spencer to make her weekly excursion to fix up with the baker, when the door pinged.

'I told you we were getting off at the wrong stop, Fiona. But you never listen.'

'Oh Mummy, it's going to be all right. We'll shelter from the rain in here until the next bus comes.'

'It's not too bad, I suppose, we shall have a cup of tea, then. I spy some danish pastries in the case.'

Their voices were very familiar, jolting her to the caressing warmth, the fragrant jasmine, garden parties and verandah evenings. Not the Jamiesons! Could it really be them? She peered out from behind the water-boiler. What were they doing *here*? Her heart leaped with a strange joy, then she felt herself turning hot with shyness and embarrassment. She wished that Miss

Spencer were here. Miss Spencer always served what she called the better type of customer, herself, and the Jamiesons would, with their expensive wool coats, leather gloves and well-made shoes, qualify.

Frances had no option but to face them herself. She walked over with a menu and greeted her customers in what she half-hoped was a voice not that of Frances Whittier, wondering if the cap which partly hid her dark hair might disguise her identity. But she was of course recognized immediately, and the subsequent disbelief and discomfort, at seeing Mrs. Whittier reduced to working in a humble tea-house, was gotten over in a few minutes. Discomfort and pity. There were no other customers, so now that the awkwardness was over, she lingered to talk, finding herself quite curious for news.

'We arrived in England just a week ago; isn't it cold here?'

'It's not cold, Mummy.'

'Not to you, maybe, but it is to me. We are visiting my sister Vera, Mrs. Liversidge. She has a very comfortable house, very warm. They have central heating *and* fires.'

How are the Arkins'? The Finches? Was Michael going to school soon? The questions about everybody poured from her and were answered.

Fiona seemed to be waving her left hand around a great deal, and at last Frances noticed the ring, and congratulated her.

'Anybody we know?'

'Oh yes – you know him quite well – Hugh Anderson!'

For the second time in minutes, Frances felt a shock travel through her, and she struggled to disguise her feelings. She must not show her distress. *'I will be mistress of myself'* she said to herself, like Elinor Dashwood in *Sense & Sensibility* - and keep her emotions for later. But it was with a huge effort that she emulated the cool, controlled Elinor of fiction.

'Congratulations!' she chirped, her voice a little too high, she thought, it must be shaky – but Fiona and her mother beamed.

'He is – em - junior manager now' said her mother – no doubt remembering the circumstances of his having succeeded to the post – she had the grace to keep her tone modest. 'He and Fiona will be married in September, here in London. We intend to stay here until then, for poor June feels the separation from all of us very hard – and Mr. Jamieson and Mr. Anderson will join us sometime in August. Then we shall all travel back together on the P&O.'

'I knew Hugh would be promoted,' Frances said, trying to keep her voice calm in the face of this dreadful news – for dreadful it felt! – 'You will, then, be living in my – our - house? Bungalow Three I mean.'

'Just down the road from me,' said her mother. 'I am very pleased about that. It will make India more bearable, now that most of the British are gone. How lucky I am that she has chosen a man from the Company, I feel very happy in every circumstance of it, given the limited families we know nowadays. Things were so different long ago, so different. Oh, the times we had!'

'I hope you will be very happy there,' Frances said. She wished more customers would come in, she wanted to escape them, to be alone, to nurse this information to herself unseen, hidden behind the water boiler and the trays of milks and sugars set on top of the counter, ready for the lunch-time crowd.

'Thank you, we will. But the house needs some changes. I asked Daddy to let Hugh move in before we were married – and he did – and I asked him for new paint inside and outside. I chose *Apricot Dream* for the outside and *Coral Shadow* for the interior.

Well, at least some of the interior. I haven't quite made up my mind about our bedroom. *Buttercup Sherbet* maybe. Oh, we are getting the roof tiled. The lounge is so small compared to Bungalow One, there is nothing I can do about that of course, but I can get rid of the piano and put a japonnier along that wall. I saw one in a shop in Notting Hill that I took a fancy to.'

Frances' heart turned steely.

'Doesn't - Hugh play the piano?'

'Oh, not now. The ants got the piano! Well, they got one leg. Anyway, I doubt very much if he will have the time to play it, even if it was all right. Daddy depends upon him a great deal. Oh, that piano has had its day. I think someone brought it over from England about a hundred and fifty years ago. We will get him a nice new piano - if he wants one. He might be more inclined to play modern music then! You have heard him play, Frances, and you too must have thought his taste far too old-fashioned.' She laughed, waving her hand around again.

'I'll have one of those danishes,' Mrs. Jamieson said. 'What's the coffee like here, Frances?'

'Dreadful,' Frances said.

'Oh, well it's tea then. Most of the coffee you get in England is unpalatable. I shall drink tea. You don't happen to have Localsh tea, do you?'

Frances shook her head ruefully.

'I thought not,' the older woman said gloomily. 'The large tea companies have a monopoly. They have the money to put into Marketing and all that kind of thing. But we are doing extremely well,' she reassured her brightly. 'We have what my husband calls a *niche* market. Half of Hong Kong, Singapore and Gibraltar drinks our tea.'

Frances smiled wryly at half of Gibraltar making a meaningful contribution to the coffers of Localsh tea. But she was being mean. The news had pained her deeply. She went behind the counter and poured boiling water into a teapot to heat it. Her hands trembled. She exhaled a long, deep breath.

The thought of Fiona becoming Mrs. Anderson was unbelievable. *Unbearable!* And ordering the piano to be gone! The piano was an antique, and in perfect working order, as long as it was kept tuned. The leg could be somehow repaired, splinted, or given a new leg - there was a very skilled carpenter on the estate. But what of Hugh - being forced to play *How much is that Doggie in the Window* over and over again to please Fiona and her jolly friends? *Yip! Yip!* It was too much! How could he stand it?

How could Hugh Anderson have fallen in love with Fiona Jamieson? 'Buttercup Sherbet' indeed! Ridiculous!

They were thrown together, that was all. The British community was small. Two young, single people were very likely to end up getting married. And – she was young; in full bloom, her skin peaches-and-cream, her dresses new, crisp and elegant. Thirty-one and eighteen. Twelve-year age gap. It was too much, she thought, conveniently forgetting the age gap between her own parents, and between her and Alec, which had been exactly that.

It was just possible that Hugh was in love with Fiona. But she doubted it. She refused to countenance that it could be so. How could it be so? She was shallow and silly! Not his type at all! Hugh was in love with *her, Frances Mary Whittier*!

Frances brought them their tea and danish pastries, then lingered and took a deep breath. Thank God, still no customers.

'Before I left, I forgot to look in the piano stool for my music,' she said carefully. 'I particular miss a book with some French compositions. There are three volumes, but I only would like one. *Gymnopédie* by a composer named Erik Satie. I was wondering if you could perhaps arrange to have it sent to me, if it wouldn't be too much trouble. It would mean a great deal to me. It brings back memories of the evenings we had after dinner, when we used to sit on the verandah and watch the sun go down.'

'Of course, Frances! Anything she wishes to have from the house, Fiona, she should have, if it is not wanted. I do miss Mr. Whittier greatly. Oh, the wines! Mr. Jamieson always depended on Mr. Whittier for a good wine.'

'Is there anything else you want?' Fiona asked her with generosity.

'Just that music book,' Frances said. She felt that if she asked for all of them, that she would have no chance at all of getting any. In any case, that was her grandmother's favourite. And – it reminded her of – but what was the point of that now? Yet, she still could not quite believe that Hugh and Fiona were engaged. Her heart rebelled.

'I'll have to write that down,' Fiona said. 'What did you say his name was, Suttee? Is he Indian? I never heard of him. I can't stand Indian music, but everyone to their own taste. But you know we shall not return until September, so I shall have to write to Hugh to find it and send it on.'

'I would be very grateful if you could do that, Fiona.' Frances felt she was scheming, something she had never done in her life, in order to remind Hugh of her. Would he think – would he see – *stop it Frances*, she said to herself.

'But I didn't know you played, Frances – I never heard *you* play.' Mrs. Jamieson said. 'I shall be very cross if I find out now that you could play, when you never played for *us*.'

'Oh, I can't play – but as you must know, I love listening to music.'

'Bungalow Three always had a piano.' Mrs. Jamieson reminisced. 'It was there when I

406

came out as a bride in 1922. Mrs. Davies used to play quite well, and after her Miss Carter, but she married a Colonel – a *full* Colonel. They went off to Madras. Then nobody used it for years, then a Mrs. Standish – a Bourke by birth – the Bourkes of Kinsabby – she *thought* she could play. She *thought* she was wonderful – but she was so short-sighted she couldn't read the music. We were forced to listen to her at every party she gave – her husband was a very mild-mannered little man with a pipe, she had him wrapped around her little finger. But she knew how to treat her guests, I will say that for her. Oh, the dinner parties Mrs. Standish used to have! She had a wonderful table, I will give her that. Oh, the steaks! Filet mignons! I don't know where she obtained them – she never, ever told a soul!'

'Yes,' said Frances, who had this litany almost off by heart, though why it felt oddly comforting to hear it again, she didn't know.

'Alec, God rest his soul, didn't play either. Hugh Anderson was the only person I ever heard play the piano. He used to play 'Gymnopédie' very well.'

'If I am not mistaken – that was the piece Hugh played at the Christmas Party,' Mrs. Jamieson said, turning her attention to her daughter. 'Yes, Gym-no-pé-die. I thought it a very odd title for a song. We all thought it very unsuitable really, for Christmas. It was like a dirge.'

'Oh, that!' Fiona said, wrinkling her nose. 'Is that it? Goodness, I don't know why he likes it! I don't think it's a dirge, Mummy, it puts me in mind of being very bored. I told him afterwards that it was very dull,' she added proudly, 'and I made him promise never to play it again.'

Frances pursed her lips. 'Not everybody likes it,' she said carefully. 'But…Hugh and I – it was a favourite - of - ours.' She took the vase of plastic flowers up from the table and set it down a few inches away from its original position, almost with a thud.

There was a pause. The door pinged and a young woman came in, drenched and shaking her umbrella so vehemently that one or two cold drops reached them.

'I do hope I haven't thrown that music out already,' Fiona said with an altered tone, as if something unpleasant had occurred to her. 'I have gone through a great deal of things in the house, and found a lot of rubbish, to be quite frank. If this book is old and dog-eared, it's gone I am sure. I can't bear anything tatty and old. I am very sorry, Frances if it was a *favourite of yours* – what a shame you didn't remember it when you left!'

'It was a very – trying time,' Frances muttered as she withdrew. 'Can I get you more tea?'

'No, thank you,' Mrs. Jamieson said, and then dropped her voice. 'Mrs. Whittier –

might I ask – does your brother-in-law – *Lord Delarbrey* - know of – I am sure he would be able to do something for you - settle you somewhere more suitable. And Mr. Jamieson would not like it known that the widow of an officer of Localsh Tea was reduced to – to – *you know*.' She looked furtively about.

Frances made no answer, just smiled to herself. Finally, just to be polite, she murmured that she was in contact with Alec's family. She withdrew behind the counter to write Aunt Margaret's address on a piece of paper to give to Fiona. She hadn't really any hopes of its being sent to Hugh. She had overplayed her hand.

There, you've done it, she thought to herself. Do they think now that there was something between Hugh and me? *And there goes my tip*, she thought with a wry smile. Tips were very important; she fed the electricity meter with the tips. She heard a little cufuffle at the table – *'she'll be insulted, Mummy.'*

'No, Fiona, we will have to leave something or we'll appear mean.' They must have debated the amount for three minutes. Finally they got up, bid her goodbye, told her it was very nice to see her again, and with what she thought was an air of insincerity told her that if she was in Town next September she must *of* course come to the wedding. She replied with shameless falsity that she would love to. They left her two shillings – it was generous.

As she drew the cold sheets to her chin that night and buried herself deep under the blankets, she thought she knew what Satie had had in mind when the figures on the urn had inspired him to write *Gymnopédie*. Hugh had given her the clue, but perhaps not even he had expanded the thought. Time passing – immortality – perhaps? The figures on the urn were timeless. They would always be; were in most probability still there, on the urn, somewhere in France

411

she supposed, perhaps in an attic, forever in youth.

Perhaps Satie had been influenced by the poem *'Ode on a Grecian Urn'* Keats or Shelley, she couldn't remember. *'Forever wilt thou love and she be fair.'* Was it even written then? She didn't know. She would go to the library and look it up. She longed to talk to Hugh about it –such a trivial matter really, yet he would be interested in what she had to say. He was lost to her now. But it was her own fault. She'd let him go. But it was the wrong time. Too soon. Why hadn't he waited a while longer? *Loss, Longing.*

But perhaps the urn was no more, and Satie's dreams of its immortality were naïve. The figures could be scattered in shards after two wars, buried deep, never to come together again.

She could not sleep, thinking about Hugh Anderson playing *Gymnopédie*, and he and Fiona to be married, and when she finally slept she dreamed of an ugly *buttercup sherbet* bedroom, and woke to hear the clink-clink of the bottles as the milkman did his rounds at five o'clock.

Hugh's engagement plunged Frances into more sorrow than she could have thought. She mechanically went about her duties, but every time she was not serving customers her heart reminded her now of this loss also. In the evening, Jenny liked to share her coal fire with her and Phyllis, so she distracted herself by listening to the many stories of Phyllis' day spent serving lunches and teas in '*The White Horse*'. Many of her customers were men and she seemed to spend her entire working day being sharp and clever and fending off advances. It amused Frances and she was grateful for a warm fender she could put her feet up on, while sparing her own meter by not having to have her heater on for hours at a time. She felt that her neighbours were very kind to her, and was touched.

The fact was that Jenny and Phyllis felt from the first that there was some great Tragedy with Mrs. Whittier. First, she spoke posh, and must had had an awful comedown. She had told them that she had returned from India recently after her husband had died suddenly on a business trip to Singapore. When Phyllis related this to her aunt and uncle, something rang a bell with Phyllis' uncle who had been in Singapore during the War. Whenever he saw any article in the newspapers about Singapore, he read it. He recalled reading not so long ago about an Englishman being murdered in Singapore. And there was something about India as well. Something like that would stick in a man's head, especially since the deceased was a brother of a *Lord*. Some searching was done, hoping they hadn't used the paper to light the fire, looking under cushions and finally in the dog's bed in the toolshed, and they found it. *The Sunday Pictorial*. Now all was revealed. Mrs. Whittier was the widowed sister-in-law of Lord Delarbre.

Phyllis lost no time informing Jenny, and Mrs. Whittier became even more Tragic to them, and pitiful too, more especially since she had been completely dropped by her rich relations. They liked to be in the company of a Tragic Figure, and their families and everybody they worked with knew of Mrs. Whittier and requested up to date news, of which they had little to supply, unfortunately, except to say that they were looking out for her, poor dear, and they didn't know where she would end up.

CHAPTER 43 Mrs. Liversidge

One day only two weeks later, Miss Spencer rushed to greet a lady customer in a mink coat who wore coral lipstick and filled the café with the scent of *Guerlain*. She ushered her to a seat and the lady took off her fine gloves and lit a cigarette in a pearl holder, asking for tea and a danish pastry. Frances could not fail to see that the wealthy customer scrutinized her.

As she passed back to the counter from serving another table, the woman looked her full in the eye.

'Pardon me – and forgive me for asking – but are you Mrs. Frances Whittier?

Frances affirmed it, very surprised, and curious as to what was coming next.

'My name is Vera Liversidge – I am the sister of Marjorie Jamieson,' said the woman. 'Perhaps you may have heard my name – ?' As Frances wonderingly nodded her assent, she went on 'I would *so* like to talk to you privately. If you are free for lunch, I would like to meet you. My treat.'

Frances was too surprised to object – she supposed that the visit from the Jamiesons had resulted in this encounter. But what she expected from this meeting, she had no idea. She had no time to think about it as they were very busy for the morning, and Miss Spencer, who had overheard, was asking her leading questions.

They met in the Rose Hotel, rather old-fashioned but quiet and convenient, just a few streets away.

'You don't mind if I call you Frances, do you?' Vera asked after ordering steak and kidneys for herself and chicken risotto for her guest.

'Not at all.'

'Well, you call me Vera then.'

Frances had more opportunity to study Mrs. Jamieson's sister, the woman who had come to India and fallen in love, and left with high hopes, only to be dreadfully let down. She had strong features, but they were well-proportioned, with large dark eyes and a firm, almost hard, line about the mouth. Her dark hair fell in bouncing curls and waves about her face, which was made up, but tastefully. Her nails were polished a glossy pink. She had taken off her fur coat to reveal a twinset of cerise cashmere, a pearl necklace, and a multi-coloured scarab bracelet. Her fingers glittered with rings.

'What is it you want to talk to me about?' Frances asked. Perhaps Vera Liversidge was just curious to know more about the woman who Alec had ended up with, after jilting her. She remembered the letter she had found and hoped she still didn't look as if she had just 'left the schoolroom'.

'I wondered if you were interested in another job.' Vera began 'Because I am perfectly sure I can find you one. Marjorie seemed very upset to find you – as you are, and we feel a certain responsibility to help you settle back into life here in England.'

Frances smiled faintly. She noted the '*we feel*' – as if Vera thought herself responsible in any way for her predicament!

'That's very kind of you – I don't know what to say.'

'I am so sorry for your loss.' Vera said then, looking up. 'It must have been very difficult.' Her pink fingertips deftly worked her knife to butter a bread roll.

'Thank you. I suppose you would like to know what happened - '

'Marjorie gave me the details. I don't need to know any more than everything she told me. Poor Alexander, murdered. I did get a brutal shock. I am sorry you had to go through all that. And then - everything else that followed, of course, must have been truly cruel and barbaric. The way Alexander *left* everything.'

Frances winced. Marj had not spared any detail, and Vera saw nothing wrong in mentioning it, which was rather impolite. *Cruel and barbaric* was what had happened to Alec in Singapore. What followed had been dreadful, yes, but Frances realised at that moment that she had dealt with it, and coped in a way she didn't know she had been capable of.

Their plates arrived, steaming hot, and Frances forgave her when she tasted her risotto, though she was a little sorry she hadn't ordered the steak and kidneys. She could not afford to eat out. Her lunch was a potted meat sandwich, her dinner in the evening a cheap cut grilled or fried, a potato and half a tin of peas or beans, followed by a slice of bread and jam, except on payday, when she treated herself to a cream bun.

'Marjorie said she never really spoke of me to *you*,' Vera said a little self-importantly, 'but perhaps Alexander may have spoken of me?'

Frances could not very well repeat what Alec had said to her of Vera.

'He mentioned you a few times' she gulped '- that you had been out to visit Mrs. Jamieson.'

'Is that all he said?' Vera looked at her with perfectly groomed raised eyebrows, a little smile about her lips. 'He must have mentioned – I'm sure it would be very odd if he had not – that we had been engaged.'

Frances was taken aback. Was Vera deluded? Or had Alec kept the information from her?

She said nothing.

Frances wondered if the desire to see her settle back in England was really the motivation for this meeting. But why would Vera bother?

Frances now remembered that once, she had mentioned Vera to Lydia Finch one afternoon when the latter had called upon her. They had had a glass of wine on the verandah, a bit early in the day but it had been Lydia's anniversary and her husband was away, so Frances had picked out a Merlot and opened it for both of them. Lydia related the details of her husband's courtship of her, and then they talked in general of men and attractions and courtships, and Frances added rather recklessly – and no doubt because of the Merlot - how she knew that Mrs. Jamieson's young step-sister Vera had been out on a visit and fallen hard for Alec, but Alec had found her quite a pest, and hadn't liked her at all. Oh dear, had she really said that? Oh, my goodness! Had that remark gone straight back to Mrs. Jamieson? Frances felt sure that it had. She thought again that the small society in Localsh Tea Estate had been rather too porous. Marj, short of things to say in letters and writing of the people she knew, may have written to her sister… *'I'm hearing that this is what Alec told his wife of you'*…Localsh Tea had as many whispers and intrigues as any Maharaja's Palace, and nobody knew what news was carried back to England.

'I arrived in Assam to spend Christmas with Marjorie and Alastair,' began Vera, without any thought of the propriety of speaking so openly - 'and Alexander immediately began to pay me a great deal of attention. He was always driving up to Bungalow One from the bachelor's bungalow. How he pursued me! While I wasn't immediately interested, he began to make me like him, and before long I had convinced myself that I was in love. After all, I was going to make Alexander, myself and everybody happy if I went along with all this. He was very serious. Marjorie and Alastair were thrilled to see us so close – Marjorie at the thought of me ending up as a bride in Bungalow Three or even Two! Three is a horrid little house, isn't it? I mean, One is the only decent house on the Estate. But I shouldn't have said that about Three. Forgive me? However, to get back to my story - we went on a picnic one day – I met this lovely Indian lady Mrs. Dutta – do you know her? - she saw how it was between Alexander and me – we had a wonderful chat, and she arranged for us to have the use of a charming little guest-house on her estate to get away from everybody. By now, Alexander and I could hardly bear to be apart. When it was time for me to go home,

we parted full of promises to meet again –
we wrote to each other - dozens of letters.
We were in love. He was coming over on
leave in the summer – and everybody
expected that we'd come back to India
married.'

Frances nodded impassively. She did not
know whether to believe any of this or not.
Vera still might have imagined Alec's love.
Alec might have just gone along with it, for
as Polly had said, men can be easily
flattered. But a decent man would not allow
it to go so far, if he had no serious
intentions. But Alec? Possibly. She had to
admit that he was capable of it.

'So we met in London, and had a blissful
reunion. We had three heavenly weeks
together, he asked me to marry him, and I
accepted.'

Frances nodded her head just the tiniest bit.
She was still skeptical.

'We had another three days of happiness, and then something dreadful happened. His brother came down from Nottingham. It seems he had lent Alexander some money a few years before, and he wanted to know when he was to be repaid. I was not supposed to know this, but I was in the hotel suite when Lord Delarbrey arrived – I quickly hid in the bathroom, and could hear everything – Delarbrey was raising his voice, and Alexander urging him to be quiet. But soon Alec himself was raising his voice too. They were saying quite horrible things to each other. Alec seemed resentful of Delarbrey. He didn't at all deny that money was owed. It was a surprise to me that Alec had needed to borrow money – he had been plying me with jewellery for three weeks, I was even wearing several pieces at that moment. Pearls. Gold earrings. An exquisite brooch – a diamond seahorse brooch. And a ring - an oval-shaped emerald set in a cluster of tiny diamonds. It was the most beautiful thing I had ever seen. That was my engagement ring.'

Frances' heart stood still at this information. She almost wanted to cry out in pain. Tears welled up at the back of her eyes, but she fought them. Thankfully Vera kept her eyes on her plate and the long pink-tipped fingers worked the knife and fork assiduously on her pie. Frances forced herself to eat.

'I remember looking at it there and then and thinking that it was not really mine, not at all, not if it had been got with borrowed money, money Alexander was not intending, if I was hearing correctly, to ever repay. He felt entitled to his brother's support and patronage.

'George – isn't it George? - left in an angry mood, and I came out to face Alexander. He was pacing up and down, smoking a cigarette. I knew it was over. It would be impossible for us to be happy. He was not who I thought he was. And not at all independent! How did he intend to keep a wife? I took all the jewellery off, placed it on the table and left the hotel. I was tempted to keep the seahorse brooch, but I'm rather glad I didn't; I should never have liked to wear it.'

Frances swallowed. She said nothing.

'I consider I had a very lucky escape,' Vera said in a pointed manner.

Frances was still silent. How could she answer that?

'Alexander wrote me a rather nasty letter. It made no sense at all. Pleaded with me to come back and then said I would be sorry if I didn't.

'Younger brothers of peers don't, in general, go to manage Tea Estates in India, it's a lot of hard work, long hours, and almost no society worth mentioning. I had wondered, you know, why he went there, and lived in a rather decrepit old bungalow with peeling paint. The War spoiled everything for him. His father would not have been so horrid in peacetime, sending him away like that to India because he wouldn't join up. He was very bitter at not being allowed his way.'

'A lot of people didn't get their way in the War', Frances said quietly, forcing herself to speak. 'My Uncle John and Aunt Margaret intended to buy a house in Weymouth and retire there, but he was killed in the Blitz. He drove an ambulance.'

'Oh, that was bad luck. Anyway, India suited Alexander in a way, didn't it? I mean, he was nobility there. Servants. Lord and Master, almost. Isn't every planter? But not here. A big spender, too. He left you in -' she looked up.

'Yes, he did, rather. But I am all right now. Or will be.'

'Look, if you will allow me to help you, I can get you another job, Frances. It will be better, I can assure you.'

'After – you separated – was that the end then? Was there any more contact?'

'I remember writing to him after I heard he had married. You see, I thought he had done quite a dreadful thing, marrying someone as young as you – Marjorie told me of you of course - who hadn't any experience of the world, and I understand you were rather on your own. I was furious with him, Frances. I knew what he was doing! He was -' she stopped suddenly.

'You thought he was trying to make you sorry?' Frances asked her sadly.

'Oh, I had no idea what he was trying to do.' Vera replied with some insincerity.

Frances smiled ruefully. It wouldn't occur to Vera that Alec would ever fall for someone like her, so it had to be that he was looking for revenge. The trouble is, Vera may have been right in her assumption. It pained her to think so; but she consoled herself quickly that Alec had, in the end, come to love and appreciate her. The End was what mattered, wasn't it? Or was it?

'Would you have ever come back to him?'

'No. Never. I knew he had no money – I didn't love him enough to marry him without it. A tea planter's salary – *a damn fool career*, as somebody said.'

'And your sister Marj knows the full story of course?'

'Oh, yes. Later that year, when I was recovered enough to think rationally, I sat down and wrote her a long letter.'

Frances mused on this for a few minutes. It was just another example of how, in their small community in India, everything flowed and simmered under the surface. Had Mrs. Jamieson enlightened the Finches, the Arkins and everybody? An explanation as to why Alexander Whittier had gone Home with the expectation of marrying her sister, and returning with a complete stranger, would have been expected, and it would, of course, have been related in a way that would put Vera in the best light possible.

And nobody had ever, ever allowed her to suspect that she had been courted and married to get revenge on the lovely Vera Padgett!

'They were expecting *you*, until only a few hours beforehand,' Frances ventured.

'Yes, I know, I was very upset when I heard that Alexander played such a horrible trick.' She didn't see anything wrong at all with what she said, and Frances did not point it out to her.

'You married some time later?' she asked her. She remembered the Christmas at the Club when Mrs. Jamieson had announced the happy news.

'Yes. I knew Perry from before. He's a Crown Q.C. Very successful. We live in Notting Hill in a rambling old house with six bedrooms and a long garden in the back. Since we have two boys, we love the garden. The house itself is simply adorable.

Victorian, and wasn't touched during the War. You should come and visit us!'

'Thank you,' Frances said lamely, not wanting to at all. 'One would think that Marj would have been rather upset at Alec, and influenced Alastair to have him dismissed, after 'the trick' as you called it. Why was that, in your opinion?' Frances didn't really need to ask, but she wanted to hear what Vera thought.

'Vanity, Frances, just vanity. Alastair likes a good wine. No other Tea Estate could get their hands on wine, and that was a matter of pride to all. And Marjorie is the same. Snobs, really, aren't they? I shouldn't say that about my step-sister. But they would no more dismiss the brother of Lord Delarbrey than they would the Duke of Edinburgh. And of course – later - there was the *Work* they were doing – the *Border Operation* – Marjorie told me all about it – not in a letter of course, in case you think she is very indiscreet. I wonder what will happen that now that there is nobody to pass information along to our people in Singapore. Oh well, the Empire is gone. More's the pity. I hope we can be friends, Frances – would that be possible, do you think?'

'Of course!' wondering if she really wanted to even see Vera again, and secretly feeling she was one-up on Mrs. Liversidge, as she knew that there was no spying operation. Would she enlighten her? She held her tongue. It would simply be spiteful and could cause trouble between Marj and Alaistair.

They finished their dinner with a cup of tea and biscuits, and as the day was fine, walked in the nearby Park for a few minutes. There was a band playing on the bandstand.

'Alexander didn't like music very much, did he,' Vera remarked.

'No, indeed not. Do you like music?'

'Very much. There was one piece of music Alexander liked though. We were at my

433

house, my father's house in Ipswich - and he was sprawled on the sofa, and looking at me but not really listening, until I played a piece called *Gymnopédie.*'

'Gymnopédie!' Frances couldn't hide her surprise.

'Yes, *Gymnopédie!* That's a very beautiful piece by a French composer.'

'Oh, I know *Gymnopédie.* I wasn't aware Alec liked it though,' she bit her lip. She felt foolish admitting that, as if Vera would wonder what they had been doing for seven years together.

'Well, perhaps it was a flash in the pan. He said it was the nicest bit of music he ever heard, and he wasn't at all taken with classical music, not at all. I had to play it half-a-dozen times there and then, just that 1st movement, you know.'

Frances thought with a pang, of the evening when Hugh had played it, and Alec had been listening on the verandah.

434

*Loss. Longing. Loss. Longing. Loss.
Longing!* Her own words pounded louder
and louder in her head. If she had only
known - ! Oh, God! She prayed desperately.

A Void. An endless Void. Alec's angry voice
floated back to her.

'We met – Alec and I met – when he was
home on his last leave,' Vera said rather too
casually. 'I wanted to see him, just for old
times sake, I suppose. I tricked him into
coming to the Connaught Hotel. And he may
have been still somewhat in love with me – I
hope you don't mind my saying that – but I
can tell you that he was faithful to you,
Frances. I was waiting in the room, and
when I heard the knock I called to him to
come in, and he opened the door. I will
never forget the look on his face. He said my
name in utter shock, and – hurt perhaps – he
seemed unable to move for a few moments –
frozen to the spot - I went to him but he
turned away and walked very quickly indeed
toward the lift and left me all by myself with

a bottle of Dubonnet and nobody to drink it with. I was very put-out, but rather admired him too.'

'I wanted you to know that,' she added generously, 'even though it does not reflect well upon me.'

...you might hear something. About the last time we were in England...

'I knew it,' Frances said in as calm a voice as she could muster. 'Alec told me.'

'I seem to have humiliated myself then for nothing.' Vera said with a little cattiness.

Frances decided she had heard enough from Mrs. Liversidge. 'I think I should be getting back to work now,' she said hurriedly. 'Thank you for lunch.' In her own mind, she thought that she had paid a very high price for it. *There was no such thing as a free lunch!*

Vera promised that she would let her know about the job, as Frances hurried off, trying to keep tears away. She worked mechanically for the rest of the evening, ignoring Miss Spencer's pointed looks and references to the woman visitor of that morning –and when she got home to her cold flat, she lay down on her bed and sobbed.

Jenny had come home early that day, and heard with alarm the heartbreaking sounds coming from poor Mrs. Whittier's bedsit. Later that evening, as soon as she heard Phyllis' step in the hall, she ran out to consult her. Something would have to be done for the poor heartbroken widow, and soon, before she had a nervous breakdown.

CHAPTER 44 'Read all about it!'

One evening about two weeks later, Frances was about to let herself in her front door when she startled at a noise across the street. She wheeled around to see a man in a hat and coat taking her photograph. He walked briskly away, leaving her in a disturbed state of mind as she unlocked the door and entered her bedsitting room.

Who was he? Who wanted her photo? Was it – to do with another creditor? Surely not. Even if they found out where she was, they must know that there was no point in pursuing her for money. One look at the grotty street and the dilapidated building would be enough to tell them that there was nothing to be gained. She thought then that he may have been taking a photo of the house, which could mean that the landlady may be putting it up for sale. It may not have anything to do with her at all.

When Jenny invited her to her fireside that evening, she told her and Phyllis, for they had a right to know. To her surprise, Jenny nodded significantly.

'You won't have to worry about anything soon,' Phyllis said soothingly.

'And if he comes looking for an interview, give it to him.' added Jenny. 'Because an interview would be more powerful than just what we told him, wouldn't it. You could just pour out everything in your own words.'

'What are you talking about?'

'*The Sunday Pictorial*! I hope you don't mind, but we know everything, and we think you are very deserving and very plucky, and we decided to help you.'

'We think it's terrible that your brother-in-law has abandoned you. This will shame him into doing something, it will.'

Frances could hardly believe her ears.

'You mean – *The Sunday Pictorial* are going to do a story about me, and about - '

'Lord Delarbrerr; how you was left a poor widow, and he hasn't lifted a finger to help you.' Phyllis said. 'It is his bounden duty to look after his brother's widow.'

'We know you don't belong with our sort,' said Jenny with generosity.

'It must have been a terrible tragedy,' sighed Phyllis. 'Was he a very handsome man, Mr. Whittier? We know he was robbed, it said it in the paper. Oh, how you must 'ave felt when you heard! It doesn't bear thinking about!'

Frances saw the headlines of next Sunday's *Pictorial* in her mind's eye.

'CRUEL LORD DELARBRE
BROTHER'S WIDOW LIVES HAND-TO-MOUTH'

She buried her face in her hands.

'It was very kind of you to do that, but you really should have asked me,' she said after a few moments, not knowing whether to laugh or to cry, and wondering desperately how the story could be stopped.

'Oh, we were going to tell you an' all,' Jenny said.

'Only we didn't think he'd come around to take your picture so soon,' Phyllis said.

'Will you give them an interview?' Jenny said eagerly.

'I shall not.'

Jenny and Phyllis looked at one another in dismay. Frances wondered how best to proceed. She hoped that it wasn't too late. How dreadfully embarrassing it would be to the Delarbres if this story ran! How humiliating to herself, to Aunt Margaret, everybody!

'I know you meant well,' she said, squirming her stockinged toes on the fender, soaking up the heat. 'And it was a very kind thing to do. But my late husband wouldn't have liked it, and I must consider how he would have felt.'

Both girls thought that the feelings of a dead man didn't matter one whit one way or the other but they said nothing.

Frances wondered later how best to stop the story. In the end, she had to get time off and take the bus to Fleet Street and ask them not to publish. They offered her fifty pounds; she refused. They said they would go ahead in any case, whereupon she boldly threatened them with Lord Delarbre's lawyer, for none of it, she asserted, was true, and they would be sued for defamation. She won.

CHAPTER 45 Wardo!

It was September. The summer had been short. Leaves blew from the parks around Frances as she walked to work from her lodgings. She had found a new job – by herself – she had never heard from Vera and concluded that the promise of help had been a ruse to meet her and tell her that Alec had been besotted with her, not the other way around, and that she had actually done quite well for herself without him.

She had moved out of her old flat, unable to bear the thought of another freezing winter there and of feeding the greedy meter for her light and heat. She'd said goodbye to Jenny and Phyllis, the wireless, the wallpaper and the curtains. She had a good bedroom in this house, it had a hearth and she could light a fire there. The bed was comfortable with clean blankets and a candlewick bedspread that co-incidentally matched her pink dressing-gown.

She worked in a restaurant run by a man from Florida. *Sunshine State Eatery* was a casual place, a popular place for tourists, especially from the United States. Again, Frances' accent had played a part in securing the job, for Americans loved a posh English accent. They were very generous with tips, and in the case of one Texan aged on the wrong side of forty-five, who came every day for three weeks, he had offered her a great deal more – his hand in marriage. She had declined politely, but it made her feel that at seven and twenty, though she had found three grey hairs so far on her head, she was still attractive. Or maybe it was just the plummy accent. Whatever it was that had captivated him, she had felt cheered.

She worked long hours, by choice. She was determined to save as much as she could. At her lodgings, her meals were catered for, and there was a cosy sitting-cum dining room with a rented television. Though it was only September her landlady was lighting a fire there for her lodgers, five girls aged between seventeen and twenty-seven, Frances being the oldest one. She enjoyed the company of the others and sometimes they went to the cinema, and occasionally, to a dance, but Frances felt ancient at the dances, though she was not always left sitting by the wall, and a couple of these had resulted in dates. But she had felt no common ground with the men. Emily, one of the other lodgers, an office clerk, told her she was too fussy. The truth was that

Frances didn't know what to talk about if she couldn't talk about India and her colours and foliage and flowers and fauna and nobody was interested in that after asking her how she stood the heat and what was the food like. Nobody cared that she had spent seven years in India. And she found to her dismay that she couldn't really relate to anybody who hadn't seen green paddy rippling in the wind as far as the horizon, or a sari shop ablaze with vivid colour from ceiling to floor. That was the heartbreaking thing with friends, men and women. She saw a lonely life before her unless she forgot India, and she could not.

September! The month Hugh and Fiona were to be married. One Saturday, she turned the corner into Jermyn Street and came to a dead stop, for she saw him. It was unmistakably Hugh Anderson. He didn't see her; he was looking into the window of a formal dress shop. Of course he was buying his suit for the wedding. Frances, hardly believing the reality of what she was seeing, plunged around and walked the other way, causing more than one pedestrian to look at her a little curiously. This confirmation that the wedding was a reality drove her spirits down. Somehow, she had hoped – but there was no help for it now. Tears flowed from her eyes. No invitation reached her of course- not that she could have gone anyway. And nothing about her music book.

September left them; October blew in, and the rain began.

Hugh was married by now. Fiona was redecorating the bungalow according to her taste. If she was like her mother, she'd be imperious with the servants. They would be slow and not go out of their way for her. She'd throw tantrums. That would make them resent her even more.

The piano, she was sure, had been thrown out, and set upon to be broken up for wood to light cooking fires. The end of the

Collard&Collard and all the joy and sorrow it had given.

She was walking one day rather aimlessly around Belgravia, when she remembered that Alec's friend, Tom Edwardson – 'Wardo' had moved somewhere near to there, to a larger house to accommodate their growing family. However, she had no interest in meeting him, but as soon as this thought came and went in her head, a voice called her name with eagerness.

'Mrs. Whittier! Frances? By golly, it is you!'

It was Wardo. He came running down the steps of a rather nice house, and held out his hand to shake hers.

'It's been far too long, Frances! I heard about Alec only some months ago – I wrote to him in Assam, but got a polite letter back from a secretary to Mr. Jamieson, telling me the bad news. I say' – in a reproachful tone

– 'why didn't you let us know about poor old Alec?'

Frances felt ashamed. She should of course have let Alec's best friend know. She muttered that she wasn't long returned from India, and hadn't gotten around to all she should have done.

'Oh never mind, I understand – it must have been a great shock – and we did move house which you probably didn't know - I say are you free next Saturday night? I – we – that is, Alison and myself would love to have you come round. Come for dinner, at 8pm. Would that suit you? Don't say no, I sha'nt accept a no, you know.'

His obvious forgiveness and warmth melted her heart, and she found herself glad to accept.

'And we can talk about the – you know,' he said. 'I'm sorry but I'm in a frightful hurry – I have to leave you now. I have a client due in – ten minutes. It was wonderful bumping into you, Frances, it made my day.'

With this warm affirmation, he was gone.

Frances didn't know what to wear on Saturday, but she cobbled together a black pleated skirt and a grey silk blouse she'd bought second-hand. It wasn't really her colour but it was in perfect condition and only cost a shilling. She had a decent black jacket and a nice scarf. She polished her shoes to a shine.

She arrived on the dot of eight. She walked, to save her money for a taxi home later. She walked slowly, so as not to appear sweaty. She carried a box of chocolates.

When they had met some years earlier, Alison had been too frazzled and busy to pay much attention to her guests. She made up for it now, with a warm hug and an exclamation that it was wonderful to see her again.

She was led into a cosy sitting-room with a blazing fire. Wardo offered her a glass of sherry.

'Shiraz, 1929' he said, noting the label. 'Alec would be able to tell us the exact spot in the exact vineyard.'

He chatted on about grapes and sherries, while Alison stood at the bottom of the stairs issuing threats to noisy little persons that if they did not get into bed immediately, Daddy would come up.

'I'm the baddie,' Wardo said with a smile. 'We have two boys and a girl. I hope I shall not have to make good the threat.' But all became quiet and Alison came back in, apologising.

'Oh thank God, only grown-up talk now,' she said, cheerfully. Frances felt more at ease with this couple than she had thought she would.

Alison soon had dinner on the table, which was served in the dining room, again with a cheery fire. Roast beef and gravy, two vegetables and potatoes. They talked of Alec, and Frances found herself remembering, for the first time since he had died, some of the happier times they had spent together, like when he had taken her to see the Himalayas, and they had stayed in an enchanting lodge by a crisp blue lake.

'Now this is a 1932 Merlot,' said Wardo, filling her glass.

'When you were at school with Alec, was he interested in viniculture then?' Frances asked.

'Oh yes. In our second year at school, we were given a project to do. '*The Industries of Medieval Monasteries.*' Alec and I teamed up. So off we went to the library, and Alec for some reason just clicked with all the information. He was the man with the ideas; I was good at setting it all down in some coherence to hand it in. The whole idea of living a monastic life, growing wine or ale or beer, studying the different

451

methods, and cultivating the different kinds, took hold of him. Our project got an A. But Alec didn't stop there; he got the bug, as they say. He began to research how wine was made in ancient times, and how St. Martin's donkey invented pruning by eating a few vines down to the ground and the following year, they grew better than ever. He thought that was hilarious. One fact led to another, and soon he was picking up bits of information that were not generally known. He used to send away for books. He wrote it all down. He wanted a wine import business; you probably know all that. But as you know he gathered enormous amounts of information just the same, which brings me to - '

'I hope you like rhubarb tart,' whooped Alison, who had been in the kitchen for a little while and was now sweeping to the table with a plate. 'And I have custard made with Devon cream!'

'Oh, well done, Alison, rhubarb!'

'I put a little ginger in it, not too much,' said Alison, sitting down again.

'Now Frances,' said Wardo a short while later as they sat in the sitting room again. 'You have been very patient; I know you will want to know about the work, and how it's coming along; it's almost finished, and I have, I am very happy to relate to you, found a publisher.'

A wail emerged from somewhere in the house, and Alison, who had just sat down, got up again.

'I'll go, darling,' said Wardo, and disappeared from the room.

'It's Anthony; bring him down for a little while,' Alison said.

Frances was glad of the hiatus. The work? A publisher? What was this about? As Wardo appeared with a tousled thumb-sucking toddler in his arms, she remembered that Alec had been writing a book. A book about wine.

Alison held out her arms to take the baby, and Wardo disappeared again, to return with a thick loose-leaf manuscript.

'Here it is,' he said with triumph. 'He sent it to me in bits and pieces over the last few years - it was quite a mess – anecdotes and histories and all jumbled together, but I made something coherent of it, and there we are. I am quite proud of it, and Alec would be too, if he was here. So, what do you say – shall we publish?

CHAPTER 46 *Melody in the Glen*

One evening about three weeks later, her landlady, ready for bed in her quilted dressing gown and hair-rollers, met Frances in the hallway after she returned from work at half-past ten.

'There was a gentleman who called to see you today,' she said. 'A Mr. Anderson. I didn't know what I ought to tell him, as I wasn't aware if you would even wish to meet him. I suggested he might leave a note. So he went away for an hour, and returned with this.' She handed Frances a letter.

'Mr. Anderson?' Frances' heart lurched. 'Did you say Anderson? Was – was he alone?'

'Well, yes. Anderson. He was quite alone.'

Hugh! Still in England, and why would he want to see her? Thank God she had been out! She went upstairs to her room. It was a card, obviously bought at a nearby newsagent's, with a watercolour bunch of violets on the front.

Dear Frances

I hope you are well. I'm back in England briefly. I took the train to Stevenage this morning and called to your aunt's address there in hopes of finding you; I had the pleasure of meeting your Aunt Margaret and your cousin Jane. Your aunt told me you were in the City and gave me your address.

I have no association now with Localsh Tea, or indeed with anybody associated with that Company. <u>Every connection there is severed</u>.

I have a job playing piano in a bar in Kensington. I play there on Thursdays, Fridays and Saturdays. Perhaps I'm being too bold to think you might wish to meet. If you do, write to me at this address:
<u>c/o the Rushy Glen,</u>
<u>108 Belling Street, W8.</u>

Or drop in. There's a nominal cover charge. I'm about to change lodgings, so there's no point in giving you my address, as I am not sure where I shall end up.

I will only be in London for six weeks. I must spend a little time in Scotland before my next position. I sail for Brazil in the New Year.

I have something for you, which I have heard you were looking for.

Hugh E Anderson

Frances sank upon the bed with astonished delight, her heart beating quickly, her mind alight with surprises, hardly believing the missive. There were several extremely important pieces of news in this. Number One: – Hugh Anderson was *not* married! That was worth savouring for well over a minute before she went to Number Two: – Hugh Anderson was not returning to India, but he was going to Brazil. *Brazil!* He might have said the *moon*. Number Three. He wanted to see her. To give her something.

She almost wished number 3 *wasn't* there. Perhaps that was the only reason he wished to see her, to return to her the music book or books that most likely he had heard of from Fiona or her mother. She wondered if her request had led to suspicion, an interrogation, an unpleasantness - and in her mind's eye she saw Fiona greet her arriving fiancé with coldness, tear the ring from her finger, throw it at him and flounce out of the room. She smiled. Her imagination was running away with her of course.

Frances' mature age and once-married status had granted her privileges denied to the younger members of the household. Mrs. Quintin imposed a curfew on the two girls under eighteen. But Frances had a key. She could come and go as she pleased.

The following morning brought a letter from Aunt Margaret.

'Dearest Frances

This might not reach you in time, but you may expect a call from one of your friends from India, a Mr. Hugh Anderson. He called this morning to the house looking for you, and we brought him in and gave him tea. We had scones just out of the oven. So I sent him back to London with your address, as in our brief meeting, he impressed me, though he was rather quiet.

But he seems a very sincere and nice gentleman. The Vicar called in (in time for

*the scones, I warrant he waited) and Hugh
warmed up when the Vicar began to talk of
football.*

Love,

Aunt Margaret

Too late, Aunt! Frances smiled. Hugh had
not lost any time!

Frances had decided not to write to Hugh,
but to go to the piano bar. She had no
shyness about entering on her own,
everybody would think she was there to
meet somebody inside.

Thursday was her day off. She could go
there about nine o'clock, which seemed a
reasonable time. Oh, what to wear? She had
to consult Emily. Frances tried on outfits to
get her opinion. Emily shook her head at
most of Frances' faded flea-market blouses
and skirts. The best thing she had was a
periwinkle blue full-skirted dress, with a
bolero attached, shell buttons down the
front, and a white belt. She had made the

dress herself. Gloves, of course, and a coat –
thank God for Camden Market, and
Piccadilly – she had proved to be a great
forager, and had a very decent dark green
herringbone tweed. Her pillbox hat, netted in
front over her forehead, she had found on a
stall, her shoes had been new but were now
scuffed from all her walking - they would be
polished within an inch of their lives. She
hoped they weren't going to let in water, or
that the bar was a posh place.

When she hopped off the bus, she found the
bar without much trouble. As she opened the
door a lively piano rendition of *'Scotland
the Brave'* met her ears, a song she had often
heard in Assam at the Club. A swift tide of
joy swamped her heart, making her feel a
little lightheaded and giddy – it had been a
long, long time since she had experienced
that ripple of pure happiness. It seemed to
whisper: *All will be well, all manner of thing
shall be well.*

The instrument – a baby grand - was at the far end of the room, and the pianist had his back to the patrons. Frances recognised the set of the shoulders straight away. The soft light caught the burnished shades of his hair. Dressed formally, his coat-tails were draped neatly behind the piano stool. A table near him was singing enthusiastically along. Tartans, coats-of-arms and old-fashioned sconces hung on the walls.

Frances chose a small round table directly under a sconce, and sat down. She was instantly approached by a waiter and ordered a sherry. Was she really here? Was that Hugh? She felt that this was not really happening.

She had to let him know she was here – she had planned how exactly – and she took out her fountain pen and a sheet of notepaper, and when the waiter brought her drink, she asked him to take it up to the pianist. He obliged, and laid it on the top, and Frances could see that hers was not the only request this evening. Cheers went up as the next request was played '*Loch Lomond*'.

A medly from *Brigadoon*… hers seemed to be the only one left. He picked it up, read it, appeared to read it again, and laid it back on the piano. Oh what a long, long silence! What was his turned back saying? Then he looked around! He didn't see her – a large bulky man with a large bulky drink walked directly across his line of vision as he looked towards her!

A pause, endless…then he began. She alone was listening. *Loss. Longing. Time. Timelessness.* Her surroundings fell away; she was back in Bungalow Three, watching him play, as darkness fell outside, the heady scents of jasmine drifting indoors and the moon rising. She closed her eyes, remembering, every note resonating with sweetness…a tang of bitterness mingled with it, because nothing in this life is all one, or the other.

It was a change of pace for the patrons and they listened rather impatiently. Who had requested such a *queerie sang*? *It wasna Scots!*

After the last notes died away, Hugh left the piano and began to walk down among the tables, looking about. She waved, their eyes met and in a moment he was greeting her, he put out his hand, she clasped it in a warm and certain ease and he sat down.

Delight and a little awkwardness at first, but the latter soon very much done away with mutual pleasure at seeing each other, he seemed struck with her – and told her she looked 'stunning' and she told him he looked very professional and joked about his formal dress. They soon got into a chat about weather, jobs, lodgings, etc. And Brazil of course – she was dying to know about that - his uncle on the coffee farm had renewed his job offer. After about twenty minutes of animated, easy chat spoiled only by the meaningful looks of his employer after a quarter of an hour, he returned to the piano.

There were two more requests on the piano, but he ignored them – instead he began the popular song *'I know where I'm going'* from the film of the same name, playing it with rather too much abandon.

He stopped playing at 11pm, and joined her again.

Hugh took her home, and they talked a little more deeply on the top deck of the number 117 – even remembering the evenings on the verandah in Assam. Before saying goodnight at her door, they arranged to meet the following day. He pressed her hands, kissed her lightly on the lips, told her how great it was to see her again, and turned for the long walk back to his lodgings.

Frances sank on her bed, her dress floating around her, and kicked her shoes off. Her feet were pinching and cold but she didn't even notice.

It was as she had thought – Hugh and Fiona had been thrown together – an expectation had arisen – but when she and her mother had returned to England to plan the wedding, Hugh had come to his senses. But what was an honourable man to do? Thankfully, Fiona had written him a letter. She had unexpectedly bumped into Mrs. Whittier – now working in a café – and she and her mother, both, had formed the distinct impression that there had been something between her and Hugh, and this before she was widowed – Mrs. Whittier wanted some music books she had left behind her and implied that they had sentimental value – the way she had spoken of one piece of music had told her everything as to why they were important to her - would Hugh care to explain himself?

Hugh had written back that there had been nothing between him and Mrs. Whittier. And he had no necessity to explain himself. But it was obvious that trust was no more between him and Fiona – he would invite her to break their engagement. She had done so. That of course was also the end of his career with Localsh Tea.

Fiona had done fine, she had stayed in England and became part of a very fashionable set of people, and her admirers were plentiful. 'She was far too young to become engaged to anybody,' was Hugh's admission. 'For both our sakes, I'm relieved it all came to an end.'

And he had wondered – wondered if there had been some sort of message in the mention of the music books – and *Gymnopédie* in particular - ? Frances had smiled and said: 'Yes, perhaps there was – I did feel – hope – you would get to hear of it – I wasn't even sure why, myself, at the time, I hoped for such a thing – you were engaged. I know that it – disturbed me to hear that you were engaged.'

'Och, the note you wrote me – it was a curt little note, Frances – I had put thoughts of you away forever.'

'I was overwhelmed at the time. My life had taken such a horrible turn – I needed to be alone, completely alone, to see my way – I didn't intend to be curt, though – I didn't intend that.'

'That's what I thought – that you needed to concentrate on settling yourself in England. I concluded that, in hearing that you had dropped all your friendships from India, that you wished to put that experience behind you, and never think of India again.'

'Never think of India again! That would be impossible, I can assure you! Utterly impossible! I love England, it is my native country – I only hate the weather – and the dull colours – even how everything has to match. Nobody would put purple with orange here, but in India they are so much more adventurous with colour. Riots of colour! And how everybody here seems –

stiff and formal, unlike the Indians. We can learn so much from their culture – I have learned, a great deal. I loved India, but – I'm sure you knew this, Hugh, Alec and I were going downhill. We were not happy, in the last two years or so.'

'I could see that,' he said in his quiet way. 'I felt for you. I tried not to let it show. Another man's wife! I actually applied for a job in Maulvibazzar in East Pakistan, but I didn't get it.'

Hugh anticipated perhaps settling in Brazil, as his uncle wished to retire and having no children of his own, had offered to make Hugh his heir if he could run the business with success.

'I don't think we Europeans have much of a future in Tea, in India anyway.' he said. 'Those who stayed on after Independence, like the Jamiesons and the Arkins', find it more difficult every year. If you stay longer than eight years, you can't send your salary back to England, it has to stay in India, because they consider you domiciled. From the Indian Government point of view, that is understandable. I can't see young men like myself going out there as in the old days to manage estates, it's something the Indians are more than willing to do. Brazil, now, would be a completely different scenario.'

'And as for Localsh,' he went on, 'I think it will fold sooner rather than later. Sales have been dropping. Farah want to buy it out. Mr. Jamieson has lost interest in the whole enterprise. As has Marjorie. She couldn't take this second disappointment -'

'Oh, of course,' Frances said, with genuine sympathy. What rotten luck, indeed!

'Duncan Arkins has been thinking of transferring over to Findlays. There's more of a future there, he feels.'

'What of Billingsworth?' asked Frances.

'Oh, didn't you know? That's rather a tragic story. He developed a yen for travel, got involved in - that funny business smuggling from Hong Kong. He was arrested at customs at Singapore.'

'Oh no, that's dreadful. Perhaps he couldn't carry it off. Or maybe he wasn't bribing enough.'

'His jumpiness gave him away on his first attempt. They couldn't but see it.'

'Where is he now?'

'Sad to say, before he was brought to trial, he was found dead in his cell. They suspect foul play.'

The long reach? Frances shivered.

'Lord have mercy on him! Nobody deserves to die like that. What happened to his wife?'

'The whole affair got into the papers, and Localsh treated her very badly. Sent her home with nothing. I heard she lives in a tiny room in Liverpool and hasn't two pennies to rub together. Her son married an Indian woman in Singapore. Her other son is a ne'er do well, something about a war injury, his wife left him and he's in and out of a mental hospital. She's on her own.'

'How horrible. I've been in her situation. I hope something improves.' She felt an odd kinship with this widow who had lost her husband in circumstances similar to her own and was left with nothing. She could not wish on anybody else what she had suffered, not even this woman. She'd had youth on her side though; there was little hope of Mrs. Billingsworth being able to remake herself. She was a woman to be pitied.

He asked her about herself – was she settled in London now, or would she be on the move again soon? She said that she had often thought about going elsewhere. 'I don't feel I am meant to stay here,' she said to him frankly. 'I don't know what God intends to do with me!' It was good to defer to the Deity when she did not want to show her own hopes. And God did decide these things, didn't He? She prayed to Him now. She felt so happy and comfortable with

Hugh Anderson. Would he propose? She would say yes if he did, yes, and move to Brazil – she would have to go to the library and find a book on Brazil, with plenty of photographs. She knew so little about it – the Amazon River – rainforests – Brazil nuts – jungles – sunshine!

Hugh had also told her that he planned to go to Scotland for Christmas to say goodbye to his family. His uncle's *fadenza* was near São Paolo; on their next meeting, he had some photos to show her.

She felt at peace about Alec. She set herself not to dwell on that whys – the reasons why he did this or didn't do that. He'd paid for his shortcomings with his life.

Rest in Peace, Alec, I am at peace. I'm getting on with my life; I know you would want that for me. I'll pray for your soul every day.

She lay back, gazing at the ceiling.

But an alarming thought struck her. Frances Whittier did not have the means to buy a wedding dress, or a trousseau, or pay for a reception. She covered her face with her hands. Poverty was horrid, perfectly horrid. Wardo was publishing the work – he had yet to think of a suitable title – and she would be entitled, he said, to half of all royalties. But publication would take a year or more, and royalties might, or might not, trickle in.

CHAPTER 47 *The Melody Goes on*

The following day Hugh dropped into her workplace at her lunch-time and as her boss expected her back early, they went to a small, crowded café around the corner for a quick sandwich. He produced the photographs – colour – of his uncle's house – a spreading villa with arched windows in rich, verdant surrounds, an odd contrast to the noisy city café they were in at that moment. It was quite grand.

'What do you think of it?

'It's even more lavish than Bungalow One. The verandah looks very nice, it wraps around the corners of the house. I wonder if it goes all the way around.'

'I think it does. I've seen some photos of the back verandah. He built the house himself. I should say – he emigrated there in 1920, and began the farm, and the house is only about 20 years old. It's got all modern conveniences.'

'What are those trees?' she pointed to a grove of large trunks entangled with vines, with wide canopies, a little way from the residence.

'Goodness I don't know! But I know there are rubber trees and palms in plenty.'

He gave her some more photos to look at – rich, lush vegetation, funny-looking tall trees with high naked trunks topped with foliage. And the coffee plants – tidy rows swirling over a hillside, covering acres and acres of ground. Like tea bushes! She smiled at him.

'You'll find out the difference between growing tea and growing coffee!'

'Of course tea is a leaf; coffee's a bean. No *'two leaves and a bud'* there.'

'Will you live with your uncle?'

'That's my intention until I -' he stopped suddenly. 'Frances, I just can't talk about me in the singular anymore – until – I know.' he stopped and put down his sandwich and became red in the face.

'Frances – you must know – you must know - that I love you.'

For Frances, the world fell away.

'I love you too,' she responded.

'You do?' He beamed happily, and appeared to be lost for words, for he opened his mouth and shut it again. Finally he blurted out:

'Then – will you become my wife, Frances?'

'Yes, gladly, Hugh. Gladly.'

They had a few moments of intense hand-holding across the table as they did little more than look at each other. But then Frances began to feel a little uneasy, and her expression became sad.

The couple, absorbed in their own feelings and the great moment that had occurred, the great decision made - failed to notice that they were being watched by another set of diners. Three middle-aged ladies were huddled at a small round table in the corner. They met weekly for lunch. Today, they had run out of news early. Always tuned to their fellow-diners, they caught the proposal, and all listened, eye-browing each other and expressing opinions in low tones. They were very good at that – it was a perfect art.

''E's a Scot,' said the heavy woman wearing a navy turban.

'Well she's as English as they come, and she's well-heeled too. Listen to her talkin'.'

A thin woman with an Irish brogue, her head covered in a polka-dot headscarf nodded discreetly toward Frances.

They observed them while drinking their tea and finishing their sweets.

'I 'ope they are very 'appy, I love to see a wedding.' said a short-nosed one whose hat was like an overturned red flowerpot with a large plastic sunflower on the side.

Now they too saw the lady's troubled expression and cast each other puzzled glances.

'Maybe her father doesn't like him,' mouthed Turbaned One. *'Wants 'er to marry an Englishman.'*

'Well EdinBorow is very far away, now isn't it really.' offered Headscarved One, who thought all Scotland lived in that city.

'Oh go on Bridie, nowhere is far away now, with the fast trains.' Flowerpotted One.

'I really didn't mean to pop the question over a mediocre ham sandwich and a cup of very inferior tea,' Hugh said apologetically. 'It just seemed like an opportunity - I promise I will re-do it, tomorrow, properly, in a nicer place – a restaurant, or in the Park, if you like.'

'Oh dear Hugh, it's not that – do you think I would care about that? But you have to know something – you must know it already - I have no money.'

'And here am I thinkin' she was well-off!' Polka-dot Headscarf said.

''E'll be off now,' prophesied Turban, her face glum.

'You won't see 'im for dust,' this from Flowerpot, with emphasis on the last word.

'Oh, is that all?' He leaned toward her. 'But I knew that, Frances. I'm sorry – I shouldn't speak ill of the dead – but the way you were left by that scoundrel - we all – except Jamieson – knew what he was up to, borrowing money, left right and centre. Gambling in those dens in Calcutta and Singapore. I could hardly stand it when I realised what he put you through.'

'So it really, really doesn't matter?'

'What? What doesn't matter?'

'My being skint.'

'Not one whit.'

'Ah sure he's a lovely lad. Wish Kitty could meet someone like that,' Headscarf.

''E must really love her, 'e's besotted really.' Flowerpot, dotingly.

'She met a scoundrel who took all 'er money!' Turban. *'Gambled it away, and somewhere in Arabia too! 'E could've gambled 'er away next, to a white slave trader!'*

'I've heard of it happenin', you know!' Headscarf, nodding, who never had heard of such a thing.

'I think' whispered Frances, 'we are being watched.' They glanced over, but the ladies were very practiced, and very quick, and were interested in nothing except their apple tart and spotted dicks.

Frances was bothered by one more concern. She had been married for seven years, and never had children. Though she was sure that had not escaped Hugh's notice, she felt duty-bound to mention that as well.

'We never tried to prevent it of course,' she said to him quite frankly. 'And I don't know which of us was – at fault.'

Hugh took her hands. 'So little the poor wives of Localsh know,' he sighed. 'But there's no harm at all in telling you. I heard that before he married, Alec had a lover – a garden girl. For five or six years. There were no children. Alec – after he met – Vera – separated from this lady. He set her up with a little house and paid her money so that she could make a life for herself; it wasn't expected that anybody would want to marry her – but she did marry, and into a good furniture shop in Sundarpur. And had a baby the next year, and another the year after that – so – what does that tell you?'

'That the men of Localsh are worse gossips that any of the women and that the women of Localsh know absolutely nothing about their husbands,' Frances said with spirit. She felt very, very relieved. Alec of course would never had mentioned this girl to her. It was just as well. It was very, very shocking. And yet, she felt that almost nothing could surprise her anymore. He, like Mr. Jamieson, had almost ruined the girl's life. Frances hoped she was happy and that her children brought her joy and that her husband never threw it at her that she had been the woman of an Englishman.

'Have you any secrets?' she charged Hugh.

'None at all – or - maybe one,' he confessed.

'What's that?' she felt alarmed.

'I knew you were very fond of *Gymnopédie* ever before I played it in your bungalow – the night – that night when you were troubled, when Alec complained about the dessert. I could hear you humming the melody sometimes.'

'I didn't even know I was humming it! Anything else?'

'Not a thing.'

Frances wrote to Aunt Margaret in Stevenage and told her that she would like to bring Hugh to visit her. She felt sad leaving her only close relative for a country farther away even than India had been, but at least her aunt was not alone in the world.

'You will look after Frances, won't you?' Aunt Margaret said when they were saying goodbye.

'To the end of my days,' Hugh promised, drawing his fiancée close.

Hugh and Frances had a quiet wedding in St. Botolphs near St. Paul's. Later that day, the couple set out on the *Flying Scotsman* for Edinburgh, and went thence to Inverness. As they neared the city, Hugh regaled her with stories of the new scenes before her, and she was avidly interested in the place where he had spent his childhood. They received a warm and hearty reception from Hugh's mother, his sisters and brothers, and a great many relatives besides. Frances felt overwhelmed – and though prepared to love each and every affectionate new relative, was rather glad that there would be a distance between them all too. They visited many branches of the family. It was a chilly Christmas and New Year, but every room had a blazing fire.

'If my uncle had a fish cannery in Greenland, would you have married me?' Hugh asked humourously one night as she drew as close to the crackling coal fire in their room as she possibly could.

'I would have had to think about that very carefully,' she'd answered playfully. 'I did have an admirer in Texas, you know!'

'I wonder,' mused Frances some days later, 'I have been thinking – I wonder if I could sell my book rights to Wardo.'

'That's your decision, love. Whatever you decide will be fine with me.'

January saw the couple board the *Andes* for the long voyage to Brazil. On the way, they studied Portuguese. And sometime during the voyage Frances remembered that Hugh had said he had something to give her. They were the music books, of course...all of them. They were in his luggage.

The End

ABOUT THE AUTHOR

Mary aka Máire Flannery is from Ireland. At one time in her life she lived in the charming town of Srimangal, Bangladesh, which was formerly East Pakistan. Srimangal is surrounded by Tea-Gardens and is right up against the Indian Assam border.

She lives with her husband Liam in the United States. She loves a good cuppa, especially if enjoyed with family and friends...

Visit Mary at www.celticjaneite.net

www.ingramcontent.com/pod-product-compliance
Lightning Source LLC
Chambersburg PA
CBHW050841030726
47503CB00007BA/2270